David Stewart

HEART AND SOLE

the road I chose

Powder River Publishing

First published June 1994

Published by:
Powder River Publishing LLC
147 N. Burritt Ave
Buffalo, Wyoming 82834

Copyright © 2021
ISBN: 978-1-7366659-2-3
Printed in the United States of America

TO MY WIFE, JACKIE
I dedicate this book to you. Thank you for being there for me.
We'll never forget that night in the truck stop.
I love you, Jackie.

With special thanks to…

My mother: Something said to a young boy in love
made a difference in my life.
My children: Each one of you is unique and you
will have your dream, too.
Floyd Haynes: You're sure one to ride the river with!
Thank you for sharing my dream.
The Opry folks: Thank you all for caring.
Miss Evelyn and Barry: I could not have faced it
without your help.
Snicker: You're a darn good dog! Now you can rest…
until our next adventure.

Contents

PART 3
ILLINOIS, KENTUCKY, TENNESSEE

Photo Credits

Foreword

(by Floyd Haynes)

I well remember that day in April, 1988, when I received a phone call from my good friend David Stewart in Gillette, Wyoming, asking me if I would act as his backup crew/public relations man on an adventure he was about to undertake. He intended to walk roughly 1,600 miles from his home town to Nashville, Tennessee. I knew David to be a determined man and had no doubt that he would succeed in his endeavor to walk those miles in order to sing from center stage on the Grand Ole Opry.

I felt privileged to be asked to perform the duties described and thought of the distance involved, the dangers and hazards of the road, and the severe and extreme weather conditions that would be encountered on such a journey. Deep inside, I knew David could meet these challenges: the grit, desire, stress, and all the bumps and knocks that must be taken in stride on the road to success.

I did take the job, and I must say that it was both exciting and challenging, taking much time, effort and dedication. I met many wonderful people and made some surprising friends along the way, including David's faithful walking companion, the little dog named Snicker. I call him Mr. Snicker. The 84-day walk and my involvement in it was indeed a high point in my life. I would not have missed it for the world.

Floyd Haynes,
January, 1994

Floyd by, Mary Anne Shields
of the Guernsey Gazette

Heart and Sole :

the road I chose

The Beginning

I could feel a chill from the ever-present Wyoming wind that slid in from the northwest, as if to say to me, "You better think twice about what you're about to do." So many thoughts ran through me as I sat alone in those final moments before walking onto a flatbed truck that was to be my final farewell stage before leaving my home town for what I knew would be the hardest three months I had ever faced in my life.

Six months earlier, my wife, Jackie, and I were home alone one winter evening. The chill factor was well below zero and in this sense it was not unlike any other Wyoming winter eve.

That night I had something stirring in me that had haunted me for years. As I sat at the piano after midnight, I said, "Jackie, let's go out for breakfast."

The look on her face was one of puzzlement because I never liked to eat breakfast. It was her favorite meal so without question she smiled and said, "Sure!" and we were soon sitting across from one another in the local truck stop.

The Jukebox was playing a George Jones song, and I stared out at the huge white flakes that covered the vastness of the Prairie and began to hum "In The Wings," a song I had written about the Grand Ole Opry. That longing feeling of wanting to sing on the Opry stage was one I had carried since I was a young boy of 7 years.

In a loving manner, Jackie asked, "What would you do to sing on the Opry?" She knew how much I loved music and knew that I longed to be a star and how I dreamed of the ultimate hope of so many country singers, to be on the stage of the Mother Church of Country Music, as the Opry is so often called.

As my eyes searched Jackie's, there seemed to be something magic in the air, and I instantly replied, "I'd walk to Nashville."

Jackie looked at me with all sincerity and said, "Then do it. Let them know how you feel."

We giggled like children, still unsure of where our conversation was going.

"What?" I asked

"Walk to Nashville! It's perfect, honey! You can do it," she encouraged

"Wait a minute, Jackie. You're getting a little carried away here. That's a long way to walk."

"Well, did you mean it or not?" she dared.

I knew at that moment that my offhand comment had become a reality to her. Yes, I would do it. To sing on the Grand Ole Opry, I would do it, I thought, although the very idea of such a long walk scared me. I remembered the surgery I had had on both knees from old sports injuries, and for some reason they began to ache as I pictured myself out on the road...

● ● ●

I took her up on her dare,' and we planned, replanned and mapped the route I would take. We knew I had to have someone ahead of me, doing my publicity and acting as a support for me

That someone was to be Floyd Haynes. He was a good man and a true believer in my dream.

In my mind, I could hear the band vamping. I knew it was my cue to take the stage. People were waiting with anticipation. Some believed I could do it. Some had skepticism in their eyes. I was gripped by fear! The moment of truth was upon me...

Dawn Delinski-Stewart

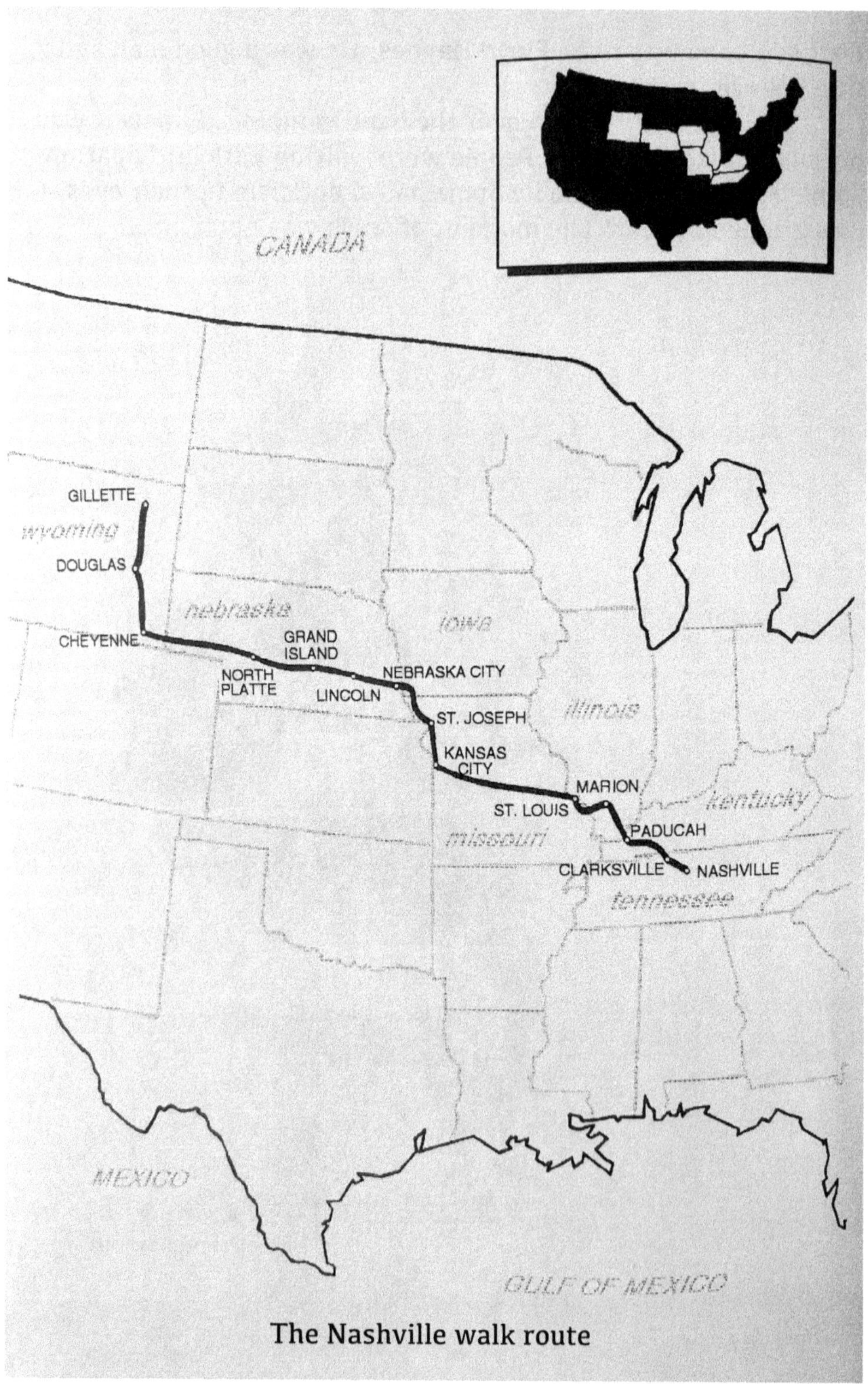

The Nashville walk route

PART 1
WYOMING,
NEBRASKA,
IOWA

1

Steppin' Out

She asked, "What would you do to sing on the Grand Ole Opry?"

My answer: "I would walk."

It had been so many months ago, on a cold winter night, when those words had passed between my wife, Jackie, and me.

Floyd Haynes of Guernsey, Wyoming, the man I had asked to be my support crew, promotions man and guardian, was truly one of a kind. Not a big man of stature — 5-foot 6-inches, maybe 140 pounds soaking wet — he had a crooked little smile that made you feel at home when you were with him. He, too, had always had a dream. His hope was to have one of his many songs recorded and marketed in a big way. This was the man I chose to be near me for the next three months.

Evelyn Jackson from Reno, Nevada, whom we called Miss Evelyn, was a different story. This dear lady had been a friend and fan of mine for about three years, and had attended the Wyoming country music festival every year with my good friend, Barry Doss. Barry, a true country music lover, lent me his mini motor home as a support vehicle. He informed me that Miss Evelyn wanted to go along and help Floyd with the driving. I was shocked because I knew how hard it was going to be on her out on the road, but I did not have the heart to say so.

The date was April 30, 1988. It was a day I would never forget. As I looked on the crowd, there were those with joy on their faces and some with doubt in their eyes. No matter the reason, they were there to see me off, and it was a happy day for me. I sang on stage at a special "David Stewart Sendoff" event. Despite the good feeling and celebration, the reality of what I had undertaken had not yet gripped me.

The cheer of the crowd was intense as I turned and took that first step to the south, holding Jackie's hand until our fingers touched no more. Our eyes met one more time, and the tears began to flow as I walked off the flatbed stage to leave through streams of flags held by the American Legion Color Guard.

Ada Tolar

Singing at the David Stewart Sendoff

I caught a glimpse of the face of my brother, Jack, over Jackie's shoulder. He was shedding tears. This was an emotion I had seen from him only a few times in our lives. Jack was the strong one and had taught me much about the world. He had many ways like our dad, and I smiled often to think of how much they were alike.

My brother, Jim, reached out and touched my shoulder, and his face was saying, "I love you brother," as tears filled his eyes. Jim was a firm man but a gentle soul, and I had learned much from him through the years as well.

I was 37 years old, the 13th child of a clan of 14. Although I was born and raised in Florida, I felt Wyoming to be my home. I was manager and co-owner of the Arby's restaurant in Gillette. I took three months' leave of absence from the job in order to make the trip to Nashville. Jackie, who also worked at Arby's, would continue working there as a bookkeeper during my absence.

My 16-year-old daughter, Dawn, who had been with me since the age of three, had to work at Arby's the day of my departure. I walked away with my heart aching at the thought of not spending private moments with Dawn before I left. She did not understand the thing I had to do. Her friends had teased her about her dad being crazy for wanting to walk all the way to Nashville without even knowing if the people at the live country music show called the Opry would let me perform.

As my dog, Snicker, and I walked away from our home town, two of my nieces trailed along, their childhood faces changing from joy to sorrow and back again.

Emily asked, "Can we go with you, Uncle David?"

I stopped for a moment and looked into their tender faces.

"No honey," I replied to Emily. "You can't go with me. This is something I have to do myself. I love you both, but this is as far as you can go." I wanted to turn myself for a moment and go with them.

"But Uncle David..." Melissa spoke through her tears.

"No," I said with choked voice as I held them both close to me for a moment. "It's time to go back."

My body trembled, and tears fell to the asphalt beneath me as I watched them go. I wanted to shout, "Come back! Come back!" But swallowed the words and tried to get a grip on myself.

The adrenaline was flowing. Floyd and Miss Evelyn had gone on ahead to start the promotion. Snicker, who was now 2 years old, had no idea where we were going. He had always been home by dark when we trained, but it didn't seem to matter to him now since this was a new adventure. He looked up at me with those small brown eyes, his head cocked at a slight angle, ever alert to every sound of the vast land — a land I had grown to love the past 11 years. There was nothing like a Wyoming sky, and I marveled at the one I gazed upon. There was a storm brewing to the north, and a chill ran over me. Somewhere on the prairie, a meadowlark called to its mate.

We had all agreed that the first two days I would return home at night to soak and heal any starting blisters. That thought gave me a moment of peace, knowing that I would be able to see my daughter and to hold her and Jackie after the first day of what I knew would be almost three months away from home. We had discussed a system of making my spot of completion each day with an orange ribbon or yellow balloons, whichever the weather would allow. I believed it would work well. We thought we had planned well, but I knew that it was really a "seat of the pants" trip.

The news cameras and some friends followed for several miles, but were soon gone. The loneliness of Highway 59 began to reach inside me, and I knew the time had come to prove myself. I could smell the sage as winter was giving way to spring, and I was glad to have Snicker at my side. His ears were perked, and his tail waved like the flags that bade us farewell. I marveled at the grace in each step he took. His round, almond eyes searched the terrain, and occasionally he glanced to our "back trail" as if to wonder what all the hoopla had been about. If only he knew this was it — no turning back.

There had been a time when this little spaniel pup was on my list of the world's worst dogs. We had gotten Snicker for Dawn as a Christmas gift. Like most pups, though, the newness soon wore off, and he was a little rascal, not caring at all where he did his business. But there was always something irresistible about the little fellow. I started thinking about my walks in training and how one day I had decided to take him along with me on a 20-mile day. We were up bright and early to the sound of the meadowlarks and out the door. After about an hour, Snicker ran right out in front of a large truck and came very close to "buying the farm." Well, from that day on, he never left my side, and we became comrades and best of friends. That day I had decided the small tan and white pup would be my constant companion on the walk to Nashville.

After starting at about 2:00 p.m. on the first official day of my walk, I only made it about 12 miles before stopping. Floyd retrieved me just before dark.

The night of April 30, I must have gone through almost every emotion possible, not wanting to leave my family but at the same time wanting to walk into Nashville so badly that the excitement raced through me.

I knew sleep was essential, but I needed to talk with Floyd. We discussed the strategy we would use over the next few days. The press had the story now, and it hit the headlines in a dynamic way that we had never imagined possible — thanks to a man named Joe Edwards with the Associated Press out of Nashville. He had called me the night before the walk and asked if anyone else in the press knew about the event.

I told him, "Not yet."

He replied, "Well, tomorrow the whole world will know." He put the story on the Associated Press wire and it spread all over the country.

The next morning (Day 2) 5:15 came earlier than I had known it to come before. The rain came down in a mist, and the cold from the north blew in piercing blows. I had learned to stretch before walking, and that particular day I stretched longer than usual to avoid confronting the elements. I held Jackie as long as I could, then hugged Dawn and Jackie's mom and was on my way.

With as many clothes as possible, rain slicker donned, I was dropped at my starting point and soon looked out at the low, hovering clouds that seemed to dwarf me against the landscape. Day 2 proved to be very trying, I had told Floyd to check on me every couple hours but to please not coddle me or I would not be able to endure. I knew I had to face whatever was to be in order to stay strong. We made the pact, and he held to it. I could see he would be a great strength for me.

The rain soon turned to snow and Snicker's little pads began to pick up ice. I carried him from time to time. We had a saying in Wyoming, "If you don't like the weather, just wait 30 minutes and it will change." This was to hold true on Day 2. The snow and wind came at me with anger, and I wanted to just lie down and quit, knowing however that I would freeze to death if I did so. My feet became so numb from the cold, and I stopped often to massage some life back into them. Snicker shivered as he fought the driving wind. My eyes watered as the cold raced over my face. The moisture froze on my cheeks before it could fall to the ground. I held my face under my shirt to avoid the bitterness, At times, I could smell the scent of Jackie on my clothing, and it gave me strength.

A dear lady named Rosemary came out and walked for a time to encourage me. She shared with me how she had been a snowshoe champion and how she kept her toes warm with lamb's wool. She gave me a medal she had won to carry for luck. Tears filled my eyes as she placed it in my hand and I swallowed hard. It was a great inspiration for me, and I made 23 miles that day before the temperature dropped to an unbearable level.

We were to stay out on the highway that night in the little camper that was to be my shelter, but soon discovered the heater was broken. Floyd and I discussed the situation and felt we'd better go back home for one more night because Miss Evelyn was at risk of getting sick. She was an elderly woman and this concerned us.

That night I told Jackie that I wished I knew how to tell Miss Evelyn to please stay behind. I knew the trip was going to be heart-wrenching, but I just couldn't do it. The snow fell all night long and I wondered if the lord was telling me something about this walk. I held Jackie as if I would never see her again.

May 2 (Day 3) came and I had been out for several hours knowing that the chill factor was well below zero and that my hands and feet were at risk of being frostbitten. I cursed myself for being out in the weather. I knew what the Wyoming cold could do to a man before he even knew he was finished. I was dressed warm and had to be careful of sweating beneath all the clothes.

This is your ultimate test, David, I thought to myself as I paused to attend to Snicker's feet, then my own. Soon you will know if you have learned well.

I finally reached my first town, the small coal mining town of Wright, Wyoming, that morning and entered the cafe to warm up. There were people who were curious about the man who said he was walking to Nashville. Some thought I was nuts; others gave me a warm handshake and wished me well. Bea Parker, the Mayor of Wright, came to greet me. Miss Evelyn and Floyd later moved out to the next town, but not before Floyd had asked the mayor to have her picture taken with me. It was terribly cold out, but she graciously posed as the wind whipped at us with fury. I was so thankful for the lamb's wool Rosemary had left for me.

I resumed my walk about 10:30 a.m., praying for the weather to break, but knowing that would not happen. I wished in my heart that I had not listened to the weather report. "That's a stupid thought," I said to myself softly, trying to build my courage to move on once more.

My legs felt very strong, but I developed a slight shin splint and began to limp a little. There was but a small shoulder on the road we walked, and the trucks and cars were spraying us with wet snow. I kept thinking: it's only about 70 miles to interstate—25 and a wider road to walk on.

I carried a pouch that was my "traveling medicine show," as I came to call it. I stopped for a spell to dry my feet and as I did so, I watched two pronghorn antelope toy with each other as the rest of the herd looked on from a nearby butte. I marveled at the way they endured the harsh elements of the land. As hard as I tried, I could not imagine what it was like for the early settlers coming West. To see Wyoming for the very first time must have been a sight to behold.

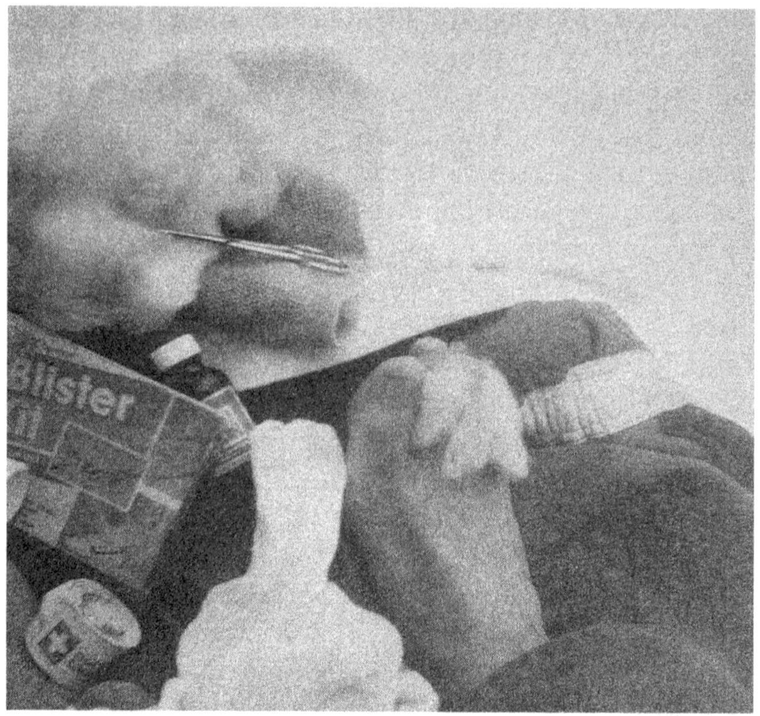

David Stewart

Foot care - blister kit and lamb's wool

I watched a herd of buffalo for a time later in the day. It brought sweet memories of a lady named Josephine Bryant, born in 1903. This woman had become dear to me in the past year, and we had visited at length about what I was to do. She shared with me how, at age 15, she and her family made a trip by wagon across the prairie from Iowa to Woyming. She walked most of the way. She told me of the many herds of bison that roamed free when she was a child and also of the stories she had heard of how many there were long before her time.

"If only for a day, I would like to have lived 100 years ago," I said to myself as I prepared to write in my diary of the trying day. She was to be another of my strengths as I placed one stumbling foot ahead of the other, wondering if I would make it.

My legs were starting to cramp up on me, and I had to massage them as well as my feet to be able to sleep at night. It sometimes felt like a constant toothache in the lower part of my body that would subside for a time but always let me know of its presence.

Day 4 came and the sun was finally in my face. It felt great. Floyd had developed touble with the camper and returned to Gillette to get it fixed. About 8 miles into my day, I spotted a young cowgirl on a four-wheeler, herding sheep. She seemed at peace as the wind blew through her hair and the sheep plodded ahead in a somewhat orderly manner, grazing at every opportunity and sometimes looking at the walking stranger.

I sat down to watch for a few moments and take some time to rest my feet. I had trained myself to stop every hour and change socks. I carried two pairs and would switch back and forth so that one pair would stay dry (or as dry as possible). After about 10 minutes and a peanut butter and honey sandwich, the young lady came to the fence line and asked if I was the one walking to Nashville. "Yes," I replied, and we talked in the warmth of the Wyoming sun that I had longed for. There was still a cold wind from the northwest, but the snow had left me. Snicker had a strong urge to chase after the sheep but knew he would be in trouble. It was nice to talk to someone in such a remote area where loneliness haunted me. I soon had to leave my resting spot and that young cowgirl behind.

It was always such a high to talk to someone on the road. Depression, however, set in soon afterwards as the miles began to work at my body, and I would forget any pleasure I had experienced earlier in the day. Walking past a place called Bill, Wyoming, I had to smile. It was only a store and a post office, but a sight to behold for a worn-out man.

I began to get concerned as night was coming on and my support team had not shown up. They must still be having vehicle trouble, I thought to myself. I sat alongside the lonely road and watched as the sun crept to rest behind the Bighorn Mountains that I loved so much. This was to be the last night that I would spend at home — I was out 70-plus miles now which meant having to get up an hour early to return to the spot where I had quit walking the day before. I began to think of the days to come.

May 4 (Day 5) had to be one of my hardest emotionally, because I knew I would no longer return home at night. I listened to the meadowlarks of early morning and began playing word games with road signs to help pass the time. I blew a little on my harmonica and hoped someone would stop and talk to me. Snicker listened well, but the sound of another human voice became a cherished item.

The weather was changing for the better but was still very windy with a cool edge in the air. The land seemed to have no end as I looked to the far horizon. The low bluffs were a spectacular sight. An eagle danced on a current high above me, with a grace that only God could bestow.

Floyd had gone into Douglas, Wyoming, and I began to see less of him during the day. It was time for a rest, and I began to write my thoughts in my diary. Two men came alongside in a pickup truck as I sat off the shoulder up next to the fence. There were few places in this open country for me to seek shelter.

"How about a Pepsi, pardner?" the one closest to me spoke.

Something hot sounds much better to me, was my passing thought.

I thanked them kindly but told them my drinking was limited to a strict diet of water and Gatorade. I showed them a couple of blisters. They chuckled and said I was either crazy or wanted this really bad. I told them how much it meant to me for them to stop and talk.

"Well, we're proud of what you're doing," the other said with kindness. We talked for a time, and soon they were another memory for me to carry to Nashville.

That night as I lay in my bunk, I thought of the last week and felt very proud that I had averaged about 23 miles a day. I knew I could do more if need be, but would not push it unless I fell behind schedule. I was getting more and more excited as I approached my first 100-mile mark.

The next morning I walked into the radio station in Douglas, Wyoming after being interviewed by a Casper newsman out on the road. The media had been great and especially concerned about my health.

"How does it feel to have made your first 100-mile stretch?" asked one reporter.

"Great," I replied with a chuckle while beaming with joy.

"Do you think you can make it all the way?" another asked with a smile.

"I think I can," I smiled back. "I only have to do what I did this week 15 more times." With that thought, I sat alone for a while and pondered what I had to do.

Miss Evelyn, a gentle but tough spirit, reassured me as she came to my side that it would be okay. Guilt came over me in waves as I thought of how I had wanted her to stay behind.

As I looked at my map, I had accomplished only a fourth of an inch per day, according to the scale on the map. I wanted to crumple it up and throw it away, and probably would have if Snicker hadn't looked at me with those eyes as if to say, "Hey, Dad, I'm out here, too." I held him close and thought of nothing in particular.

2
The walking cowboy

The folks in Wyoming were sure proud of my quest and let me know it. The Holiday Inn put me up for the night when I arrived in Douglas on May 5 (Day 6) and treated me to a hot tub to soak my aches and pains, which seemed to be mounting by the mile.

A new day came with the previous night still sweet in my mind. It was 6:00 a.m. straight up when my foot touched the cool asphalt. The morning was beautiful as I looked torwards Casper Mountain. The air was still very cold, and my feet ached with every step as I walked up that long ramp to Interstate 25.

Highway 59 was a secondary road and so narrow that I always felt an ever-present danger. A unique and exciting feeling came over me as I contemplated new territory and a new direction.

The wind, still blowing, was finally at my back as I entered the new stretch of pavement. My thoughts raced to Bitter Creek and to Elmer, a man of the Wyoming land. He'd often advised me, "Keep the wind at your back, pardner."

"Well, it's at my back for a spell, ol friend," I whispered to the north, hoping somehow he could hear.

The terrain was changing as I turned southerly toward Cheyenne. An hour into my walk, a trucker slowed to a snail's pace on the opposite side of the highway, rolled down his window and started singing a line from my song, "In the Wings." My heart began to pound as he gave me the thumbs up. At that moment, I knew my record was being played over the air. I felt really proud to know that Floyd had succeeded in getting radio stations to play the song I had written and recorded about the Opry. I began to envision myself on that 63-year-old Grand Ole Opry stage, singing straight from my heart to all the country music fans.

As the trucker pulled away he yelled, "Good luck, Walking Cowboy." It never registered until sometime later that this man had dubbed me "The Walking Cowboy." I never knew his name but I don't think I'll ever forget the warmth in his eyes. His voice seemed to echo for miles across the open range as his rig pulled away and grew ever so small against the horizon. His words lingered with me for a time, making the next few miles seem short and sweet.

I was soon back to reality — especially the reality of the road that lay ahead of me. There was an ache in my shoulder that began to gnaw at me and did not leave me for even a moment. When first departing from Gillette, I had asked my Maker to give me one day at a time. Each day I would sing Christie Lane's song, "One Day at a Time." It gave me great strength over many a mile. That day I was to try and walk 22 miles. It never ceased to amaze me how I could be on such a wonderful high while visiting with people and then sink into such a low depression as the loneliness of the highway later took its toll. I had my diary, which became a part of me. I stopped to write whenever depression set in.

I came to grips with the fact that I was on a journey without a definite ending, and it scared me. I would be alone except for Snicker. Floyd had his job to do and I would only see him and Miss Evelyn if Floyd thought the weather was bad, or at night when we would rendezvous. My shoulder felt heavy and cumbersome, and I was soon trying to crack my back against a fence post. I sat alongside the road and held Snicker as I talked to Jackie in the wind and wept a quiet tear. Sometimes I didn't even know what made me cry. Waves of emotions would run over me, leaving me crying one minute, and laughing and playing with Snicker the next. He seemed to always understand.

"If only he could rub my shoulder for me, he would. I know he would if he could," I said, rolling my shoulder against the metal post. I knew my shoulder would get better if I could just keep going. Then maybe the miles would get easier.

Water was not a problem for Snicker at this point . There were some small watering holes along the way, and I was teaching him to drink from my water bottle. I would hold it over his mouth and let it drip onto his tongue. I carried dog biscuits in my pouch. He soon got used to peanut butter and honey sandwiches I carried and eventually grew to love them. I also carried almonds in my pouch. Snicker loved them as much as I did.

Teaching Snicker to drink from a bottle   Dawn Delinski-Stewart

I would have to have a "power meal" at about midnight every night. Loaded with carbohydrates, the food gave me a lot of energy by morning light. I hadn't lost any weight yet.

The sun felt particularly good after the days I had just gone through. I sat and enjoyed its warmth as I wrote in my diary and tended to my feet. Some of my blisters were healing, and I learned that a product called New Skin worked well. I always took time to massage and care for my feet. They were my wheels, so to speak, and I invested a lot of time in making sure they were okay.

I lifted my head to the sound of a dove, cooing on the wire above me, and realized what a wonderful experience my journey was to be — how close Snicker and I would become and how in tune we would be to every creature we encountered along the way, from the smallest insect to the young hawk in flight. I felt a peacefulness come over me that I could not put into words upon the page where my tears had fallen just moments before.

Another day came to a close, this time at the Lusk exit, and I had a great reception and barbecue with some dear friends. We sat around and pulled on the guitars until about 1:00 a.m. I was so keyed up by all the excitement from the people in this small town that my exhaustion seemed secondary. As I looked around the room at all the friendly folks, I knew it would be hard to face the solitude of the road once more. I could not help but wonder what it would be like once I entered territory where no one knew me.

Those thoughts lingered until at last I slept. The next morning, I awoke around 6:00 and had breakfast with members of the Chamber of Commerce staff before I hit the trail once more. I had to carefully monitor what I consumed for breakfast. Fried foods were out as they would only slow me down.

Being able to go to the bathroom was a problem because the country was so open with nowhere to hide, but how soon we adapt to such situations...

The day felt almost like summer, so I dressed in shorts for the very first time, then began walking south once more. Floyd and Miss Evelyn waved goodbye and were on their way to another town. My shoulder still nagged at me but not with the intensity as before. About an hour and a half later, I could feel a slight breeze coming at my back. The clouds began to change to a ghostly gray color. I remember an old saying about the temperamental Wyoming weather. In the West, you can sometimes sense the danger in the skies. I began to hear an all too familiar sound. I knew I had heard this sound before. In that moment, I knew: "Hail, it's hail!" I shouted, with fear in my words.

The wind suddenly turned from a slight breeze to an angry old man, belting me with ice that stung. Gusts of more than 50 mph, I later learned, swept my pup and me like a huge wave of water. Snicker was suddenly blown over a steep embankment. As I reached for him, another gust toppled me over, and we both rolled down the hill, clawing to get a grip. I soon recovered and spotted a culvert of about 3 feet in diameter. Grabbing Snicker, I raced for the shelter. My legs and arms were numb from the cold air, and my breath was coming in short gasps. My mind was clouding with fear.

"What if they come looking for me," I wondered in panic-stricken thought. "I didn't mark my spot with an orange ribbon," I said to Snicker, holding him close for warmth. "But how could I?" I snapped with anger at being swept from the bank so quickly.

We must stay here, I thought. I tried to evaluate the situation; I needed to think clearly. The wind suddenly shifted and blew through the culvert, creating a refrigerator-type effect, chilling me to the very bone. My hands and legs looked like they were turning blue.

"What do I do?" I shouted, hoping someone might hear, yet knowing it was futile on the lonesome prairie. I could not stay put — that was for sure. The temperature was dropping too fast, and I didn't know how long the storm would last. The hail gave way to an icy sleet so I grabbed Snicker, raced from our cover and scrambled up the bank. There was no support team in sight. I knew they were miles away and probably didn't even know of my situation. The sun could be shining where they were. We were on our own!

I had tied my sweatshirt around my waist that morning. It had a hood on it, so I quickly put it on while in the shelter of the culvert. My legs were getting very cold. I soon spotted a new concrete drainage tunnel under the interstate about 100 yards down the road. Running as fast as I could, trying to keep up my circulation, I scrambled down the bank and ducked into the tunnel. I had once again failed to tie a ribbon to a mile marker so I quickly raced up the hill against the driving wind, wrapping the ribbon.

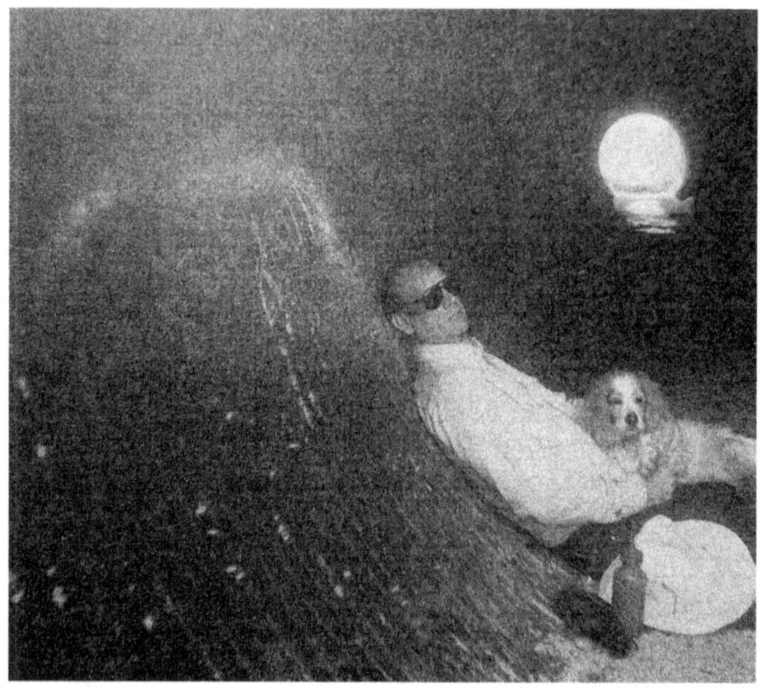

Dawn Delinski-Stewart

Shelter from the storm - in the drainage tunnel near Glendo

Back in the tunnel, well out of the wind, I felt safe but knew I had to find warmth or a better place for cover. I made several dashes out in the open, retrieving small brush, some pieces of an old fence post and anything else I thought would burn. Fortunately, I had some matches in my pack, and I soon had a small fire going in our cave. The tunnel was at an angle that kept out the driving wind. I held Snicker close against my legs, and his body helped warm me. He shivered against my freezing body. I could see my fire would not last long. I built it close to the wall of concrete and it reflected enough heat to help us overcome the cold for a short time, but wood was scarce, and the comfort would soon be gone. I ate every sandwich I had for energy and rubbed warmth into my legs.

"Oh Snicker," I said, "why did I have to be so stupid and wear shorts?" I knew better and had told myself not to until I reached Nebraska, well away from the chance of a freak storm.

"Lord, I need your help to get out of this one," I prayed softly. "I don't want to die out here!" I spoke a little louder. If only I had dressed in warm clothes or at least carried my long johns.

I felt helpless as I held Snicker close and wondered if I would get hypothermia and how it would feel. Maybe the storm will be over soon, I thought to myself.

I decided it was time to start moving and get my circulation going again. As I emerged from the tunnel, the wind had eased a bit, but there was still an awful bite to the air. I walked as fast as my legs could carry me with Snicker racing along beside me. I hadn't gone 100 feet when all of a sudden, there it was! I could see the camper coming at me. It was Miss Evelyn. I began to run torward what I knew to be safety.

Suddenly, she stopped about 200 yards from me on a hill. I could not understand what she was doing, so I began to run torward the vehicle. I could not see Miss Evelyn in the camper, and it was rolling down the hill. I ran alongside and saw that she was lying down between the seats trying to open the side door so that I could get in.

"Miss Evelyn," I shouted and banged on the window. "You're rolling, you're rolling!" I screamed even louder.

"I'm trying to get it open!" she gasped from within. She was so concentrated on getting the door open for me that she had no idea the truck was rolling .

I banged harder on the camper as I ran alongside trying to get her to look up. When she finally did, it startled her so much that she jammed on the brakes. The truck stopped instantly, and my head slammed into the side mirror. The impact knocked me to the ground. As I sat up, Snicker licked my face, wondering what new game this might be.

"I'm so sorry, David. I didn't know I was moving," she said with tears ruining her make-up. "I only wanted to get you inside."

She continued to cry as I tried to shake off the blow to my head.

"I know you didn't know, Miss Evelyn. I'm ok," I smiled, trying to console her. "It's actually kind of funny when you think about it."

"What are you doing?" Floyd shouted at Miss Evelyn. "Didn't I tell you this camper would blow over and to stay put?"

"I had come to find David. You were nowhere around," she snapped through her tears.

"I told you that until we dropped my car in Guernsey, I would check on David when the winds were blowing. We cannot afford to have the camper turn over, and these winds are too strong to be out here," he said with a tone of voice I had not heard from him before.

"I was only trying to help!" she retorted again.

I could see a battle coming on. "Hold it, you two, hold it. Let's get to shelter!" I said, trying to soften the moment.

An hour later, sitting there curled up in a blanket, I was still cold but happy to be safe. I made a vow to myself then and there never to make a mistake like that again. I learned from my support team that because they had been many miles ahead of me at Glendo, they had no idea I was in such danger.

Miss Evelyn had seen the sky and had started worrying, so she took it upon herself to find me. We had discussed my wearing a walkie-talkie but soon dismissed the idea because of the added weight, and the range was only a couple of miles anyway. My people were always beyond that range.

We rested for a time in the little community of Glendo. I felt as if I had been through a terrible battle but had come out a winner. In the little town, I met a most interesting man, Mr. Ed, as he was called by many. He was a writer and we developed a friendship that day. In fact, my support team and I met many different people such as Howard, who owned the local station and motel and who gave us the cabin for the night. We were treated with tremendous courtesy by the Glendo folks. That night, we dined with them and shared a little music.

Serena, a small, attractive woman, gave me a book of songs she had written through the years. On the front cover was a little leprechaun, stirring a pot with musical notes boiling within. Another person had carved me a small truck from wood. Then a special little man with hands swollen from arthritis handed me a book, titled 'Odious Odes for Fisherman,' by Ed Stone. On the first page, the little man had written, 'To David: A young man with a dream and the courage to pursue it."

"Thank you," I said, with admiration in my heart.

He smiled at me and confided, "Tonight I will write of the Walking Cowboy."

Dawn Delinski-Stewart

Resting on the Wyoming prairie

3
Country Love

The folks in the tiny lake community of Glendo held a reception for me, and we sold some records and T-shirts that night of May 6 (Day 7). It made me feel good to know that the people cared enough to buy my record and that we could now afford to pay for the gas in our support vehicle.

My aches and pains were eased for a while as I sang on stage with some of the local musicians. It's amazing how people can help suppress misery for a time with only a smile or a kind word.

That night it seemed especially hard for me to get to sleep as I lay and thought of the day. I hurt all over and pain shot through me like small lightning bolts, one followed by another.

My thoughts kept drifting homeward to my mate, and memories rushed over me, sending so many emotions through me at once that it was hard to "get a grip on." I could see her at the typewriter, working hard to let people know of my heart's desire.

She had sent out many letters across the country and over seas.

I wondered what her thoughts might be. I drew in a deep breath, in hopes of capturing a faint smell of her. I pictured her long, flowing hair and her small frame of only 5 feet. Her passionate eyes lingered in my mind, and I longed to stroke her face gently. Her smile was only the threshold of her beauty. Every part of me ached for her.

I tried to keep from calling home every day because it was so expensive. Sometimes I just needed to hear Jackie's voice and for her to reassure me that everything was going to be okay.

I had talked with my doctor about the trip and asked him about my physical condition. He assured me that physically I was fairly sound. I might have to watch my knees closely, but if I didn't push too hard, I should be okay. His main concern was for my emotional being as I got farther away from my loved ones and closer to the unknown outcome of the trip. "David, you must be careful of your state of mind," he said with deep concern. Dr. Becker had treated me for many years and was a dear friend. His words had already come back to me many times as my emotions ran amok.

Will they let me sing? Will they know how much I love country music when I get there? Will they know how much the Opry means to me? Will they even care? Those questions haunted me many times a day, yet I was not even one-sixth of the way through the journey. I was certain of one thing — no matter the outcome, my love for country music would be known.

As I lay in a pool of worry, Snicker nudged my hand as if to say, "I'm here, my friend." I checked the little guy's pads to see if he was getting raw spots, but everything looked fine. I had started massaging his muscles after the long days, and he really seemed to appreciate it and began looking forward to those times.

I wished I knew what he was thinking. Did he wonder where we were going? Oh, I had told him often enough, but I wondered what he really thought. That question weighed on my mind until finally I drifted into a daze as the wind roared and seemed to grow stronger. The last thing I remembered was Floyd saying, "You did well today, David."

The haunting howl of the wind shook me awake at 5:30 a.m. the next morning, May 7 (Day 8).

"David, the wind is really hard out there today. Maybe we should consider resting today," Floyd spoke as if almost apologizing.

"No, Floyd. Remember the deal we made? If I stop for the weather, I'll get soft and never make it. You promised me that you would not coddle me," I said, all the time wishing that I could concede and not face the menace that beat me down step by step.

I could tell he was concerned about my emotional state. "Please dress warm, and remember your marker if you leave the road," he advised me with a pat on my shoulder.

After a great breakfast with some of the townsfolk, I was anxious to be on my way but scared of what lay in the next 20 or 30 miles.

Two miles out of Glendo, I was leaning headlong into a driving wind. I had worn coveralls and was working so hard to move forward that I began to sweat and get cold, sometimes shivering uncontrollably. Every hour I sought shelter under a bridge or culvert to recover and gather my thoughts. Each time I moved on, I thought that this bad weather would be over soon and bright sunny days were near. Somehow I had managed another mile.

I looked up to see the dust storm coming across the prairie right at Snicker and me. With nowhere to go for shelter, I picked up Snicker and held him inside my coveralls as the storm hit us straight on. I covered my face and kept my head down, knowing it wouldn't last too long and that if I could push forward, I would walk out of it. Visibility was bad so I got down well off the road and walked next to the fence line.

The storm was gone almost as quickly as it had come upon us. I felt drained and could taste dirt between my teeth. It had filtered its way through my bandana. Snicker's little eyes were beet red as I'm sure mine must have been. I longed for a toothbrush. I removed water from my belt and rinsed Snicker's eyes and then my own. I knew Floyd must be going crazy, not knowing if I was ok or not. I had told him not to bring the camper out on the highway to check on me until the wind had died down. We could not take a chance of it being blown over, and he knew I would seek shelter. After his bout with Miss Evelyn over the camper, I did not want a repeat.

Several hours had passed when I looked back and saw Floyd coming down the road with a cement block on the hood of his car. When he pulled up next to me, I laughed and asked him if he thought the block would keep his car from overturning.

"No," he smiled. "My hood latch is broken, and I don't want the hood to rip away in this wind."

His little machine had seen many a mile, and I was glad we would soon leave it behind. Floyd's home was on our route, and we thought it best to take his car there for the three months we would be gone.

"This wind is somethin' awful, David. Is there anything you need?" he spoke above the wind in a loud voice.

"Just a little luck and a lotta prayers, my friend," I said, trying to make the best of it. I found in the short time I had been on the road that no matter how hard it got, I seemed to endure.

Floyd was soon back at his job of contacting the media, and I was sitting along an embankment out of the wind that still howled. It was easing more and more as the day wore on and I wore down. The feeling of removing my shoes and socks grew to be a special ritual for me, and I cherished it.

I saw a young hawk rise and fall with an air current. "How far can he see?" I wondered. I figured I could see for about 50 miles as I looked torward Laramie Peak in the distance. Surely at his altitude, he could see many times farther. A hawk's eyesight is very keen, with the ability to see way beyond human capabilities. None of this really mattered — my mind just seemed to be throwing out trivial thoughts.

I began to try and ignore the mile marker signs. They seemed to make the day go very slowly. If I could only take my mind off each individual step and think of something else. I started sweating again and smiled at the thought of sunshine, but the sun refused to shine long at all, and soon the temperature was chilling me with every step.

I walked toward a little rest area with covered shelter.

When Floyd found me about an hour later, I was sitting beneath a hot-air hand dryer in the rest area, warming my cracked hands. It may have been a comical sight to see me sitting there, but the warm air sure felt good, and I grew to appreciate those hand dryers more than most!

I knew that Nebraska was a little more densly populated than Wyoming. The towns would be closer together. I had mapped the trip out an knew exactly how far between towns it would be. Still there was a mystery around every corner. My thoughts were starting to cause me to babble, keeping me busy, and I didn't seem to notice the road that much.

My thighs and calves were beginning to grow and harden. I had to chuckle a little as I thought back to my training and how one day my pastor had called and asked to go out walking with me. "Sure, Jerry," I said. "I'd enjoy having the company."

The next morning before daylight, we headed east out of town with Jerry's wife, Nancy, driving us to our drop-off point. I always liked to be dropped off outside of town so that I had to walk home. That particular day, Jerry wanted to walk about 25 miles. "No," I laughed, "you're not used to it. Let's only go about 15 miles out," I said trying to convince him that I knew best.

He was feeling his oats that day and won the argument. We were dropped off 23 miles from town. The day was like any other approaching spring. It was early April so we thought pants and a sweat shirt would be sufficient. As Nancy pulled off and the taillights of her car became two small specks against the distant skyline, I wished softly, as I'm sure Jerry did, that I had dressed a little warmer. Jerry did have a baseball cap on his head and my sweat shirt had a hood that I wrapped around my face as tight as possible.

"We'll get warm when we start walking, Jerry. The sun will be up in an hour or so," I spoke like I really knew what I was talking about.

"I hope so."

That old sun stayed under the clouds all day, but that's Wyoming weather for you.

Twelve miles into our walk, the semis were blowing us

backward with every step we took (they seemed to be coming in a never-ending line that day). One blew Jerry's hat completely off, and it tumbled down the road in the stream of the truck's suction. Jerry raced for his hat as he yelled to me, "I lost my hat!"

I turned to look back at Jerry; his poor legs were cramping terribly, and he hobbled more than he ran. Then I stepped on a rock that was protruding at the shoulder of the road. "Aaagh!" I wrenched in pain and went to my knees. Jerking my shoe from my foot, I examined myself to see what damage I had done. It felt as if I had broken something. There was no physical evidence except for a reddening spot that I was sure would turn black and blue before the day's end.

Five miles later we must have been a picture to see. Jerry's legs were like jello. I had to chuckle at him because he had wanted to go so far. I looked like Chester from "Gunsmoke," trying with every step not to put any pressure on my instep.

I began to worry because it was only a little over two weeks before my actual journey, and I was starting to lame up. It made me aware of how easy I could be hurt when I was alone. To make matters worse, within about 5 miles of town, we could feel the air change and started seeing light snow flakes that soon turned to heavy snow! We were freezing cold and hobbling.

A pickup truck stopped to see if we needed help. "You guys okay?" the driver questioned.

Jerry said, "Yes, we're okay." He really wanted to make those last few miles without giving up.

I told him I thought we should take the ride to town before the weather turned worse. I knew he was sad and I felt that way, too. This was only practice for me, but to him it was a great challenge, yet I was pretty sure he was as glad as I was to see the truck.

"We made it over 20 miles," I said to Jerry as we warmed up in the lumber store at the edge of town and waited for Jackie to come get us.

We had gone directly to the hot tub at the local spa to soak. Jerry slept well that night, and we talked of him going with me again soon.

That was a great day, I thought, while still warming my bones.

• • •

The blast of a trucker's horn snapped me back to the present. I jumped a little as I came into the reality of the moment. It was like driving down the road and not realizing how fast the miles were passing by.

I loved to think of home and memories of good friends. Those were my favorite times because I didn't find myself thinking of the pavement, or trying to decide how many gallons of white paint they had used between the Douglas and Guernsey exits.

"You wanna call it quits for the day?" Floyd asked, as I sat in the rest room, warming myself under the hand dryer.

"No, I want to make it to the Guernsey exit. You go on ahead. I'll see you at day's end. Just make sure you're near me when the sun drops."

"I'll be there, ole buddy," he quipped from the side of his mouth as he cuddled Snicker. Floyd had developed a love and respect for my little friend who was marking the miles with me, and often would call him Mr. Snicker. I had great respect for the pup myself.

The cars were few and far between. I waved at each one and, in most cases, someone would wave back. I was nearing the Guernsey exit and had made close to 20 miles. I felt pretty good about it. Floyd hadn't been around since leaving me at the rest area. I knew it was Guernsey — his home town. He was really trying to make things right for me. He wanted a good reception

Snicker and I sat down for my hourly "changing of the socks" routine. Between two of my toes, I spotted a blister that looked ready to burst. I had another one on the top of my big toe. This blister stayed moist, kept getting irritated and would not heal. I caressed each toe as if it were a small child in my hands and rubbed each one ever so gently. Many times after sitting down, I would stiffen up. The first few steps were almost robotic until my legs could function again. I would stoop and grasp a pole to hold onto while I stretched. I found this to be very important. Snicker amazed me by walking right beside me even though he was never on a leash.

I began to ponder the days to come. I worried a lot about the cities and how we were going to make it through all the busy traffic. "One day at a time, son. That's all you asked for."

I had not seen many reporters lately. For one thing, there were no large towns around, and I felt sure no one wanted to stand out in the blasting wind to talk to me. As I thought of my loneliness, I looked back and saw a car coming on the opposite side of the highway. It was far away and I ignored it for the time being. The car soon became what I thought at first to be a hallucination. It looked like my Jackie driving, but no, it couldn't be. Jackie didn't do much driving, especially over long distances. I looked again, long and hard. "It is her, Snicker. It's Jackie!" I yelped with excitement, causing him to dance about. I found new strength in my legs and rushed across the median to the other side of the interstate. As we embraced, the tears welled up inside me, and my heart began to pound till I thought it would burst.

She was enticing. Her face glowed with excitement as she told me of the calls she had been getting from radio stations and newspapers across the country. My skin tingled as we touched. I was so glad to see her but knew she would have to leave me soon, and it hurt to think of it. The past days had taken their toll on me, both physically and emotionally, and I knew Jackie could tell, for I saw it in her eyes.

That night Jackie stayed with me. We held one another and talked of my state of mind. I told her of how my days were going, and she listened with concern on her face. I shall never forget falling asleep that night in Jackie's arms with such peace of mind, convinced that I would make it. A man should be thankful to have a companion such as I had — a true friend and lover. She had a gift of encouragement, and I was truly blessed. As I looked into her sleeping face in the early morning light, I thanked God for her once again.

It was soon Sunday, May 8 (Day 9), the day I was to rest. I got up bright and early, as I was accustomed to doing, Jackie and I visited a local church while Snicker rested and regained his strength. I had a hard time resting and was wanting to walk. It was as if I could not sit still, my mind focusing on one thing. Monday would come all too soon, and I knew a day of rest would do me good. My brother, Jim, and his wife, Betty, came late that day for one last farewell. As Jackie pulled away, heading north torwards home, I stood at the side of the interstate waving until I could see her no more. Then I waved again.

We had been treated with true Western hospitality in Floyd's home town,and he was surely proud of it. The morning was clear and there was a "forever" look in the big, blue Wyoming sky. High above me, I could see an eagle as I began to slowly move out, occasionally looking back as if to catch one more glimpse of my beloved. I began to weep, and I wanted to talk to her so very badly. I remember that she had brought my small tape recorder out to me, and I removed it from my pocket as I watched the eagle get closer to the ground. Turning it on, I said.

Jackie, I love you and I miss you so much.

Snicker stopped and perked up quickly. Just ahead on the side of the road was a snake. "Heel. Heel," I commanded Snicker as I moved onto the interstate to make a wide circle around the reptile. He didn't want any part of us either and slithered off into the grass. The eagle, I soon learned, had been watching this same creature. After moving a safe distance from the snake, I sat down to watch the bird of prey for a spell. In a movement that would marvel any man, he swooped down into the sagebrush and came up holding the snake between his talons. With a wing span of more than 5 feet, he climbed upwards with his pillage dangling beneath. I had a small camera, but without the zoom lens it was impossible to capture the moment on film.

A reporter soon drove up from the next town, and we talked at length about my past few days. I told him of what nature was letting me see firsthand.

I walked with renewed strength in my legs after my visit and felt very good about myself and what I was doing. The hours passed quickly and soon it was almost noon. I had found that if I got started at 6:00 a.m., I could have almost 20 miles in at noon and would be able to rest when the sun was straight, overhead, although of late the sun was a welcome sight at any time of day.

Floyd was soon out to check on me. My shoulder was giving me a lot of trouble so I asked him if he could crack my back like I had shown him to do. I laid down on the side of the road, and Floyd placed his knees on my back and began to press down on my shoulders. We heard the brakes screeching on a motor home that was passing by, the door flew open and a man came running torward us with a First Aid kit. He thought Floyd was administering some sort of CPR and that I was seriously injured.

"What can I do to help?" he stammered, out of breath.

We all had a good laugh after Floyd explained who I was and what we were doing.

The man shook my hand and held it firmly. "I have been reading about you, young man, and I admire what you are doing. Good luck to you and God bless you." Later, after he and Floyd were gone, his words stayed with me like sweet notes from a bird.

My mind began to wander and I thought of Helen Ullery. Helen was the founder of the Wyoming Country Music Foundation. I smiled as I thought of this lady and her love for country music. She was to have been part of my support team but illness would not allow her. I knew she was with me in heart and spirit as were so many others.

I walked 35 miles and could really feel it in my legs and shoulder. I had fallen several years before and hurt my knee and shoulder. The shoulder pain often flared up when I was tired or tense. It felt as if a sharp object was in my back.

As I walked down the long and narrow road into the town of Chugwater, Wyoming, I was scared and felt a need to have people around me. My next stop would be Cheyenne, where I was to turn east and leave my home state. The thought of this seemed to bring back the haunting winds that I had faced all day.

"Snicker," I muttered, as I surveyed my surroundings. "I'm all in, boy."

I slumped against the wall of an old store that had been closed for some years, or so it seemed. He lay his head upon my thigh, looked up into my eyes and breathed a worn-out sigh.

Jackie Stewart

Rest

4

I Can Do This

Sitting in the cold by the roadside, I waited for 5:30 a.m. Chugwater, Wyoming, would soon be only another memory. The date was May 10 (Day 11), and I prepared myself for the weather, hoping to never find myself helpless in the elements again. A ground squirrel scurried across the road as I sat and stretched, taking my time to work on every muscle I could. He stopped to observe me for a moment, then disappeared. "Hello, little fellow," I said in a hurry to see if he would look back.

Snicker wanted to give chase but sat still and whimpered low. He knew I would not approve. I gently stroked his head and began to massage his legs. I could tell he, too, was sore from the previous day, as he moaned with every stroke.

My knees felt as if they had been worked on with a club. They were swollen and tender to the touch. I started my day with a prayer to my Maker, thanking Him for the day and for giving me strength for the previous one.

The traffic became heavier as I moved out torward Cheyenne, hobbling a little as if I were aboard a rocking ship and had not yet acquired my sea legs. Each truck that came my way rocked my full attention. I soon learned which ones would blast me with wind more than the others. The ones with the wind scoops on top hardly affected me at all. The ones with the flat fronts and no scoops sent me reeling about, sometimes losing one step for every two I took. Those were some of the times I wondered, "Can I do this?"

There was a tender spot in the arch of my right foot, the same spot that I had injured while walking with my pastor. It wasn't a bad pain, just one to be wary of. I had to watch where I placed my steps and to walk in a rhythmic manner, rolling one foot ahead of the other, which kept me from slapping my feet against the pavement.

Jackie Stewart
Tending the sore spot, outside Cheyenne

"We'll never make it to Cheyenne tonight, Snicker. Just too many miles, buddy," I informed him, as if he really cared. It did not matter to him where our day ended. He was content with any spot that I chose to make our home for the night. I knew we could not take another hard day like the previous one without risking injury that could put an end to my objective.

The sun that came up on this Wyoming morning was turning the blue sky a radiant orange as if a master painter was starting to fill the canvas with the most beautiful scene. The sun that I watched slowly rise was the same one I had wished to come for so many days, and I wondered to myself if I would soon be cursing its tormenting heat and praying for a cloud to cloak it.

The mule deer stood with their ears up, listening and watching me carefully, ready to dash away if I made a wrong move. Looking down, my feet seemed to be moving in a rapid manner. I knew this was only an illusion. The silence of the early morning was soon to be interrupted by the sound of a new day developing.

Snicker stopped abruptly, nose in the air, tail erect, as if to say, "I see something." Surely he did. Less than a 100 feet from us. I spotted him; he was crouched low, ears back, not moving at all, in hopes we would not see him.

"What good eyesight you have, my friends, you both spotted each other at the same time." I said it for Snicker's benefit but truly thought the young red fox saw us long before my faithful companion saw him.

I knelt close to Snicker and said, "Good boy, but you cannot harm him. He is not hurting anyone, Snick."

His whole body shook; he whined in a low, whimpering voice. Suddenly the fox jumped up and was running all out. Snicker sprang into action and gave chase before I could stop him. I watched as the young fox toyed with my friend until Snicker's tongue was hanging low from his mouth. As he slowly walked back to my side, I said scornfully, "Snicker, that was bad, but I must say fun to watch."

I sat down and let him rest a spell, trying not to pet him. Instead, I scolded him so that he might not do it again. I was afraid that if he got used to chasing the animals, he might dart out in front of a vehicle. I had no fear of him catching or hurting any animals, but I did know that soon we might run across nesting birds or young rabbits, and I did not want him to bother them.

As I sat still and went through my hourly ritual, I began to think of Cheyenne. Fear crept up in my spine like the wind that had been with me in the past, and I felt my throat begin to dry. This was where I was to meet Mr. Sullivan, governor of the great state of Wyoming. What would he say to me? What would I say to him? I had been friends with the former governor but did not know Mr. Sullivan. It was also getting close to my last day in my home state, and I didn't want to cross the state line. The feeling had been with me for some days, and I could not suppress it — no matter how hard I tired. "Maybe I'll just sit here and go no further," I grunted in a pitiful voice that caused me disdain. I could feel a deep depression coming over me. There were certain times of the day I could not control the darkness that seemed to cover me like a heavy cloud from nowhere and then make me sink so deep into myself that I just wanted to lie down.

A pickup truck slowed to a stop alongside where I sat. Three men were in the front seat. The man in the middle looked like a huge grizzly; his hair was long, and he had a beard that hung low and showed signs of graying. The driver wore a hard hat and smoked a cigarette. I wanted that cigarette, but fought back the temptation to ask. The man closest to me was the youngest, with bright blue eyes and a Gene Autry smile. "Howdy," he said with a ring in his voice.

I was always leery of strangers and of the ever-present danger, but these men did not seem evil.

"Hello," I replied, longing for human contact.

"Are you the Walking Cowboy?" asked the man in the middle who had leaned over the younger fellow.

"Yes, sir, I am." The Walking Cowboy story was spreading like a raging fire. I suddenly realized what my mysterious truck friend had done by coining that phrase back near the start of my walk.

"We been hearin' about you on the news and wanted to stop

by and wish you luck," the younger one said with increasing excitement.

A tear lingered on my cheek, and I quickly wiped it away. They didn't know it, but they had just lifted that dark cloud of emotion that was about to engulf me a minute before.

"Thank you for stopping," I whispered as I handed them the address of the Opry.

"Do you need any money?" asked the one with the beard.

"No, sir. Thank you for asking, though. All I need is your prayers and the kindness you have shown today." I smiled, shaking each of their hands firmly.

The Opry is the oldest show in Nashville. Opry performers are well-established entertainers — people with a name. Since the Opry's policy is to only hire known artists, I hoped to acquire enough publicity from my walk and performances along the way to be allowed on the Opry stage. Floyd and I requested people we met along the way to write to the Opry and urge them to give me a chance to perform there.

"You can write the Opry, if you will," I said to the men.

"You bet," the young man blurted.

The third man nodded his head in agreement, swallowing hard as if he might cry.

I thanked my new friends again and departed. Looking upward with a smile on my face, I said, "Thank you, God." I truly believed he had a guardian angel watching me.

Those men said they were going to write to the Grand Ole Opry for me, as did so many others, and I was sure they would. Western folk are an honest breed of people and a hard-working bunch, and when they tell you something, you can count on it.

I began to think back when Jackie and I had moved west. We were adventurous, sold everything we had and headed out in an old Plymouth. That was years ago and now Wyoming was home and an important part of us. I had learned how hard and unforgiving the Wyoming winters could be and how a spring storm could fool a man as it had fooled me earlier in the week.

I looked over the prairie that seemed to have no end and thought about what a beautiful place Wyoming was. The land was covered with sage and grassland, with very few trees except for the mountain areas and along the creek bottoms. The old homesteaders had planted "wind rows" to protect their land from the northwest wind. A ranch in this country was not measure in acres but by sections. It was miles between neighbors, and there were not many ranch houses visible from the highway. Occasionally I would see a lone horseman checking his herd or, if I was lucky, riding the fence line. At times, I longed to be in the saddle.

Physically tired and emotionally exhausted, I quit walking 16 miles from the capital. I stayed with some friends that night and was glad to have the warmth of a bed. So many times I was asked why I had come so far south before setting east. People knew it was quite a bit further and did not understand why I would add extra miles to my trip.

I wanted to visit Cheyenne for several reasons. I wanted to meet with Governor Sullivan and thank the local DJs personally for playing "In the Wings" and telling my story. Floyd had also set up quite a few interviews with Cheyenne and Denver press.

The sun sank to the west and was soon casting a glow from behind the mountain. The sky was splattered with shades of purple, blue, orange and even a hint of pink around the edges of the low clouds that hung in the sky like the trail left behind by a huge jet. I smiled and thought of how I could carve one more notch in my gun for another day behind me.

The cool nights were nice for sleep, but as morning crept up, that same coolness was not wanted. Soon another day was upon me.

"Why don't I jump around like Snicker every morning?" I asked myself. This guy had so much energy that I wondered where it came from.

Floyd and Miss Evelyn were getting on each other's nerves now, and I felt more trouble starting to brew.

"This is no place for a woman. The further we go, the harder it's going to be on her!" Floyd would say to me.

I knew he meant it and that he was right. So far, people had housed Miss Evelyn and treated her like the lady she was, but soon we would be on the back roads of Nebraska with no one to ask for a room and with no money for motel rooms. The mini-camper was only meant for two, but I did not have the heart to tell Miss Evelyn that she couldn't come along. She had been very supportive and wanted to help out, but I knew the tension of the road would get to her.

My legs felt so very heavy — maybe because of the butterflies in my stomach — anticipating the press in Cheyenne. I had already been told they were waiting to see the man who would walk across the country in hopes of singing on the Opry stage. That last mile to the capitol building seemed like it would take forever, not unlike being on a long trip away from home and driving the last ten miles.

Snicker performed in town like a trooper. He heeled right up next to my left leg and walked in perfect formation, tail erect and proud. With cameras flashing and reporters asking questions after question, I could see Governor Sullivan coming my way. My heart pounded like a giant hammer, and I was sure it could be heard. I was sweating at the palms like an oversoaked sponge.

"Hello, David. How do you feel?" he asked as he handed me a soft drink (and it was a diet one at that).

"Fine," I replied as I took the drink from him with nervous hand, hoping I would not drop it. "A little weathered, but fine."

He presented me with a Wyoming pin for my hat as he shook my hand. With TV cameras rolling, I said, "Thank you very much, **Governor Herschler**." Oh, no! I did it! I called him by the former governor's name! It just rolled off my tongue. He laughed as I fumbled to correct myself, my face flushed and red from the embarrassment.

"That's okay, David. You've been working hard."

Reporters soon were shooting questions again and the governor excused himself and said, "Do Wyoming proud, David."

I pleaded with the newsmen not to air the part where I had called him by the wrong name.

The governor smiled and said, "It's okay, David. Don't worry about it."

Soon all was still; reporters and news teams gone. A few people stayed around for a while to see me off, and I began to walk through this town called Cheyenne, heading for I-80. I would be able to stay on I-80 until the Nebraska line and then would switch to highway 30. In Nebraska I would not be allowed to walk on the interstate. We were aware of this type of information for all the states I would cover, thanks to the letters Jackie had received from each state.

May 12 (Day 13) was my first day heading east, and I felt new excitement. It would not be long before I would conquer one state and cross into another. It was a 6:00 a.m. and I knew Floyd would be out within the next few hours to get me for radio interviews. I enjoyed the interviews but hated to lose time on the road. I seemed to be driven by a force to move on all the time.

Eight miles from town, I stopped to investigate a small card on the road. It was a credit card, a gas card to be exact, with a lady's name on it. This is strange, I thought. Why a credit card way out here? I had been finding new things on the road, some tools, rubber straps and at least a penny a day. I always picked them up for good luck.

"Remember to give this card to someone, David," I uttered to myself as I looked around for some visible means as to why it would be on this roadside.

"I wonder why this card got lost, boy." I nudged Snicker, as if he might have the answer. He only looked at me as if he wondered why this should even trouble me. After all, this was an adventure, and anything could happen. Soon Floyd came to get me, and we headed for the radio station back in town.

After the interview, I was about to walk out of the radio station when I remembered that I had the card and gave it to the DJ who had told everyone of my story. Floyd soon returned me to the solitude of the highway, and I began to think about the card I had found. It didn't take much to get my mind off the road; all I had to do was think of things like this. I had a Walkman radio on my belt and was listening to the station that had talked with me earlier and heard the announce the lady's name and mention the lost card.

Within the hour, a man arrived and parked along the highway as I sat fixing my shoes.

"Are you David Stewart?"

"Yes, I am," I replied slowly.

"I'm from the sheriff's office," he said as he showed me his badge. Fear ran through me like a hot poker; a lump gathered in my throat. Oh, god, I just knew something had happened to Jackie or my daughter, Dawn.

"What is it?" I cried out. "What's wrong?" I was starting to crumble inside, and he sensed that he had alarmed me.

"Nothing, nothing, David. I just want to ask you about the card you found."

"My...my family," I stuttered, "I thought it was my family."

"I'm sorry. I didn't mean to alarm you."

"It's ok, sir. It's just that my emotions are on edge these days."

"I can understand why. What you're doing would tear anybody's feelings."

We talked for some time, and I learned that the card I had found belonged to a lady who had been killed in a car wreck some time ago and whose purse had never been found. They thought if I could show them where I had found the card, it would help in their investigation of the missing purse. I knew exactly where to take him because it was next to a billboard along the highway. No purse was found, and he soon let me off where he had found me.

"Thank you, my friend, and good luck." He waved as he pulled away.

Affirmation, I learned, sure helped move me onward, and I was thankful for the people like this man and the many other who had already befriended me.

Noontime found Snicker and me sleeping on and off underneath a bridge. The heat was starting to get to us more and more. I had longed for these days, but now they were wearing at me. I would soon change my habit of walking through the heat of the day to resting in the afternoon and walking later in the evening. It was a peaceful feeling to lie beneath a bridge and drift in and out of sleep. My pup's little furry face was soft in my large hand. He trusted me totally. I could feel this trust between us as I stroked his ears while he relaxed and took it all in. I had remembered to hang out my orange ribbon on the highway and didn't move from my haven for several hours.

Coming around and trying to move after a nap was very tough on my legs. They cramped up. I knew it was my fault. I should have stretched when I stopped as well as when I started out. Some friends from Lusk came by to wish me luck. They knew I would soon be out of Wyoming. I hugged them and thanked them for everything and shed tears when they left. I don't believe I had cried so much in all of my life as I had in the past 13 days on the road.

Twenty miles east of Cheyenne, I decided not to go any further. My legs would not respond, and it was time to back off a little. My body seemed to tell me when it had had enough.

Water was starting to become very precious. I tried to drink heavily in the mornings before leaving so that I would not dehydrate. As I lay and rubbed my tired feet that night, my body surrendered to an early sleep.

Pine Bluffs, Wyoming, was just a small place on the map and was the last town in Wyoming that I would see. I was heading straight at it with a determination to cross the line into Nebraska. As I approached the small town, I looked back over my shoulder several times as if Jackie would come along at any minute and rescue me from my insanity. Yes, I knew it now. I was insane for doing this. Nobody cared. My steps were slow and methodical, and each one was harder than the one before it. Why was this happening now? For days I had been looking forward to crossing the state line, and suddenly I dreaded the very thought. The cattle along the fence were gazing at me as though I was something they had never seen before.

"I am!" I shouted. "I'm a crazy man. You've probably never seen a crazy man before."

I sank to a sitting position and began to sob harder than I had ever done before, grasping for breath with every wail. Lying back, I looked up at the bright sun above me and wondered if the early settlers just laid down and died sometimes as the crossed this hard land. Soon my mind was in my past and there I was, standing on a makeshift stage of the old planks, held up by concrete blocks, guitar in hand pretending to be Hank Williams. That was my dream then — to sing in the Grand Ole Opry. As a small child, this was a part of me, and now here I was walking torward that hopeful day. I could feel my insides easing from the pain of the wrenching sobs, and I began to smile and say to myself: "You can do this…you can do this."

As I crossed onto Nebraska soil on May 13 (Day 14), I smiled and said to Snicker, "I can do this!"

Jackie Stewart

We can do this, Snicker.

5

Into Nebraska

No one knew of my breakdown before crossing into Nebraska. It wasn't included in my diary. I really can't say why. Maybe because it was such a private time in my life. Maybe I was ashamed of crying. I really don't know.

My first encounter in Nebraska was with an elderly couple by the name of Tibbits. They had a son who lived in Gillette, and he had told them of my walk. Lo and behold, they came upon me early one morning.

"We're going to see the doctor, son, and will be back at our farmhouse in about an hour. It's only a few miles down the road. Would you come by for lunch with us?" Mrs. Tibbits asked.

I said I would love to stop but would only be able to stay for a short time and then have to be on my way.

Her smile was so warm as she looked at me with tender eyes and said, "I pray for you every night, David."

That took me off guard an I felt a lump in my throat as I

said, "Thank you, ma'am. I really need your prayers."

Their place was a gracious house that sat back in the trees with a flower garden out the back door. The house was old but sturdy and had a feeling of love and warmth as I entered. I believed both these folks to be in their early 70s as I listened to them talk. I never asked their age, and they never mentioned it.

For all Snicker knew, we had arrived at our destination. He lay down next to me as if it was our new home, and he was content to stay. I had the same feeling stirring within me and knew it would be hard to leave the warmth of a family. I looked at their past, reflected on every wall that was visible to me. I listened intently as they told me of their lives together and shared their iced tea and cookies with me. I tried not to eat those cookies since I was avoiding sweets, but they were homemade and so very good.

"You sure do have a nice place here," I said as I stood and looked out their back door.

"It's home and has been for many a year," Mr. Tibbits replied with pride in every word.

Floyd had to take Miss Evelyn to the beauty salon on a daily basis so she could have her hair done. He would get upset when her hair appointments required him to neglect his promotional activities. This day was no exception. He had once again begrudgingly taken her to town to have her hair fixed. Afterwards, they joined me at the Tibbits' home.

"I'm gonna have to get back to work," Floyd finally said, munching one more cookie.

"You're always in a hurry," Miss Evelyn replied. "David can use this little rest."

He looked at her, not saying a word. I knew that when we were alone, he would tell me that she was driving him nuts.

"She's right, Floyd," I said, sitting back in a chair that felt as if it were made for me. I agreed with her in order to keep the peace between them.

We talked with our hosts for about another half hour until I knew I could linger no longer. "I must go," I finally said.

"Thank you for coming by to see us," Mr. Tibbits replied. "Sure hate to see you go so soon, son."

"Be very careful, David," Mrs. Tibbits warned in a loving voice as she gave me a farewell hug. For fear of depression, I never looked back toward that farmhouse.

They had left me with a good feeling that I wanted to keep, if only for a time. I hugged Miss Evelyn and bid Floyd goodbye as they drove away. I looked around and felt good about being in Nebraska. That part of Nebraska resembled Wyoming with its sage and up-shooting buttes in the distance. I looked northwest to where I thought Gillette might be and thought how nice it would be to grow old with Jackie and share all the things in store for us.

The lady at the farmhouse had said she prayed for me every night. This brought back my thoughts about the guardian angel, and a chill flowed about me.

I had only stopped for a short while, but because it made me feel as if I had lost so much time, I walked longer than I should have before changing socks. The blisters appeared before I knew it, and a rage came over me that I had once again been so dumb. I have always prided myself with having good common sense, and mistakes like that make me feel stupid.

Sitting there eating an early lunch and doctoring my raw feet, I looked out over a large pond of water and saw a pair of mallards on the wing. If only I could fly . . . I watched them glide into the water, leaving a wake behind that soon turned into a ripple and was gone.

There were more trees along this route than I was accustomed to seeing. I saw a squirrel shinny up one, his coat shining brilliantly in the sun. Snicker's head was bobbing in every direction as the wildlife seemed to increase minute by minute around the huge watering hole. My dog lay over on his back as I began to pick cockleburs from his fur. Every so often he would curl his lip at me in a threatening manner, letting me know I was pulling too hard — never biting but clearly giving a warning. The temperature was creeping into the 80s and soon Snicker was asleep. I dozed off, too.

I awoke feeling disoriented and had to think about where I was. I was stiff but refreshed. I stretched long and hard before we moved out for a town called Kimball. Floyd was very depressed when I reached him. He told me in an apologetic tone that the newspaper was not coming out for an interview, I could finally see how difficult it also must have been for him. He was working very hard, and the rejection really depressed him.

It felt good to be able to lift Floyd up instead of him always having to lift me up. "It's all right, Floyd. It's only one town out of many." He quickly got on the phone and started calling ahead to the next town. I trembled every time I saw him using the phone long distance. I knew it was necessary to let people know of my quest. I had given him a telephone credit card and he used it wisely, but I couldn't help wondering how we were going to pay for everything. It did seem like every time we were down on money, something good happened to us, and this made me think of home and my daughter, Dawn.

On May 15 (Day 16), a Sunday and my day of rest, Floyd woke me early and said he had interviews lined up with TV, radio and the press in about three or four outlying towns. I cringed at the thought of using my rest day this way but knew he was right to arrange it such. We ran ragged all day, and I finally lay my head down at 9:15 p.m. in Kimball, Nebraska, knowing Monday morning would soon be upon me.

I was over 300 miles into my walk and could feel the toll it was taking on my knees, especially my right one, as I looked out on that Monday morning. I had bandages on both knees. It gave some relief, but mostly stability. I talked more and more into my recorder. It became a good way to cope with each and every mile.

Early that morning I looked at the map and the schedule I had made of where I should be every day. I was one day ahead of schedule according to my calculations. The little towns appeared further apart on the map than they actually were. I was glad they were close together because I could refill my water often. I worried that water would soon be harder to come by.

The railroad ran along Highway 30, and the trains traveled constantly back and forth. The engineers seemed to know me and waved as they went by. The counting of the train cars became a welcome way to fill my time.

Shortly after 8:00 p.m., I passed a small farmhouse. Just beyond the edge of the house, I saw a huge German Shepherd at about the same time he saw Snicker. The dog's teeth were bared as he came running at us.

It happened as if in slow motion: I grabbed Snicker in my arms and turned to face the charging animal with a stone I had snatched from the shoulder of the road. He was within 20 feet when I thought of turning to run but knew that would be a mistake since there was nowhere to go. I could feel Snicker shiver in my arms. He made a feeble attempt to growl. I knew the large dog could hurt him if I let him down.

I was about to let go of the rock when a shrill voice echoed across the farmyard. "No!" was the word I heard, and the dog stopped and sat down not more than 5 feet from me. He never took his eyes from us as he growled low and vicious. His master, a heavyset woman with rosy cheeks and hair pulled back in a bun on top of her head with a scarf tied at the back, approached. "No!" she said once more as she came closer with a stick in her hand.

"Thank you, ma'am," I said as calmly as I could. My legs were like jello, and I wanted to lie down but held fast to Snicker, not knowing what he would do. Her dog growled once again, and she smacked him with the stick. "I said NO!" He turned and slowly walked back to the house.

"Thank you," I said again. She never spoke, just looked at me with cautious eyes, as if to say, "Be gone before I let him have you."

I turned and walked away, looking back to make sure the dog was still in check. Some time later my heart was still pounding, and Snicker was still looking over his shoulder.

Hours came and went that day, and I thought of that dog often and of the lady who had saved our hide. Even though she never spoke, I was fond of her. I walked on slowly, began to drift in time.

Before leaving Gillette, in fact the night before my departure, I had received a telephone call from Bill Berlin, a broadcaster with WSM, live from the Opryland Hotel. His call came at 1:30 a.m. I awoke from a sound sleep to, "Hi! I'm Bill Berlin and I want to interview David Stewart."

"I'm David," I replied with a voice that sounded as if I had swallowed a ball of cotton.

"Are you really going to walk to Nashville?"

"Yes, I am."

He put me on the air live and we talked for a while. He wished me luck, gave me a toll-free number and told me to call him from the road. Unfortunately, he went on the air at the time when I needed to sleep. Floyd had already made contact with him several times.

The broadcaster was on my mind heavily as I plodded along the lonesome road. In the distance, I saw a man with the hood of his car up. A boy stood at his side. The sun was really belting down the rays as I slowly and cautiously approached them. I looked at my waistline and realized I was starting to lose weight. I wondered how this could be, as much food as I put in my mouth. I munched on a sandwich as I approached the two strangers.

"Hello," I said to the man and the young boy, who I assumed was his son.

"Hi," the man replied.

I could tell he was a little nervous about me. "Having trouble?" I asked.

"Can't figure it out."

Now, I was no mechanic, but from the sound of his car and the heat, I suggested he might have vapor lock. That meant nothing to him. There was a small pond nearby, and I took a Coke bottle he had in the car and retrieved water, poured it over the gas line and repeated the process once more. As his car fired over, I could see the relief come over him.

"Thank you so much," he yelped.

We talked a bit, and I told him where I was going. He said he had heard the story. As he bid me farewell, he said he would call the Opry for me. I asked him not to, explaining that a letter would be much appreciated.

• • •

I owed a lot to the man they called Scrap Stewart — my dad. He had taught me to respect my elders, not to cheat your fellow man and to remember always to keep sight of who created you.

My father, being a very hard man when it came to discipline, gave me the will to make the journey I was on. He was long gone from my life, but his words would remain with me forever. He used to say to me: "Son, make sure what you want to do is right; then go ahead."

The first time I heard Davy Crockett use those words in a movie, I thought he got them from my father, but as I grew older I knew that they were words my father had learned and passed on to me.

He always felt that idle hands were likely to become troublesome hands. "Son," he would say on a Saturday morning when I wanted to sleep, "go out back and chop your mother some wood." Well, I had that old woodpile stacked high enough for three winters, but it made no "never-mind" to him. At least once a month, he had me dig up a sewer line for repair or paint one of the apartments that he rented out.

I soon stopped for my noon siesta and drifted off to sleep thinking about my dad.

• • •

Late afternoon, around 3:00 or 4:00, was a good time to start out again. The sun was at my back and not so hot as when directly overhead. I turned on my recorder as I had so many times and began to speak . . .

It is stifling now in this flat land. The hills have disappeared behind me now, but the trees seem to be increasing somewhat on these back roads that bend ever so slightly now and again but for the most part are straight as a string.

Two miles east of Potter, Floyd discovered a campground and came to tell me of our nest for the night. "It's a beauty," he said, giving me fresh water. "There's a shower there, too." He smiled, knowing how welcome those words would be to my ears.

"Where's Miss Evelyn, Floyd?" I asked with concern.

"She was tuckered out, David, so she stayed at the camp where it was cool."

I was glad he was taking care of her needs. He had a great deal of patience for everyone.

"You're not all that far out, only about an hour the way you travel," he barked, amused at what he had said. I could not help but laugh at his humor.

"That's all right, Floyd. I'm walkin' there, but you're walkin' back," I said with a big grin.

He winked and spoke with that crooked smile that was a part of his great character. "We'll talk about that in Nashville!"

The place he had chosen was secluded with tall trees that offered much shade. I would indeed be happy there for the night. We were pretty low on money again, and while Floyd made camp and Miss Evelyn rested, I sat under one of those magnificent trees, strummed my guitar and relaxed my weary bones. Some time later, Floyd came and told me that the people at the local restaurant wanted to hear some music. What a wonderful time we had with those people. Before the night was over, we had sold almost $100 worth of records and T-shirts. There was a couple there who had been married for more than 40 years. I sang a special song to them that I had written called "The Best Part of All." They were truly an exceptional couple. My walk had put me in touch with many wonderful people and made me realize what a truly great country we have.

It was a new day and the thoughts of the night lingered with me. It was like watching a movie in slow motion as I walked. I had always been a person who enjoyed nature but, like so many, had gotten used to modern transportation. We whiz by everything in such a hurry that we often miss the little things. Taking my first rest of the day, I watched as a spider worked hard to spin a web in a piece of low brush, high enough off the ground to capture insects that happened to stray into its lair. The spider continually worked away until every fiber was perfect.

As I sat intently watching, I began to sweat at the thought of this little creature, and I backed away a little as it brought back memories. When I was but a young lad of about 6 years, I was fishing on the Ockechobee Lake with my dad and a friend of the family, Charlie Shuck. The old cabin in which we stayed was without modern-day conveniences. We washed our dishes in a tub and had to go to the outhouse for our business. I hated that old outhouse. I would sneak around the side of the cabin when no one was looking and relieve myself, not wanting to go near the outhouse. It was run-down, and I could always see spiders lurking in the cracks.

Late one night I had the calling as all young boys do. I woke my dad and told him I had to use the bathroom. He started up, but Charlie said, "I'll take the boy, Scrap. Got to go myself any-way." Then to me, "Come on, boy. Let's get it done."

Charlie was a gruff old codger and very selfish about most everything, but we all loved him, and he was part of the family. I don't know why I loved him. He never showed signs of love, or none that I could distinguish as a child. He held the flashlight as we walked down that narrow path. I was ever aware of snakes and things that lurk in the dark.

"Go on in, boy," he said as we walked up to the old building that served as a bathroom.

"Can I have the light, Charlie?" I asked in a shattered voice.

"No, damnit to hell, I don't want to be out here all night. Get on in there."

I had the impression that Charlie was a little afraid of the dark, too, but would never dare say so. As I sat in the dark, trying to get it over with and be as brave as possible, I felt something hit my shoulder. I let out a squeal.

"Charlie!" I cried as I jumped up, trying to get my pants up and push open the door at the same time. "Oh, God," "the door is stuck!"

I heard Charlie laughing on the other side as I pushed for what seemed an eternity. Suddenly the door flew open and I toppled to the ground face first, still digging at my hair and back, trying to get it off me. I could picture that spider, and I knew he must be huge because I had seen spiders during the daylight hours, crawling about as if they owned the place.

Charlie picked me up by the back of my shirt and stood me upright, laughing all the while.

"Better get yourself cleaned up, boy. You're a mess! "

I wished him dead at that moment, tears down my face in streams. He was a mean old man, and I wanted to tell my dad.

"I hate you!" I cried as he entered the outhouse, still laughing at me.

"Boy, that weren't no spider on you. Just your silly imagination."

Well, my imagination still runs away sometimes when it comes to spiders, and I keep my distance. Charlie always swore he never held the door closed, but to this day I still believe he did.

Now Charlie was a long time dead but not by my wish. I had grown to love him even more over time and spent many more days fishing alongside him. I often argued with him, and there were a few times where he showed a sign of love in his own way. I remember asking him once when I was about 16 if he had held that door shut on me. He just smiled and went on fishing.

As I looked down to watch the lone spider that had made me think of Charlie Shuck, I realized it was gone. "Where is he?" I asked, but Snicker was off somewhere in his own dream state. I quickly jumped up, looking back once more to see if the spider was back in its web. Some fears never leave you, no matter how old you get. For the longest time I kept feeling as if something was crawling on me as I walked that day on a back road of a new territory called Nebraska.

6

Goodbye, Miss Evelyn

As I embarked torward the desolate East, the memories of the night before helped send me at a smooth stride down the road once more. I had stayed on an extra day at the campground because my knees had begun to swell again. I was a day ahead of my planned schedule, and it did us good to take another day of rest. What a great bunch of people they were at the camp. They fed us good and proper, and I sang for our supper, so to speak. We laughed and talked with those folks for hours. People were dancing and singing, and for a while we all forgot our troubles.

I had walked no more than 2 miles on the morning of May 18 (Day 19) when a man who identified himself as Jim stopped and talked to me about how he would have liked to have done something to realize his ideals like I was. He placed $20 in my hand. Trying to hold back a tear, he said, "Ain't much, but maybe it'll feed ya a time or two." I thought of him often as I moved on east. He touched my heart in a very special way. I was a stranger to him, but only for a spell. Now he, too, was living my dream with me. It was a magic feeling.

The morning sun was in my face. I tried to wear sunglasses, but all too soon I had a headache about my temples as if the glasses were pressing against me like a huge vise. My hat was my best protection so I pulled it low over my forehead. The hat was very special. It was creased down the middle just the way I liked, sloping to the front. My 4-inch brim was turned down at the back and front while the back of my crown had a little mule kick in it. The hat fit me as though I had grown right into it.

On many occasions, I forgot to hold the brim as large trucks came by and my hat went flying through the air. I'd made quite a lot of backtracks to pick it up out of the bottom of a ditch and

Ada Tolar

Guarding the hat

often had to shimmy over a fence to get it. I was sure by the time I reached Music City, I'd need a new one.

"Maybe I won't need a new one at all if I don't get to sing." That horrible menace of doubt hit me with a jolt.

Here it comes, I thought with trepidation, that depression that creeps up so unexpectedly when I'm thinking a sweet or happy thought. How could I have let my guard down so unsuspectingly?

"Think of something, David. Anything! Anything but those negative thoughts," I cried.

I could feel my legs starting to swell, or so it seemed, and all of a sudden the blisters on my feet became ever present to me. They were hurting more than I had imagined they could. I knew what was happening but could not control it.

It was time to stop for a break, and to think positive thoughts.

I held Snicker as I sat down off the road by a little stream that flowed at a pleasant pace and made a sweet rippling sound. There was a small bird feeding along the edge of its bank, hopping about and picking up anything that seemed to please him. I found those types of surroundings would help my mental state more than anything, so I began to seek them out and use them to my advantage as I traveled.

Suddenly I had the strongest desire. My knees were hurting as well as my feet. As Snicker drank from the cool oasis, I shed my shoes and socks. I dangled my feet in the cool stream which was some 3 feet wide and 2 feet deep. In fact, it seemed more like a drainage ditch than a stream, but the sound and feel we're soothing. Soon I had both legs in the water and was splashing water over my knees like a young boy without a care in the world on an afternoon adventure. The young bird flew above me to a branch.

"I'm sorry, my friend. I didn't mean to startle you," I said looking up. Lying back in the tall grass, I watched Snicker search for mice or whatever little varmints he could find. The bird kept a wary eye on the hunter, in fear of becoming the hunted.

"He won't harm you," I assured. He cocked his head as if listening. I was very familiar with bird behavior because I had parrots at home. The bird screeched at Snicker in an attempt to warn him away. He hopped back and forth from branch to branch before realizing we were not going to leave.

"I need the rest, little bird," I spoke to his tail feathers as I watched him fly away. I knew he would return when we left, but for now I could not move. As I lay still in the peace and comfort, I began to think of my mother.

She had no idea where her youngest son was, only that he was somewhere on a lonely road in country she had never seen. Her father had been run down years ago on a road like the one I was on. She was but a child herself, and I knew she carried that within her. She had pleaded with me not to make the trip when I told her of my plans. She had never learned to read a book and could only write her name, but this woman, born Annie Elizabeth Coleman, was a true Southern lady, and I would fight anyone who ever said any different. She was a survivor. Married at a young age, she bore six children. She was divorced from her first husband, then married my father, who also had six children from a previous marriage. Some of my father's children were older because there was a 28-year difference in age between my mother and father. She bore two more children, my sister and myself. This made for the clan of 14 children.

My mother taught me a lot about life by just getting through a day without having had much education. As I grew older, I would often ask her if "she would let me help her learn, but she was a stubborn woman, set in her ways. "No," she would say. "Ain't read in some 40 years and don't know why I would need to start now." She didn't know anything about the town her son had come to some years back. She didn't understand why I wanted to do this thing until I reminded her that she was the one, when I was but a child of seven, who had so often said, "Follow your dreams, David."

I had tried to phone her about 10 days earlier, on Mother's Day, but couldn't reach her. I'll call her soon, I thought to myself. Real soon.

A few hours later, I walked into the town of Sidney, feeling as if a heavy load had been lifted from me and happy to have laid on that bank with thoughts of my mother,

I searched with my eyes for someone I might recognize in the . small town but saw no one who even looked familiar. I had no idea where Floyd and Miss Evelyn could be. I nodded to a man who walked by, and he did the same. I read a sign that said "Home Cooked Meals" and wanted to go in and sit at a table. I laughed at myself for the thought.

"You're busted, David. Floyd has whatever money we've got," I mumbled as I stared at the sign again. I leaned against the wall of the building and slumped down slowly. I had placed some distance behind me and was happy. Thoughts of my mother had nourished my heart. I closed my eyes for a moment.

"Hi," came a small voice. "Are you a real cowboy?"

"Howdy," I said to the little fellow who stood before me with a curious smile. "I'm David Stewart." As he bent to scratch Snicker behind the ear, I added, "Some folks call me the Walking Cowboy."

He looked about 9 years old and wore a plaid shirt with one sleeve buttoned wrong. I smiled because I myself buttoned my sleeves wrong on occasion. He had dark brown eyes and hair just as dark. He wore tennis shoes and jeans that were worn at the knee. He kept his left hand in his pocket, something I suspected he might have learned from his dad or older brother. "Is that close enough to a real cowboy?" I asked in fun. He nodded as he became more interested in Snicker than whether or not I was a cowboy.

"Come here, Jimmy," I heard a woman say as she came from the hardware store. "Don't you be runnin' off like that." She gave me a look as if wondering who I might be, and I'm sure it frightened her to see her son talking to a total stranger. Jimmy scurried after her, and I heard him tell her that I was the Walking Cowboy. She stopped and looked back at me once more as if she had heard my story. I smiled and waved to Jimmy and he waved back. I looked at his mom and she smiled. I gazed again at the sign across the street, then lowered my head to rest and wait for Floyd.

Lying in my bunk that night, I began to use some horse liniment that I had brought from home. I rubbed it on my knees to relieve the pain a little. I began to write in my diary:

*Today was a little over 20 miles. I can afford to
back off a little because I'm still ahead of my
projected schedule. I keep telling myself this, but never follow my
advice.*

*I found a few ticks on Snicker and myself tonight. Little, small
red ones. Worries me some because when I was a small boy I had
tick fever once and was near death. I know that is one of my
mother's worries about me being on the road.I don't know the
times she has warned me to check for ticks.*

In the distance I saw lightning dance across the skies, illu-
minating the dark horizon. The wind had a mysterious sound as if
something was brewing. A rain drop ran slowly down the window,
and I felt my eyes growing heavy. Snicker moaned in his sleep as
if something was chasing him. I missed Jackie and wrote her name
on the fogged window. I took up a pen and began to write Jackie a
song.

*Darlin', you are always on my mind
I just crossed that ole Nebraska line
Though by miles we a far apart
I'll hold you in my heart
But I'll be blue, until I hear from you.*

I grew weary and soon fell asleep with the verse in my
mind.

May 19 came early, or so it seemed. It had rained all night
long, and the camper had leaked above my bunk, leaving the foot
of my bed soaked.

"It don't much matter," I smiled as I pulled my slicker on
and prepared to leave. I seemed to be growing callous to the elements.

"Well, Snicker, it's up to you, ol' boy. Do you want to go out in this?" I asked. He wouldn't have it any other way, so we set out in a drizzle of rain that actually felt good after the days of heat we had just come through. Snicker didn't seem to mind getting wet at all. Floyd had offered me hot coffee, but I had never liked the stuff.

The old Highway 30 was not traveled much except for some trucks that appeared to be hauling rock of some sort. A double railroad track sat about 30 yards from the road and was constantly busy with trains going in each direction.

"We've come some miles, boy. Let's pull up under that ol' trestle," I said, wet to the gills. We hunkered under a rock trestle dating back to the early 1900s where the tracks crossed over a dirt road. Breaking out lunch from under my slicker, I removed a towel I had stashed in my pack, first drying my face then working at Snicker's wet coat. He couldn't avoid the temptation to shake in my face. It had begun to rain hard, and lightning flashed all about us. I had just passed a little place called Lodgepole and wanted to get to Chappell, about 9 miles further, but felt mighty nervous about the lightning. Gathering a few dry twigs and brush under our cozy hideaway, I soon had a little fire going for warmth. I believed the Indians were right about building a small fire and sitting close to it. It made sense to me. I was beginning to feel like part of nature at this point. I understood the elements a little better with the passing of each day. I was cold but had plenty to eat, and the fire soon began to dry us. I removed my recorder from my pocket . . .

I guess it to be about three o'clock. The violence of the lightning rips through the sky as I peer out. Not a creature stirs. The rain is falling in heavy sheets, and I wonder if Floyd is having any luck with the leaks in the camper. Snicker is curled up next to me and, as I look into his small brown eyes, I wonder if he wonders where we are or where we are destined.

I can't help but think about Miss Evelyn. I know that she is miserable. She has spent so many hours riding shotgun and waiting while Floyd goes about his business of promotion from town to town. I have been fortunate not to have been around during their arguments, and I'm sure they have had a few. I haven't even had time to visit with her. Being so tired when I quit walking, I usually sponge bath or shower if we're lucky enough to find a truck stop or campground near where I quit for the day, and soon am asleep or just don't feel up to conversation.

Whittling on a stick before pitching it into the fire, I thought of the early settlers who had traveled the same trail many years before. I thought of some places in Wyoming that a wagon could never cross because of deep gorges and valleys. "I suppose that's why they had scouts who traveled ahead," I said to myself. I felt the need to speak into my recorder once more . . .

In this place, I wonder how many old hobos sat under this same trestle and watched a similar fire in their day or touched this cold stone wall that I lean against.

I removed my knife and etched "The Walking Cowboy" into the rock.

Lightning crashed about me like jagged glass thrown in fury across the sky, and I began to count, "One, two, three," before the thunder rolled and echoed on and on as if it would never stop. "The devil's wife is beatin' him with a fryin' pan tonight," my mother would tell us as children. That was something she always said when it thundered. Snicker took every opportunity to catch some sleep. I watched the little guy and learned much from him. He occasionally jumped at the thunder but soon drifted away to wherever dogs go when they sleep.

At 5:30 p.m., I emerged from my safety and set out for my resting place for the night. The rain was now only a mist. The thunder had rolled over the horizon, and distant flashes of lightning appeared around the black clouds that had traveled off to the west. Nature stirred around me little by little as if wary of another storm.

Walking came easy in the cool air. The mist felt good upon my face. I started out at a brisk stride, sometimes splashing puddles like the child that stirred deep within me — that adventurous boy who loved being with his dog and wondering what the next day might bring.

I soon discovered that the flat ground I was on was much better for my feet than the hills I had crossed in Wyoming. Maybe because I had learned the warning signs, the blisters were fewer and further between. I learned that walking downhill created more trouble for me than walking uphill.

I grew to enjoy walking uphill because I could lengthen my stride, bend my knees freely and trudge along ever so gently as if rowing a boat in perfect rhythm. Downhill seemed to pinch my toes, and blisters soon blossomed. It was good to walk on flat land for a spell.

I walked into Chappell, Nebraska, at an easy pace that day as the sun sank low in the sky like a giant fireball, splashing wondrous colors across the horizon. There is nothing quite so magnificent as a Western sunset, I thought, shivering as the coolness of the night came upon me and chilled me even more.

So many thoughts filled my weary mind as I sat alone past midnight. Floyd had been long asleep, as had Miss Evelyn and my faithful buddy, Snicker. As I slipped out into the night, Snicker awakened ready to go, not understanding why I wasn't waiting until the sun came up. "Lie still, boy," I whispered to him. "I'm only goin' out to think awhile."

Sitting under a tree with the rain coming down softly, I wasn't cold anymore. I seemed to be numb to the cool of the night. Sometimes I could feel a drop run down the front of my shirt, slip through my slicker and chill my chest for a moment. I don't know if it was raindrops or tears that occasionally found their way down my cheek and into my shirt. I felt silly sitting in the rain, smiling at times, crying at other times and not understanding where the emotions were coming from. In the distance I could hear the sound of a train whistle, and I started to sing, "The midnight train is whining low, and I'm so lonesome I could cry."

That's it, I thought. Lonesome. That's how I felt. Even though I had people around me at times, I still felt lonesome. I missed Jackie and Dawn very much, but there was more to the loneliness than that.

Never in my life had I experienced so many emotions in a day's time, day after day. The strangest part was not being able to identify certain emotions. I wondered how many emotions a person could experience. The night was very still and dark — darker than any I had ever known — but peaceful in a mysterious way.

I saw the curtain move slightly in the camper and knew that Floyd was concerned about me but that he would never intrude on my privacy. He knew that I needed to gather the strength to face another day.

"Another day? Can I really face another day?" I murmured aloud. I got physically stronger every day, but it seemed sometimes that my head was playing tricks on me. I was scared of what would come, but I had vowed to take one day at a time. As my mind pondered on facing another day, I realized that I was walking on the old Oregon Trail.

"Patience, what patience the pioneers who settled the Western land must have had. How many nights did one sit alone as I am and wonder what tomorrow might bring?" I spoke into the night.

The sun still would not show its face as another day came. At 7:00 am. I was still on the floor where I had crawled in and fallen fast asleep beside Snicker.

The rain continued to beat down, and the wind picked up as I stirred, stiff and sore. I smiled at Floyd who was trying every way possible to stop the rain from coming in on us. I could see his patience wearing thin even though he tried to conceal it.

"Can't patch the darn thing, David," he said out of the corner of his mouth with his head cocked slightly. "Roof's too darn wet."

"I know, Floyd. Don't worry. The rain will pass soon."

I looked from Floyd to Miss Evelyn and knew without asking how miserable she must be. The heater in the camper did not work, so Floyd warmed the engine and turned on the heat up front for Miss Evelyn.

"Miss Evelyn, I know this must be hard on you and I'm sorry."

She smiled and asked me how I felt.

"I'm okay. I'm doin' okay, Miss Evelyn."

Miss Evelyn and Floyd were wearing on each other more and more, and I wondered how long Miss Evelyn would want to remain with us.

Looking back down the road through the rain, I trembled at the thought of leaving shelter behind. Floyd would make his calls, do laundry, then come looking for me. I was thankful that the wind was at my back instead of blasting me from the front. I was dressed warm and had plenty of food for Snicker and myself. I had fashioned Snicker a makeshift slicker from a garbage bag, but it was evident that he would rather be without it. He sure was a tough little guy.

Before leaving the town of Chappell, I made a collect phone call to Tampa, Florida, to WQYK Radio and spoke with a lady by the name of Louise Gore. She had made contact with Jackie and asked that I call her at the station. Louise was my source of greatest strength that day. She gave me words of encouragement that enabled me once again to face the elements that seemed to be trying to beat me down.

I took shelter quite often the 20th day of May. The wind and rain just wouldn't let me be. It took all I could do to make 15 miles before calling it a day. That night I felt as if I had been walking uphill all day on the flat ground of Nebraska. I wrote in my diary:

Two days have passed me by, and the rain continues to haunt me mile after mile. My feet have become so wet that blisters are ever present, and I am continually seeking a dry culvert or bridge where I can stop to docteor them. I worry about infection.

May 21st was wet and nasty as I trudged onward torward Ogallala, Nebraska. I knew that this day would not yield many more miles than the previous one. My knees were sore and swollen, and the constant wetness seemed to compound the misery. I stopped often to tend my aching knees and feet. Around midday, I came upon Big Springs, a combination truck stop and bus station. It looked like a good place to rest.

Foul weather in Nebraska

Floyd Haynes

While I was inside warming myself, Floyd and Miss Evelyn arrived, and I could tell the air was thick with anger. Floyd sat next to me at the counter and told me that he could no longer tolerate babysitting Miss Evelyn. He was tired of having to take her to and from the hairdresser. I could tell he was really angry so I did nothing but listen. I knew it was futile to try and calm the situation. Moreover, I did not have the strength to deal with it. I let him rave on until he calmed down and, without any more words between us, he went back to the camper.

I waited a while before going out and when I did, Floyd was on top of the camper tossing Miss Evelyn's bags to the ground. I tried to stop him, but he insisted it was for the best. I attempted to talk to Miss Evelyn about it, but she would not tell me what had occurred between them and asked me to please get her a bus ticket to Reno. I did as she asked and obtained some boxes from the station attendant for everything that would not fit in her bags. My heart ached as I kissed her cheek and departed for the road once more. Floyd gave her a hug and told her he was sorry but that her departure would be good for all of us. I believe she felt the same way. I walked on toward Ogallala with her on my mind, and that night in the campground, I wrote of her in my diary.

*Miss Evelyn has left us and returned
to Reno by bus. I was sad to see her
leave, but relaxed not to have to
worry about her anymore.*

As I wrote, I heard a car approach. It was Jackie. She had driven from our home to come and see how I was faring.

"Where's Evelyn?" was the first thing she asked me.

"She just went home by bus today," I explained.

"What happened?"

"I'm not sure, but when I came out of the truck stop at Big Springs, Floyd was tossing Miss Evelyn's bags from the roof. When I asked him what was going on, he told me Miss Evelyn was leaving. You should have seen it, Jackie. Floyd was up on the roof ladder in the rain, soaking wet. He said Miss Evelyn was in the camper packing and that I was not to discourage her because it was time for her to go home! He said, 'Don't get me wrong, David. I love Miss Evelyn, but it's getting too hard on her, and we're both becoming uncomfortable.' I went into the camper and asked Miss Evelyn what was going on. She said she was ready to go home. She was pretty upset but told me not to worry and that she was not mad at me.

"Probably was for the best," Jackie said, knowing I was troubled by the situation.

Jackie had come many miles to check on me. She laughed at the way we were living. She told me I would become sick from living in filth.

The morning air was filled with moisture, and Jackie talked me into sleeping longer. The day lingered on, and I was at peace with Jackie near me. The road seemed far away for the time being. Floyd went about his business as usual and seemed glad that I was resting. He had been very concerned about the condition of my knees. I wondered if he had called Jackie and asked her to come. Jackie and her mom cleaned our camper and listened to my stories of the past weeks until the day was dwindling. I finally decided to walk through town to the east side that evening, and Jackie joined me in the rain.

The next morning, May 23 (Day 24), I was on my way out of Ogallala. Jackie decided to walk with me despite the rain that continued to fall. We talked much about how far I had come and how far I had left to go. I told Jackie of the new songs I had been working on. I also told her with concern, "The media has not been around much and I know this discourages Floyd a great deal, but we are now in a rural area and it must be expected."

Jackie listened to my every word but soon had to stop and let me go on alone. I had already made 19 miles when Jackie once more came out to walk with me.

"You have an interview with KOA tonight," she told me. That really boosted my morale, for I knew KOA was a large Denver radio station that reached many people.

That night I sang a song I had written for Jackie and her mom called "If You Can't Feel It, Baby." I told Jackie I would try to record it in David City and then send it to her.

"Where'd you get that title?" she asked.

"Somethin' Floyd said one night in conversation," I replied and Floyd grinned sheepishly. We talked until I felt too tired to talk anymore.

Jackie's mom, Betty Miller, had come along with her from Gillette. This dear lady had been very helpful. She worked day after day stuffing envelopes with letters to DJs across the country. It was a comfort to know that Jackie was with me for a few days and would walk and talk with me at times. I could tell her my innermost feelings.

The next day, leaving Sutherland, Nebraska, behind me, I set my sights on North Platte. I had many uplifting thoughts, especially after an interview with Rollye James of KOA Radio. Rollye had an evening talk show and did an interview by phone with me from the road. She asked her audience to write to the Grand Ole Opry on my behalf, and I talked to lots of people who called in over the air. We mostly talked about my aspirations, and they told me about theirs.

"Fifty-five years ago today, May 24th, Jimmy Rodgers recorded his first record," were the words I heard a DJ speak as I listened to a small radio I had found along the highway.

The rain changed to a constant mist and was not annoying in the least. Snicker was soaked through and through, and I apologized to him occasionally for subjecting him to so much misery. His little round eyes showed tremendous love as I sat and talked to him. I would never forget the tenderness in his face or the way he gently placed his small paw on my thigh as if to comfort me when I cried.

Not since my youth had I been so close to an animal. As a boy, I had lost a good friend in a dog named King. "Oh, he was a smart one," I said as I looked into Snicker's face. "And then there was my golden retriever, Chivas. He was truly a gentleman." None of that seemed to matter to Snicker. He had lost interest in my babbling and was ready to venture further east, as he shook the water off the best he could.

We walked on, leaving traces of my memories on the side of that lonely highway.

7

Across the 100th Meridian

That night of May 24, Floyd got us a room with three beds for only $7.50 in North Platte, Nebraska. I don't know how he managed to talk the owner down to that price, but it was more than fair to us. The hotel accommodation made the stay for Jackie and her mother all the more pleasant.

The next morning, we decided to take the day off and do some interviews that Floyd had lined up for me. I felt like the time off was needed and that it would not matter what day I got to Nashville, as long as I made it. I also knew that I would not make it if my knees gave out on me. Jackie made a doctor's appointment and also an appointment with a massage therapist who worked on my knees and shoulder. Neither one of them charged me for their services, and I felt much better thanks to their help. We kept the room another night at the same price.

As I stood outside the hotel the next morning, Thursday, May 26 (Day 27), the sun had been up long before me, and the sounds of nature that I had grown so accustomed to were lost in the rush of traffic going in many directions. My eyes were focused on the taillights of only one car, the one heading west and growing ever so small against the backdrop of a new town. I watched until I could see the taillights no more. Then I knew she was gone.

My dearest Jackie had once again bid me farewell and had headed home to resume her constant task of letting the world know how much I yearned to sing on the Opry. I felt Snicker's pads rest against my outer thigh as he gently raised up on his hind legs, placing his head against my left hand that hung limp at my side. My right hand was still waving goodbye, but Jackie was gone! I felt empty inside, as if someone close to me had just died.

"Why did she even come?" I said, feeling abandoned and alone. "I can't take this." I thought she might hear me and return to my side. I knew I had to get control of myself, but my insides were turning as if I had eaten poison. "Get it together, man. Get it together."

I bent and held Snicker close to me. He did not understand the sudden mood changes, but was always delighted to get some tender attention. "I could not make it without you, boy," I said, trying to forget about what was ahead and knowing Jackie would not be out again until I was close to Nashville.

"I miss you, honey," were the words I sent after her as I finally turned away.

Shifting my thoughts to the east was very hard, and my feet seemed to be glued in place. If only I had gotten in the car with Jackie, I would be home in about 8 hours. I cursed myself for ever leaving home.

"Home, that's where I should be, Snicker, and so should you!" I shouted with a raspy voice that echoed through the morning streets.

I knew that my earlier realization was true: I would not be able to see my wife again until my journey was nearly at an end. I had not yet quite made it a third of the way — close, but not yet to the one-third mark.

Jackie had only been with me for a few short days, but in that time she had me visit a doctor who X-rayed my knees, gave me a prescription for anti-inflammatories and stressed that I not walk so many miles a day. The doctor thought my legs would be okay if I followed his advice.

I also visited a massage therapist. She worked on my shoulder, trying to relieve a pinched nerve which had been making the shoulder feel numb and heavy by the end of each day. Thanks to all the tender care during Jackie's visit, I was feeling better now.

As I stared at the blacktop that stretched out before me, I knew that the way my body felt was to be only a temporary relief and that the pain would grip me once again when I was alone. I had already started to feel the loneliness once more, although Snicker was at my side. I longed for and needed family to comfort me. We as humans have the ability to adapt to hardships, but when comfort comes along, it can make us weak and I felt that weakness come to me. I hated myself for breaking down, but learned that my body needed to release those emotions to keep me going. I could not explain why. I began to write more of a song for Jackie, stopping when necessary to write it down. I finished a verse and chorus and then set out for Brady, Nebraska.

• • •

On May 27 (Day 28), I walked out of the small town of Brady at 7:20 a.m. That put me about 500 miles away from home. The rain had run off to the west or maybe the north — I wasn't quite sure and didn't care. I was just glad it was gone. I knew I'd pray for it to come again, but it had been wearing me down. The sun was a welcome sight, taunting me with warm, wonderful rays that I had, for many days, longed for. I knew that the sun could be just as unforgiving and even more treacherous than the thunder and lightning storms that were soon to be memories of days gone by.

I had been through Gothenburg early and was on my way to a place called Cozad when I had to stop once again to rest. I glanced at my young pup sitting beside me and was filled with horror. Ticks! Hundreds of ticks covered him! The heat — the dreadful heat — had brought them out like maggots on a dead carcass, and we were to be their prey. Brushing as many as possible off my companion, I began to feel them crawling on me. I was very fortunate that the traffic was sparse on that back road I had chosen. I sat upon the asphalt, picking ticks and crushing them with rocks as fast as I could.

I was still in the battle that seemed to be slowly turning to my advantage when I looked up into the face of a young man in his early 30's, or so I presumed. He had a glowing smile and a friendly manner about him. I was mad at myself for not hearing him pull his vehicle up behind me some 50 feet from where I sat. Not very smart, I thought, hoping his smile was authentic.

"Hello," he said with no detectable accent.

"Howdy. Ticks, so many ticks, all over us. You better be careful."

That smile was still there and so very genuine, as if he had been born with it. "Yeah, they're pretty bad this year. My name's Ralph, Ralph Wall. Are you the Walking Cowboy?"

"Yes, sir, I am." Someone cares, I thought with genuine gratitude.

I hadn't encountered a reporter on the road in quite some time on these long stretches of nowhere and don't know why I assumed he might be one.

"Sure would like to visit a spell and take a few shots of you."

"Be glad to have the company."

"Tell me about yourself, David. Why did you attempt this long walk?"

"All my life — well, at least since I was seven — I've wanted to sing on the Opry."

He listened intently as I went on. "I love country music. I played in front of a crowd when I was 16. I've been pursuing my goal for a long time."

"Do you think they'll let you sing?"

"I got to make it there first, Ralph, then I'll ask 'em."

We talked of many things as time passed. "What does your family think of what you're doing?" he finally asked.

"I have two sons by a former marriage and haven't been around them much. I don't know what they are thinkin', but I know in time they will understand. I miss them and hope they might come to Nashville when I make it. My daughter feels okay about it. She's been kidded a lot about it, but I think she understands. Heck, my sons might be taking a ribbing, too. They're both livin' in Florida, and I didn't tell them I was doin' this."

"Are there problems in that area, David?" he continued.

I studied his face. He was really wanting to know a lot about me from the inside out.

"Yeah, there are, Ralph. I haven't been a father to my sons, and it really digs at me sometimes. Their mother and I could not agree on much, and I've missed out on a lot of good years with them. I was too stubborn and so was she. I was married a second time, but not for long. Jackie and I have been together for almost 13 years. I sure am glad I found her. I lived the night life and a fast life for a lot of years, and I don't want to waste anymore. I am learning so much about myself out here. It's hard, but I'm gonna make it!"

"Who are your favorites in country music, David?"

"Well, my favorite singer is Merle Haggard. As far as writers go, I love Harlan Howard's work. He's really a master at his craft. I also admire Don Shlitz and David Chamberlain. They're both darn good writers. Dolly Parton is, too."

"What about your all-time hero in the music business?" he looked at me with anticipation.

"My all-time hero would have to be Hank Williams. I used to try and sound just like him."

A further image came to mind as I was answering his question. "Another master of songs that I admire is Bob Seger."

"He's not country, David."

"I like lots of different music, but I love country."

Three hours later we were still talking of our musical passions. He had visions of owning his own TV station. Shaking his hand, I finally told him, "I must go on now."

With moisture in the corner of his eye, he said he understood.

"I admire you," he said in a gentle tone of voice.

"And I you, pardner. Good luck in all you do. . . and follow your dreams."

He turned several times and looked back at me, waving some, but mostly just staring after me as I moved away. I thought maybe he would have joined me on my walk if I had asked him to. I liked this man, and I knew he would make it.

My father used to tell me, "If you never tell anyone what you are thinking, they'll never know," and, "If you don't go after what you want, chances are it'll never come to you." I had begun to understand my father more and more as time went on. I wished many times that he was still alive for me to tell him so.

I had to stop and stretch a few times those next few miles after Ralph had gone. I got really stiff and sore sitting and visiting that long, but it was ever so nice to have talked to this man. That night I realized my mind was drifting back to our conversation as I lay in my bunk, rubbing my right, then my left foot, repeating the process again and again until the pain seemed to subside for a spell.

We stayed in the park that night, and Ralph came to visit me once more. I had had another interview that day, but the one I'd remember was with the man with a vision of his own.

● ● ●

My eyes popped open as if I had been hit with a cattle prod. It was light out, and I knew I must have overslept. Groping for my watch, I saw 6:05 a.m. Darn it. An hour late, I thought. I was normally up by 5:00 a.m. and had almost 20 miles in before the sun would start slowing me down in the hot afternoon.

The Motrin that I was taking for my knees was making me oversleep, or maybe I just needed to. No matter, I had to move along. Floyd, too, had slept late, and that was unusual.

"Hey, Floyd, you gonna sleep all day?" I said in a joking tone. He rolled over and smiled, rubbing his tired eyes and trying to get the kinks out. When Miss Evelyn was with us, I found the floor to be a comfort at times because the bunks were so short, and I had to curl up to sleep. In any case, it was nice to have a bunk of my own now.

• • •

"Cozad, Nebraska, the 100th Meridian" read the sign above my head. I stepped over the imaginary line and back again, then over once more. How childish of me. Snicker was not quite sure what this back and forth ritual was but was eager to join me. I reached for my recorder . . .

> Today is the first day of my journey that I have
> not had diarrhea. Feels good. My body must be
> finally adapting to the foods I'm eating or the
> water I'm drinking or might be just plain tired of
> it.
>
> My emotional state is one of happiness today, and
> it feels good. Loneliness is not so prevalent
> anymore. The people who come out to encourage
> me sure do make a difference

Although Jackie had gone, she had left her smile in my heart. All I had to do was bring it out.

I pondered over the 100th meridian and wondered if a forefather of mine had crossed the same line and what hopes he might have had.

The sun glared in my eyes like a giant beam from a huge flashlight. Pulling my hat low, I trudged ever forward, thinking of nothing but my next step. Then I began to wonder — how many steps had I taken and how many would it be at my journey's end? I began to calculate in my head and estimated roughly over a million steps. This excited me for a few moments until reality hit me full in the face. One million steps. I'll never make it, I thought. "Yes, I will!" I shouted and began to pick up my pace.

I had memorized every town I was to go through and knew my route as if I had been on the trail before. "One day at a time, Sweet Jesus," I sang as I plodded along. These words became a part of me, my theme song, and oh how they helped me get through a day.

As I walked into the small town of Overton, Nebraska, I saw those familiar grain elevators that stood tall, up and down the line of little railroad communities I had been passing through for many days. These sleepy little towns have such warmth and personality, I thought as I glanced from building to building. I sat beneath a tree, stretched my legs and watched the town begin to light up as the sunlight melted slowly into the sky. I heard a door slam to the right of me, and a dog barked in the distance. I smelled bread baking somewhere and wanted to search it out. Some folks looked my way, wondering who the stranger might be. I heard the sound of the bell on the gas pump across the street. It was a sound I had never paid a mind to in the past.

"That's me, boy. I'm all outta gas."

A man passed, nodded at me with a smile, pressed ahead as if he had a destination and was soon out of sight. I wondered where Floyd might be and where I would lay my head for the night. Snicker was already stretched out and asleep next to me. As I stroked his head, he moaned ever so softly, as if to tell me he was hurting everywhere.

"I know how you feel, my friend," I said as I rubbed his head and began the long task of removing the ticks from him and then myself, wondering if they would be what did us both in.

My days were measured in miles, not hours. The hours did not matter, as long as I could achieve the miles I needed in the day. Whether it was 12 or 16 hours to walk 20-plus miles no longer mattered. I began to understand why they have no clocks in Las Vegas and was glad that I used the sun to detect the time of day whenever possible. I carried a watch but tried not to depend on it. As I thought of the miles and the tick population, I spotted the little camper. "Come on, boy, home's found us."

Bedded down in the camper, I picked up my guitar and began to sing and play softly, hoping not to wake Floyd. Playing was good therapy for me as it helped me express my deepest emotions.

Floyd soon turned in his bunk and smiled. "Real nice, David."

"I appreciate you, Floyd. I know you've been working hard for me, and I haven't been the easiest to live with, my friend."

With care in his words, he said, "I know you're hurtin', David. I know you're hurtin' bad, so don't you worry about me. You just keep concentrating on your task and let me worry about everything else."

Floyd drifted back to sleep, and I thought of the days we were nearly out of money, waiting on Jackie to wire us a little or trying to sell some records, and how our food supply was low at times. One particular day, Floyd cooked me a can of peas. Knowing I needed the food, he gave it all to me and poured the juice from the peas over some bread and crackers for himself. We both went to bed hungry that night, but Floyd more than I. The very next day, we made about $90 in sales. We ate well that night.

My morning ritual of stretching, praying and making sure I had everything I needed for the day had been interrupted with a new routine: the task of preparing Snicker and myself for ticks. Floyd bought me some powder and dip. It worked for a while, but the ticks still seemed to prevail. As if by habit and nothing else, I turned on my recorder as I watched the sun come up on May 29 (Day 30) . . .

There were no showers to be had last night, so I'm feelin' a little grubby and stiff this morning.

The sun was beautiful as I watched it slowly peek its way over the horizon. It reminded me of the birth of a newborn child — so new, magnificent and without guilt. The birds sang their morning songs to me in perfect cadence with my steps. As one left off, another would take over, ensuring that the music would never cease. Some of those little feathered creatures followed along for a time, lighting on a fence post and watching me with great curiosity.

I was still in cattle country. There were some nice farms along this area, with their share of crops, but the cattle were there, too. Off in the distance, I could see a water tank like so many I had seen in the past. I believed it to be a place called Elm Creek. Sometimes I felt as if I had been walking in place when I spotted a familiar sight like the water tank, thinking it might be the same one I had passed hours earlier.

I felt a hot spot on my right foot and was soon in the shade investigating.

"Oh, no, Snicker! Look at this!" I pointed at my right foot which had a bleeding raw spot that I had not even felt developing. I knew he did not understand why I was pointing this out to him, but he sat still to watch me care for the thing that had made me so angry.

"This ain't good, boy. I can't keep lettin' this happen," I grumbled, mad at myself. He lay his head next to me as if I were mad at him. He had a way of humbling me. "It ain't your fault, boy. It's mine. Here, let me see your paws."

After spending about 45 minutes doctoring my wounds, I was again about my business. I could feel the pain with every step and found myself stopping often to tend it. The wind blew out of the south. It made my steps tougher to take, and I found myself walking awkwardly to avoid the pain in my right foot.

I stopped in a place called Odessa and played some music at the Odessa bar. Everyone in town who loved music seemed to be there. John and Betty, who owned the place, passed the hat for me. I had a good time, even though I was exhausted and still had some miles to go to get to my next stop. We made some good friends in that place before saying "so long."

Two miles from Kearney, Nebraska (a sight I was so wanting to see), I heard the sound of a horn, then a car came to a stop ahead of me. Before I could make out the driver, I saw the Wyoming license plate and felt a rush come over me.

"Howdy," a voice came from up ahead.

"Well, I'll be," I shouted. "Bill and Hazel!"

These folks had driven all the way from my home town to see me. I couldn't hold back my tears as I embraced these two special friends. We sat for a spell and talked of my trip thus far. I told them I would meet them in town and was soon standing and waving at them with a big smile. My spirits had been lifted once more. "Thank you, Lord," I humbly prayed. "You seem to always know when I need it the most."

I wept as I walked those last 2 miles to town. They weren't tears of sadness but tears of joy that these folks had come over 500 miles to encourage me.

8

The Attack

I stood in silence, watching Bill and Hazel's taillights fade into the rain as they headed back to Wyoming. They had seemed to understand my need to walk to Nashville. Others thought me crazy for trying to walk 1,600 miles just in hopes of performing in Nashville. I recalled how happy I had been the day I walked out of Gillette and how that happiness had turned sour as the hardships mounted. I knew it would not be too long until the present joy within me, from seeing these two friends, would grow dim and that lonesome cloud would begin to engulf me once again. Doubt was already in my mind about whether I would be allowed to perform even if I did make it. Brushing the thought away, I blew a note on the harmonica and took an awkward step to the east.

It had been one month for me on the road, and Memorial

Day (Day 31) was upon me. The wind continued to ravage my face, and often I looked over my shoulder to see if maybe my friends were back for one last goodbye. It was cold. Now, more than ever, I longed for home and my spouse.

Slowly I moved out, trying to fight the loneliness within. Shelton, Nebraska, was miles ahead, and it would be home for the night. Snicker was at my side and looked up as if to say, "I'm here. Don't forget me!"

"I'm sorry, boy. I know you're with me."

He was wet to the bone, and I knew he had no particular goal, only a love for his master, and that was his motivation. The big letter 'A' popped out of the sign as if thrown at me, and I was soon looking for B, then C and D. I played the game until I exhausted myself trying to get through the alphabet because it caused the time to pass and the miles to diminish. Soon I saw a new sign: "Welcome To Shelton."

The search for Floyd was short. He had found a good camp, and I knew I would soon be warm. As he filled me in on his progress, my mind could only think of the events that had passed this day, and I began to hate every inch of soil that I had placed a foot on in Nebraska.

"I found you a place to play some music tonight, David," Floyd broke the news as easily as he could.

"I can't, Floyd. I'm all in."

"You have to, David. We need the money, and these people are countin' on you being there. You just rest some, and I'll fix ya something to eat."

I wanted to tell him about my day, but the words would not come, so I rested instead.

• • •

Midnight passed as I put my guitar away. I played in a place called the Vault. We earned a few extra dollars from the local bar where I sang until I was raspy. Lying back on my bunk, I tried to ease my weariness as I let my shoes drop to the floor.

Floyd was moving about in a hurried frenzy, his small frame

rocking the camper back and forth.

"David, we're almost a third of the way, and you need to take it a little slower from here on out. You're pushin' it too hard."

I sat up and began to speak, but could only cry out as Floyd's boot heel smashed down hard on my foot. The pain was so bad that I could hardly get my sock off to look at the damage, and when I did, I grew sick inside at the sight of my swollen toe that was turning a gruesome color.

"David, I'm sorry. Can I get you anything? I feel so awful."

Looking into his eyes, I could see his misery. "Yeah, I could use some aspirin, Floyd."

"I've got Tylenol," he said, as he handed me water. "I'm sorry, David. I'm so very sorry. How you gonna walk?" he stammered as he packed my foot with ice.

"Listen, I don't think it's broken, just badly bruised. We'll be in David City in a day or so to do that show with Bud. If it's not better, I'll see a doctor there."

"I feel so stupid! I'm supposed to be takin' care of you, not hurtin' you like this. I'll just die if you can't go on," he cried.

"Stop it, Floyd! I'm gonna be okay. Look, it's not broken."

I could tell that did nothing to satisfy his grief as he removed his glasses and twisted his face but said no more.

The rain came all night long, and I tossed and turned for most of it. My face grimaced at the light of 6:00 a.m. Floyd was already up making sandwiches and checking my equipment. He looked at my foot long before speaking.

"You okay?" he finally queried.

"Yeah, I'm okay, buddy."

He knew I was not being truthful as I slipped my shoe on so very carefully. My toe was completely black and looked awful.

"Well, my friend, at least the roof didn't leak. You did a good job on it," I said, trying to cheer him up.

Trying my hardest not to limp, I moved out into the cold dampness. The pain in my foot intensified every other ache that I had, and I knew the day would be grueling.

"Lord, you gotta get me through this one," I said, looking back at Floyd watching me, with only pain where his familiar smile should be.

"To endure . . . to endure" were the words I spoke to the stillness about me, as my body moved forward and my mind stood still. I knew that my friend, Bud Comte, was in David City waiting for us. He would know a doctor if I needed one.

Bud had been a good friend through the years, and it would be good to see him. He had a 16-track recording studio, and I wanted to record "I'll Be Blue" for Jackie. I could hardly wait to send it home to her.

The morning moved slowly, and Snicker grew sick and began to vomit. I could see him growing weak but could do nothing much to help. Floyd had passed me hours before on his way to a new town, and we would not see him until nightfall, somewhere east of Grand Island.

"Well, dog, you're sick, and I'm miserable. Heck of a pair we make."

We stopped beneath an old bridge, and I examined my toe.

Snicker collapsed where he stood. As I looked out into the misty rain and hummed a little of "I'll Be Blue," I knew what I had to do. Removing my pack, I pulled out everything I thought I would need and slipped my knife from my pocket. Cringing at the thought of what I faced, I touched my dog gently, and he looked at me as if he understood what I had to do. My stomach was weak as I slowly began to drill a small hole in my toenail. The pain became so intense that I felt as if I might pass out, but I knew I had to relieve the pressure.

I had learned this little trick from my father when I was a youngster. Several times in my life I had a smashed thumb or toe, and he would drain the blood from beneath it. I could hardly stand to let him do it, but I always trusted him to know best. While my thoughts were of my dad, I felt the pressure start to release as the blood trickled out the small hole I had wormed into the nail. My stomach was still turning over and over as I poured iodine on my foot, trying to hold my hand steady.

"Oh, God!" I cried softly, wanting to be back in Jackie's arms and away from all the pain. "What next?"

I felt so empty and cold. I began to shiver and wished I had a fire going, but I felt too weak to search for dry wood.

"Come here, Snicker."

He looked at me as if to say, "I'm sorry, but I'm a mess, too," so I repeated the command until he slowly came to my side.

"Oh, Snicker, I know you're sick, boy, and I'm hurtin' more than ever."

I felt mad — mad at Floyd for doing this to me, yet knowing he would take all the pain on himself if he only could. I was even angrier at myself for being on this back road where nothing stirred and loneliness prevailed.

I held Snicker close to me and pulled my slicker around both of us. The pain in my toe was bad, but I could feel a relief from the pressure I had drained off. I took a couple of Tylenol, gave one to Snicker in a piece of bread and soon we both drifted off as the rain fell softly outside our shelter.

The sleep we had was much needed. We were out for 3 hours without stirring. I felt disoriented when I awoke. Looking about, I tried to recall where I was and why I was there. Stiffness was all over me.

My wound was better, still very sore to the touch, but not throbbing like before. My dad, I thought with nostalgia, he's been gone for over 15 years now but is still helping me with life. My thoughts raced back in time to the man whom I loved so very much. I used to think he was cruel when he gave me so much work to do as a child, but wisdom does come with age, and now I know he was only teaching me.

My father, "Scrap" Stewart, was born Charles Manning Stewart. He just wouldn't quit at anything. He would take on whatever came his way. He also used to tell me about patience.

"Be patient, son," he would say. "Things don't happen overnight. You have to work at it." I used to feel this was just some corny cliche that I was sick of hearing, but now those words ring true to me. I was sure learning patience on my walk. "Thank you, Dad," I whispered. "I miss you."

I stepped gently and carefully on my wounded foot and headed out toward the small town of Wood River, en route to

Grand Island. Wood River would be our refuge for the coming night. Snicker was feeling somewhat better but still looked pretty peaked, so I carried him on my shoulders from time to time, despite the excruciating pain in my foot.

The countryside around me was dismal and gray, and I had a chill about me for most of the miles I trudged. I passed through the little town of Wood River, stopping only long enough for a quick sock change and a bite to eat. Everything seemed to move in slow motion this day. By late afternoon, I walked into Grand Island, pain-stricken and exhausted.

Floyd had arranged for a small press conference with several reporters at a local restaurant. I answered questions and played a song for one reporter who seemed to want to see if I could carry a tune.

After the press left, I still had a little daylight left and walked on through Grand Island, then changed highways to old Highway 34 heading east. That night of May 31, in a campground east of Grand Island, I went to sleep with my father still on my mind.

As I moved out on the first day of June (Day 33) toward Aurora, Nebraska, I limped even more, trying to avoid the pain. This only caused new hot spots that would soon be blisters, and I knew that was dangerous.

Walking on, my eyes began to roam the vastness about me. My senses were on guard constantly, yet Snicker heard things I could only imagine. I needed a rest and so did he. We left the road and were about to settle in when Snicker grew uneasy about something. As his ears came up and I heard his mournful whine, my head snapped around to our back trail, and I saw two large dogs quickly closing down on us with teeth exposed. Sweeping Snicker up in my arms, I felt every muscle in me tense up. My throat went dry. I could not move, could not run. Fear grasped me.

Don't run! I thought. Don't run! Don't put Snicker down or he's a goner. What do I do?

I remembered the last attack and the lady who had saved us, but this time there was no lady.

I screamed "NO!" at the top of my lungs, but they came on with death in their eyes. My only escape was the drainage slough to my left and below us. I threw Snicker into the murky water and jumped in after him.

The pair moved into our refuge, growling and snapping at the air. The big black one was the leader and the aggressor. One eye was cloudy as if he might be blind on that side. The brindle with the notched ear was following his lead. Snicker was struggling to stay afloat and began clawing at my side, trying to get into the safety of my arms. I pulled him close and began screaming and splashing with my free arm.

"Go away!" I cried. "Git!"

This only made the black dog more aggressive and, without warning, he lunged into the water, causing a wake that camouflaged him long enough to make a grab at his 20 pound prey. I pushed Snicker aside and grabbed the vicious animal who was intent on killing the weak — today he had chosen my best friend.

The black dog turned on me, and I kicked him in the rib cage with all I had. This did nothing and, once again, he focused on Snicker who was trying to get away. I knew it would be his death, for now he was boxed in between the attackers. I lunged for the black one and pulled him over backwards. Lashing out at me, he tore my slicker, but I held on tightly trying to avoid his gnashing fangs. The mud was sucking at my feet.

"Snicker!" I cried, as I pushed the huge dog beneath the water. He heard my cry and turned back, and I prayed that the brindle would not take to the water after him. My grip was growing weak, and Snicker was trying desperately to get to me. The beast struggled loose and went for Snicker. I fumbled for my knife and finally got it open, almost losing it from my grasp, as I clinched the hide on the dog's neck and cringed as his mouth closed down on my pup's shoulder.

He shook Snicker like a rag and jerked free from my grip again. I slammed my fist hard against the powerful jaw, and he released his grip, but only for a second. Then he lashed out again. He was going to kill! I pulled on his ear as hard as I could pull and beat at him with all I had, but he would not let go again. With desperation tearing at my soul, I wrapped my left arm under his neck, and with my right I drove the blade deep into his throat and jerked upward as hard as I could, slashing a deep wound in his wind pipe. I felt him grow limp as I pulled him back against my chest and grew sick as the mud turned red with his blood. He rolled on his side and took his dying breath which escaped from the gash I had ripped in his throat. I released my grip and went for Snicker.

"Come here, boy. You're okay. He's gone."

I pulled Snicker close to me and backed away from the pool of crimson. But it was all over me, and I could taste the bile coming from the depths of my stomach. I was numb at the thought of what I had just done and tried to rationalize my actions. I could do nothing else, I told myself inwardly.

I had learned at an early age, while hunting with my brother, Jack, how to cut a wild hog's throat. Many nights we went out chasing wild boar with nothing but a good knife, a piece of rope and a few gritty hounds.

We had also hunted many a raccoon in the light of a full moon. I had been told stories by old Charlie Shuck about dogs taking to the water after coons. He used to say an old coon could drown a good sized dog in the water. I had taken our attacker to the water, to our advantage. Even though all these thoughts were passing over me, I still felt like my stomach was turning inside out.

The brindle brought me to my senses with a threatening Growl.

"Git! Git outta here or you're next! Git!" I screamed.

I felt a rock beneath my foot in the mud, as I stumbled further back, anticipating another attack. I shifted my knife, and my right hand shot below for my next weapon. I hurled the rock as my fist broke from the water. He was fast and had sensed the danger. He leaped, but not quite fast enough, as my arm came through. The crude stone took him full in the side with a thud. He went down hard in the slick mud with a curdling groan. He slipped as he struggled to get up, but regained his footing and fled to the brush. I knew he was hurt, maybe bad enough to stay away.

I could only hope so.

Snicker was clinging to my left side. We struggled out of the water and lay still for a moment. He was bleeding from his shoulder, and I knew we must get away. The brindle might come back, and there might be more to this pack of demons.

An hour later, I stopped to rest. My blisters were turning to raw meat in my wet shoes, and Snicker was feeling like 100 pounds in my arms. It was then that I saw the place across the highway, and it beckoned me. It was a man-made tunnel, about 4 feet high, that ran under the road. I lay Snicker inside and gathered as many dry twigs as I could. I held my knife and kindled a fire, thankful that my matches were still dry in their plastic case.

Snicker was breathing hard and did not even have the strength to lick his wound. I knelt beside him and felt his shoulder. He whimpered. I could feel something within the skin. Using my smallest blade, I began to work slowly, and soon the broken tooth of the black cur came out. The wound drained even more, and I began to dry it and soon had it dressed as best as could be. It was a deep puncture, but it would heal. He was in minor shock and needed rest.

Snicker looked into my eyes as I lay back against the cold, wet wall. I saw the fear and confusion in those small brown eyes, and I knew he saw the pain in mine.

"It's okay, boy. You're gonna be all right."

He seemed to accept that and gave in to sleep. I knew that my life had been changed forever and that part of me was back in that bloodstained hole with the animal whose life I had ended. Stroking Snicker's head, I gazed at the old Cutler knife in my hand. My dad had given it to me, and I wondered if he would have done the same as I. I folded it, put it away and tossed a few twigs on the fire. Snicker moaned softly in his sleep.

As I curled into the fetal position trying to warm my body, my eyes went to the entrance, and there he stood. I had heard nothing. He had come in silence. His brown body was soaked from the rain, and he appeared to be sick. I reached out and touched Snicker's side, but he did not stir.

The creature watched my every move, and I rose upon my

elbow as slowly as I could. I stared into his inquisitive eyes and I rose upon my elbow as slowly as I could. I swallowed the bitter taste that had been in my throat for most of the afternoon. He took a step closer, and I noticed the limp. With all the strength I had, I reached deep inside myself for compassion.

"Come on in, little sparrow. There's no one here will harm you. My name is David, and this tan-and-white fellow is Snicker. I don't know if he's gonna make it. You can share our fire as long as it burns."

He turned and looked out at the gray sky, then back at me.

9

That's All It'll Take

On June 2 (Day 34), I made it to York, Nebraska. Along the way, I had a close call with some joker who tried to run me off the road. Partly because of that, I decided to interrupt my walk at York and go to nearby David City to rest for a few days. I needed to get the last few days off my mind. Snicker needed to heal, and I knew the time with friends would be good for me.

Floyd and I were excited about doing the show with Bud's band. The show made us a little more money for the road. Bud, in his fatherly manner, had slipped some extra money in my pocket. When I tried to protest, he said, "You'll need it. So don't argue with me."

The people of David City made me an honorary citizen of the town. They treated me well, and I ate like a horse. Snicker stole the show when he walked out among the audience from the stage the night we performed. He was a ham and loved the attention. He did his best not to be sick, but I could tell he was not up to snuff. I recorded Jackie's song at Bud's new studio and mailed it to her. Bud was a good friend, and I was glad we took the time off.

I was reluctant about returning to the road but knew I must, so on June 6 (Day 38) I was back at York, heading toward a place called Seward.

Reality has a way of jumping at you like a dark creature from the shadows, and that reality hit me square on the chin when I left David City. The much-needed rest was over. I thought of the people we had visited in David City, and now here I was once again on the road that I dreaded so much. I fumbled for my tape recorder . . .

> *Snicker is feeling somewhat better, but I feel ill at ease about his health. It's not quite right. His wound has started to close and is not infected that I am thankful for. Although he tries his best not to be sick, I still know he's under the gun. I made some good friends in David City. I'm glad I took the time off and was able to spend it with such good folks. Bud told me that his daughter and son-in-law would be out to meet me when I arrive in Lincoln.*

Early that morning, I stretched long and hard but still felt somewhat stiff from the time off in David City. I didn't mention my encounter with the wild dogs to anyone. It would have made Bud and Floyd nervous if they found out.

In Wyoming, packs of dogs would often kill sheep and cattle. I knew how vicious such dogs could be. My brother, Jack, had warned me to be careful of them. He was the rancher in the family and had seen firsthand how they could kill. My friend, Elmer, who was also a rancher, had once told me that a pack of wild dogs was worse than coyotes because wild dogs aren't afraid of people. He also gave me some fatherly advice about being careful. As I walked eastward and thought of Wyoming, I pulled out my recorder . . .

The rain has left me once more. I wonder how long it will be before I'm praying for it to come again, for I know that all too soon the effects of summer will be upon me. I worry about the extreme heat and how it will aflect me and my little friend.

The medication I'm taking seems to be keeping down the swelling in my knees and even seems to be relieving my shoulder somewhat, but it makes me feel a little sluggish. Nebraska must be the longest state I've ever seen. I 've been walking in this state for over three weeks now and still have close to a week left. I'll be glad to be in another state and to turn south once more.

I pocketed the recorder and set my sights on a new place. The day proved to be hard in more ways than one, but we made it to Seward on schedule. As I sat in the dim light of the camper, I began to make notes in my diary:

Shall soon be changing highways again in Lincoln. The anticipation of virgin territory keeps one foot in front of the other. The miles from York to Seward today seemed to go by fast. I don't know if it's because of the rest I took or the eagerness to once again move on.

"How ya feelin', David?" Floyd asked with concern.
"I feel pretty good, Floyd. Do you wanna walk a little with me tonight?"
"Yeah, I do, buddy. Let's go."
Floyd and I enjoyed walking a few miles together in the evening, just to chat and share our thoughts. It was one of the ways we relaxed at night. Sometimes during the day, Floyd would walk

walk with me for about a mile, then return to get his vehicle Soon he would pass me by on the road, go about a mile and wait for me to catch up.

On this particular night, the moon was bright and we could see very well. We decided to walk around the Nebraska town that was to be our home for the night. Snicker stayed in the camper to rest. I gave him an aspirin before leaving him alone.

I spoke after some time: "I'm scared, Floyd, scared of what's to come. We'll soon be in another state. I'm feeling depressed about leaving Nebraska, yet I want to cross that state line so very badly. I guess it's silly, but I know we will soon be too far away for anyone to come out and see me."

Floyd didn't speak. He only nodded with a smile of reassurance and listened as I spoke.

The little town reminded me a lot of Gillette with its old brick-front buildings along Main Street, some giving way to more modern styles through the years. There was a lot of history around us, and we wondered who was here ahead of us and for what reason they might have come.

I began to think of when I had wandered westward. My reason had been simple enough. In 1977 I was out of work. I had become a sprinkler-fitter by trade and had been laid off for quite some time. My prior aspirations of a music career had played out earlier, before I moved to Florida.

Jackie and I met in Florida. Never had I encountered anyone like her. She had a gentle and mysterious way about her and the most beautiful smile I had ever seen. Falling in love with her was a blessing for me.

My brother, Jim, had moved to Gillette, Wyoming, several years prior and so had The String Stealers, a band that I had played with for a long time. The town was booming with coal and oil. Jim and Betty were the true pioneers of our family.

One night as Jackie, Dawn and I sat at my mother's house in Bradenton, Florida, the town where I was born and raised, the phone rang. It was Jim.

"Hello, David, is that you?" We had a bad connection, and Jim was a little deaf in one ear — due to his years in the Navy, listening to jet engines, I suppose.

"Yes, it's me," I said loud enough for him to hear.

"Would you like to come to Wyoming?" he asked with a lilt in his voice. That lilt seemed to often be with Jim, and I was pleased to hear it.

"Well, I don't —"

Before I could finish, he interrupted with, "Hold on. There's someone here who wants to talk to you."

"Hello, David?" came a meek voice that I recognized right away.

"Hello, Robert. How are you?"

Robert Rosier was the father and leader of the band I had played with for so many years before they had all decided to head west.

"There's work here, and we sure could use a singer," he said with that little grin I knew was on his face without even seeing it.

"I don't even know how to spell 'Wyoming,' " I laughed into the phone. "Wyoming's a long way from the South."

He laughed and said, "I know it is, but it sure is a pretty place, and you know how hard it was for me to leave the South."

"Yeah, I do, Robert. That was quite a feat. Have I got some time to think about it?"

"We need you pretty quick."

Jim came back on the line and told me he had a job waiting for me. I told him I would call him back and let him know. I gave the receiver to my mother who immediately began giving her eldest son a good talking to about trying to get her youngest son to leave the town where she felt he should stay. She carried on for some time with Jim while Jackie and I discussed Wyoming.

"I grew up in South Dakota," Jackie said in a serious tone. "It's cold there, and I'm sure it's cold in Wyoming."

I had never been out west, and in my heart I was aching to go. Jim and Robert had made it sound so grand, and Betty's letters

always painted a beautiful picture of the new country that they
now explored. She talked of mountains and streams, antelope
and deer. That was where I wanted to be.

Jackie agreed, and we had a yard sale. We sold everything
we felt we didn't need and some things we should have kept. Soon
we hit the road with $1,500, a golden retriever named Chivas
Regal and a black cat we called Brandy.

• • •

"It's gettin' late, David. You better get some rest," Floyd
finally broke my chain of thought.

"Boy, I've just been a driftin', huh? What time is it?"

"It's after midnight."

"After midnight? I recorded a song once called 'After Midnight.' It was a song about —"

"David," he interrupted. "We're a ways from the bunk, and
we need to head on back. You need to rest." He yawned, cup-
ping his hand over his mouth to hide the yawn. I had no idea we
had walked so far.

Back in the camper, as I lay in bed pondering the day, I
started thinking about Floyd. He is a good friend, I thought, glancing his way. He just listens as I go on about nothing in particular.

Snicker nudged my hand which was dangling beside my
bed. He looked at me with those sad eyes as though he had read
my thoughts.

"You're a good listener, too, boy," I said as he encouraged
me to pet him. "Get to sleep now. Tomorrow's a comin' at us." I
spoke softly, trying not to wake Floyd. As I gave in to exhaustion,
I suddenly realized that tomorrow was already upon us.

Lincoln looked like a giant of a city to me as I approached
from the northwest. I had been through so many small towns of
late that it was overwhelming to see such a large place. Overwhelming as it was with its heavy traffic, I was happy to be
there. I soon sought out Highway 2, my route through a new
and exciting place that I hoped to pass through only once on
foot.

Mick and Renee Kovar were a sight for a tired man's eyes as they pulled onto the shoulder.

"We came to walk a little with you," Mick said, as I hugged them both. Renee was Bud's daughter. They had made Lincoln their home.

"Sure good to see you," I said and then smiled with joy. Renee had already turned her attention to Snicker while Mick and I talked about music.

"I've got you an interview at the station where I work," Mick said with his huge smile as we broke into our stride down that Lincoln highway.

"That's great, Mick. Thanks so much."

"You deserve it. You've come a long way."

That meant a lot to me, coming from Mick. He was one of the finest musicians I knew. When he sang a song, he could warm the coldest of hearts.

We walked until night was nearly upon us, talking of the days behind me and of those I had not yet faced.

"How far did we walk, David?" Renee asked as we sat down to wait for Floyd.

"We did about 8 miles," I said with a grin, knowing she was happy about the time the three of us had shared.

"Eight miles! That's great! Eight miles, Mick," she said as she gently took his arm. He smiled at her with love, and she at him, causing my heart to drift homeward.

As they bid me goodbye, or I should say "good journey," Mick said, "I'll see you tomorrow," and gave me a little pat on the shoulder.

"You bet," I said loud enough for all of Lincoln to hear. I gave Renee a hug, knowing I would not see her again in the months ahead. As they left me, I felt that emptiness coming back.

"Well, good buddy, we'll be in Missouri soon, and the press is lovin' your story," Floyd said.

"I don't want the folks at the Opry to think I'm some kind of a nut."

"They won't. Once they talk to you, they'll know you're sincere."

"Think they will, Floyd? Do you really think they will talk to me?"

"I'm sure of it," he declared with unwavering certainty.

"I can't talk to anyone at the Opry until I've made it there," I said with a nervous feeling about me. "I want to make it; then I'll feel I've earned the right to ask to sing there, but not until then."

"I understand what you mean and know how strong you feel about it. We better head for a nesting spot. You look like you could use a little shut eye."

He could not have spoken truer words. The day had taken a lot from me, but my friends had softened the blow.

"Do you mind gettin' a late start tomorrow?" Floyd asked as if baiting me.

"Why's that?" I asked, letting him lead me to the meat of his reason for asking.

He turned to me with that little grin and a sparkle in his eye.

"I've got you some interviews lined up first thing in the morning, and it might hold you up a bit."

"You do, huh?" I said in a teasing tone.

"Yes, sir, one in Iowa, one back in North Platte and the one with Mick." He was beaming all over as he spoke.

"How are we gonna be at all those places at once?" I questioned with a devilish grin.

"By phone," he said with pride. For many years he had worked hard for our country music foundation in Wyoming, never expecting anything of monetary value, only the satisfaction of doing a good job. Now he was on his way to Nashville.

This was a dream come true for him.

"You've worked hard," I said after a silence.

"That's what I'm here for," he said as we slowed to a stop. I wanted to tell Floyd about the dogs, but could not.

"Well, I sure do appreciate you, my friend."

"Just keep on walkin' and bein' yourself, David. That's all it'll take."

"The Walking Cowboy. What a handle, huh?" I said as I crawled out of the camper, stiff and sore from head to foot, and walked toward the sign that advertised food.

"It might just be something you'll always be remembered for, David."

I pondered what he said. Neither one of us spoke for some time until finally I said, "I think I can still make Palmyra tomorrow, even with the interviews."

"Wherever you get to, that's where we'll be. Walk what you can and no more," he said with a hint of fatherly advice in his words.

June 7 had been a good day. My spirits were at a peak as I gazed out the window into the darkness. "It's been a good one," I spoke beneath my breath. As I reflected upon the events of the day, my thoughts raced to the coming one, and I wanted to think no more.

10

Frank and the Fat Man

The words "June the eighth, nineteen and eighty eight" were written at the top of the page that was to start a new day (Day 40) west of Lincoln, Nebraska. I had made some good miles the day before and was eager to be on the road. Soon the sounds of the city were behind me, and I was at peace with the countryside. The morning was beautiful. Streaks of amber and gold graced the blue sky to my east. I was glad to once again be taking a back road to new horizons.

I walked with great big strides and found myself talking about many different things that did not matter because there was not a soul to listen. The only sound was a farmer's tractor in a nearby field.

"Why am I doing this?" I said to Snicker, but he never looked my way.

"I walk and I talk, I talk and I walk, I walk and I . . . Snap out of it!" I screamed so loud that Snicker jumped and cowed down as if I had beaten him.

"Oh, Snicker, I'm so sorry, boy," I said as I knelt down and tenderly touched his head. He looked at me with uncertainty in his eyes as to what I might do next. "It's just me, ole boy. Nothing you've done. My mind's playin' tricks on me again." He was shaking all over as I rubbed him and held him close. "You get a bath today, fella," I said with excitement in my voice, hoping to change his mood.

A young couple we had met some days ago in the tavern in Odessa had asked us to stop and see them when we got to Lincoln. "I work in a vet's office in Lincoln. If you bring Snicker I'll give him a nice bath," she had said as she gave him kisses and talked to him in baby talk.

"Remember the girl who promised you the bath, boy?" I asked as if I thought he might answer. This did not impress him one bit. In fact, I knew he didn't like baths. "You'll love it, and you need it," I said boldly before breaking into a cheerful stride.

"Today I will trade a day of my life for a new experience," was a thought I pondered over for quite some time. "I hope it is an experience I will long remember," I finally said aloud.

Snicker cocked his eyes toward me only slightly, as if he were skittish of me.

"I wish you could talk, Snicker," I said softly, and his ear twitched at the sound of his name. As I uttered that statement, I realized that even though Snicker never had and never would talk, he communicated well with his eyes and his motions. I smiled and winked at my little friend, as he looked back to see if I was there, like he had done a thousand times since we left home.

"Did you wink back?" I blurted out. "Of course you didn't." I looked closer at the speckled-faced pup's eyes that turned once more my way. "Well, maybe you did, maybe you did."

Floyd took Snicker to the vet for the bath as I continued to walk. I made Floyd promise to bring him back as soon as he was bathed. I knew they would be gone for several hours.

After a while, I began changing my socks and tending to a hot spot that had menaced me since early light. There was a slight breeze that made me want to seek shade and sleep for a time. I might have done just that if an old Ford pickup had not pulled over.

"Hello," a man said with a thundering voice as he got out and limped my way. "My name's Sam."

For reasons I will never know, I felt no fear or danger from the man who approached me. I could see plain enough that he was an older man. He wore a white T-shirt and bib overalls. His hair was graying, but I could not see if he was bald on the top since he had on an old felt hat that covered his head.

He wore the shoes of a working man, and his jaw had a slight bulge on one side. I was sure he had a plug of his favorite tobacco in there, and it made my mouth water.

"Howdy, I'm David Stewart."

"Are you the Walking Cowboy I been reading about?" he asked with a big smile, as he spit and confirmed my thoughts.

"Yes, sir, I'm him. Do you have any more of that chew?" I spoke all in one breath. I had not had a chew of tobacco in a while, and he had tempted me.

"I sure do," he replied with a laugh, as he cut me off a plug.

"About half, that's all I need, sir," I said as he handed it to me.

"Save the rest for later then," he said as he folded his knife and slipped it back in his trousers.

"You've taken on a chore, ain't ya, son?" He sat down alongside me in the rough grass.

"Yes, sir, I believe I have," I replied as I looked into a face graced with wisdom.

"Where's your dog?" he asked outright.

"He's gettin' a bath back in Lincoln. He'll be out soon."

"I'm on my way to Lincoln to pick up a few parts. I've got a little farm near the line. Been seeing and hearing about you, so when I come up on you, I figured I'd say hello." He continued to talk as if he'd known me forever.

"I'm sure glad you did," I said with a bulge in my cheek.

We talked of nothing in particular, just two men passing the time. Soon he bid me good journey. I hated to see him go and watched as he drove his red Ford away, becoming a blur against the distant sky.

"Well, your buddy's all clean!" Floyd shouted, releasing Snicker, who came running to me.

"Thought I'd left you behind, huh?" I said to Snicker while listening to Floyd's approaching footsteps. He had a way of slapping his feet on the ground when he walked and could not keep from using his right hand when he talked.

"He looks a bit better," he said using that right hand in a pointing motion.

"He looks better, Floyd, but you look like heck. Are you feelin' okay?"

"I'm feeling mighty peaked," he replied with a hollow look in his face.

"Did you take anything?"

"No. I don't know if it's the flu or whether I'm just plain tuckered out."

"Find some shade and get some rest," I ordered.

"Can't. I've got to get to Nebraska City and talk to the paper and call Channel 7 in Omaha."

"Get some rest. I won't even be in Nebraska City until late tomorrow, and that's if I'm lucky." I spoke with enough authority for him to know I was serious.

"Mr. Snicker's been a little sick, too," he said with tired voice. Snicker seemed okay for the time being. We left Floyd on Highway 2 so he could rest.

We walked until we were 20 miles from where we needed to be. "Gotta pull up for a rest, Snicker. I feel a blister comin' on," I said as I looked for that perfect resting place. We had been walking for over 3 hours, and it was time to stop. "I wonder how Floyd's doing, Snick?" I said as I climbed up a 12-foot bank.

We found a nice shade tree that hung over the fence and ' offered us a tempting spot for a nap. There was a small farmhouse to the northeast, some distance away. "Wonder who lives there, boy?" I said to Snicker as he drank from my water bottle. He had learned mighty fast that when there was no visible water for him, this was his method of refreshment. He didn't waste much.

I had not been asleep long, or so it seemed, when the sound of a motorcycle brought me to a sitting position. It crawled to a stop beneath me, and two men got off, leaving their machine running. This could only mean they might be in a hurry to leave. The man up front was downright fat, with as much hair on his face as upon his head. His belly showed from beneath his shirt. He spit into the wind and cursed as it blew back at him. The one at the rear got off first with ease and was well built. He had only a day or two of beard and dark hair that was pulled back and tied with a scarf. He removed his jacket and draped it over the back of the bike, as if to hide the license plate, but it was getting pretty hot out, so maybe that was his reason for doing so.

"Howdy," I said, with nervous breath, looking down the embankment and thinking how glad I was to be up there. I had an uneasy feeling, and Snicker began to growl low by my side, which only intensified the mood. For the longest moment, they held their eyes on me, the fat one glancing to the road at times, then back. Their eyes were unkind, and this was my clue to be careful. I was a thinker, and I began to work things out in my mind.

"Howdy," I said again, trying to get a clear picture of these two guys' outlook on life.

The fat one looked again at the road as if a little nervous, then snarled. "Give us your money, man. Don't give us no shit!" he shouted, as if to test my strength. I did not expect this but had been warned by more than one friend to be cautious on the road. This was something you read about that happens to somebody else. There I was, face to face with it.

I could see that the fat man was only a mouthpiece for the one with cold eyes who was staring at me. The sun soon broke a sweat upon his brow and, as I looked long into those eyes, I knew that if this man were in a war, there would be no prisoners. I stood slowly, trying to keep my legs under me. The fear was mounting inside me, and I knew I must control it. I felt for a moment that I would get diarrhea any time. I was trying my best not to let the cold one see my fear but knew as I looked at him that he did know. If you cage an animal and put his back to the wall, he might do anything to survive. A man in this same position would do the same if pushed, and I believed this man would study his prey before being careless.

Unlike his eager companion, the muscular one was a cautious man. The fat one would have charged up the hill at his leader's command, never thinking of what I might do. Although the fat man was a threat, my attention still lay on the man who studied my every move.

My legs had become stiff from sitting, and I did not feel very agile. Sweat poured from my brow, and the palms of my hands were clammy. I looked back toward the road I had traveled that morning. "Please come, Floyd," I spoke beneath my breath. "No!" I continued with only lip movement. "Don't come. They will only hurt you, too," was the thought that made me weak in my stomach. I knew if he came, it would only be worse for us both because he would stop and try to defend me.

"Hey, listen," I said, trying to be authoritative. "I don't have any money, so just get on your bike and leave me alone!"

The fat man laughed. "He's scared, Frank. Look at him. He's scared."

The one he called Frank whipped his head around and glared at him, as if he might strike him for saying his name aloud.

I used the brief moment their attention was away from me to my advantage. I quickly stepped over the barbed wire behind me. Snicker reacted almost at the same instant and leaped be'tween two strands. My foot came to rest upon a limb that had fallen from a tree in past days. I knelt and retrieved it in a swift motion, but my hand trembled as I tried to grasp it firmly.

"What good do you think that'll do?" the heavy-set one jeered at me.

I turned my eyes to Frank again, wishing I could hear his voice. I wanted to break and run, but my legs were not with me. I looked at the one who threatened me out loud and said, "I'm going to bash your fat head if you come over this fence, mister!" then moved my eyes back to the boss of this pawn who had taunted me. "Then it'll be just me and you, pardner," I continued, hoping for a reply of some kind or to see if he'd make a mistake.

He said nothing but stared at me, lighting a cigarette and dropping the match in the dry grass. I hoped it would start a blaze and offer me an escape, but he stamped it out, without looking down.

What do I do? What do I do? I thought in anguish and felt the cold of a Northern Wind crawl all over me as I stared back into those dark eyes. I knew my position was a pretty sound one, and I could surely get the fat man, who I knew would come first. The other would bide his time. With my free hand, I unzipped my pouch and felt for my knife, unfolding it with my fingers and leaving it concealed.

I glanced at the farmhouse, only to dismiss the thought for fear of bringing harm to someone there. I looked at the wire between us and knew I could use it to my advantage. I had seen the damage barbed wire could do to a man. I began to back up a few steps as they advanced toward my position. "Run, David, run," kept racing through my head, but Snicker was growling and standing his ground.

I saw a white truck from the corner of my eye and turned quickly. It was slowing down. Help was here! "Should I cry out?" was the question that engulfed me. Yes, yes. I have to, but the thought was in vain as I watched the truck turn north on the gravel road that led toward the farmhouse.

As I looked at Frank, he smiled at me, as if to say, "Go ahead and run. We'll get him, too."

It's the farmer, I thought, as the driver looked upon what I hoped he would see as danger. I whimpered low to myself. "Please keep goin', please, Mr. Farmer." He glanced back once more, as he drove toward home.

"Maybe he'll call the law," I exclaimed, as I turned to my

offenders with club in hand. Anger was building within me for these two who had harm in their minds for me and anyone else that got in their way. I knew as I looked at him that Frank had thought what I had spoken. He knew there was a chance that the man might call the law and that maybe I would not be as easy to take as he first thought.

"Let's go!" Frank snapped, with fury in his voice.

"But what about . . ." and the fat man's speech was cut off.

"Let's go, damnit!" Frank ordered as he turned away.

I wanted to curse him as he walked to his machine but held myself still. I felt as if my bladder would release at any moment, He looked back at me once more before pulling away, leaving his coat to hide the plates. The fat man gave me the finger and cursed me and my mother. Frank only stared. Then I thought I saw him smile. I stood long in that spot, my body still shaking. My hands were unsteady and my heart felt as if it might stop at any time.

I wondered if the man in the white truck might be my guardian angel as I watched him come part way up the gravel road and stop. I was on his land or so I assumed, and he was a cautious man. I stepped over the fence and waved to him. He did not respond, but watched until I was gone.

"Well, I think maybe I could have taken them, boy," I said some 30 minutes later, still looking back at my trail. "What do you think?" I said with a shaky voice. "Probably a good thing you can't talk. You'd tell me just how scared I was. Thanks for stickin' by me, boy. You're one to ride the river with."

"I will never forget the one called Frank," I said into the wind. "Those cold eyes — I'm glad they're gone."

I paused to look back once more. "He would not have been satisfied with money, my little friend. No, sir, he was evil itself, and I hope we don't have to face more like him," I said with a bad taste in my mouth, as if I might lose what was in my stomach.

I decided that I would not speak of it to Floyd. I wanted to in the worst way but knew I could not. He would only try to stay close to me and would not get his work done. Trying to babysit me all day would be stressful for both of us.

"No, I'll not breathe a word of this to him, Snicker. This is between you and me."

As the miles fell behind us, I felt that the evil pair would not return, at least not this day. I trembled often at the thought of Frank and his companion — but mostly of Frank. Those cold, piercing eyes almost put me to my knees in fear, a fear which I had never experienced from another human being. The thought of alternative outcomes of the situation chilled me to the very bone. "Could I have taken them?" I wondered over and over.

Inside there was the Clint Eastwood part of me that wanted to believe I could have.

"Thank you, Lord," I whispered. "Thank you for the fact that I now only have to wonder if I could have. Thank you for carrying me when my troubles are the darkest."

That thought took me back again to my loved ones. We were stranded in a snowstorm on Highway 212 on our way home from Aberdeen, South Dakota, in the early spring of 1985. A snowplow cleared the way for us and some other cars for a few miles, as far as the county line.

"You can't leave us!" a man close to the plow cried out in the desperation that we all felt.

"I've gone as far as I can go," the driver said. "I'll call ahead and get help for you."

We wanted to believe him as he pulled away and the snow came down heavier and heavier. The driver of a motor home took the lead and pushed on until he could go no further. The road was a solid sheet of white that showed no trace of a clear path. We could see the lights of the vehicles that approached us from the west and began to pass the word. "They called for help!" someone shouted. The man had indeed called ahead, and we soon had a four-wheel vehicle hooking onto our bumper.

The men who were helping us had consumed a few drinks and seemed to be enjoying this storm, which could have taken many lives that day. They pulled us at speeds of more than 50 mph through the blinding snow, or at least it felt so. We fish-tailed from side to side so badly that I could hardly keep my car on the road. I was mad at myself for letting this happen to my family but knew the storm would have otherwise buried us in time.

I fought the wheel to maintain control behind this crazed person whom I had placed in control of our lives. Jackie's voice was filled with fear as she tried to speak words of encouragement to me. The excitement and desperation were evident in both our voices, as Dawn, with assurance in her voice, gently said from the back seat, "Why are you guys acting like this? You have always said to have faith in the Lord. Well, he'll take care of us." She was right, of course, but sometimes it's hard to understand this when danger is near. Fear has a way of overwhelming the human spirit. Children who are not haunted by past fears can teach us if we just listen. We made it safely into the town of Faith, South Dakota.

As my mind came back to the present, I pondered over what had happened with Frank and the fat man. In the distance I glimpsed a young hawk on the rise. I sat down to watch for a spell and my thoughts returned to my daughter. I felt the tears welling up inside as the sun began its evening ritual on the far horizon. Basking in the silence, I watched until it was no more.

11

Through Iowa

I fully intended to look up the definition of "loneliness" when I finished my walk. I wanted to see if Webster's hit it on the head or not. I now knew what loneliness was but didn't know if I could find the right words to describe it.

Floyd had been sick with fever and vomiting. I worried about his health. He constantly had a cough and brushed it off as allergies. Maybe so, but it made a body worry. It was very late on June 9 (Day 41) when I made it to a place called Syracuse and found Floyd so very sick along the roadside.

"Think maybe we could take a day off, David?" he asked weakly.

"Yes, we can. We're still ahead of schedule, and you need to weather this out."

I could see he was relieved. I began telling him of Channel 7 coming out to interview me and thought about telling him of the two varmints that had tried to corral me earlier.

"I've got a great idea. Let's take the day off tomorrow and go to Nebraska City for a rest. I can make it there by noon. We'll go to Auburn for the rodeo, then return to Nebraska City and start fresh from there the day after tomorrow. By the way, Floyd, I'm changing my route."

"What?" he asked as he sat up. "You can't!"

I wanted to tell him why — I was afraid of seeing the two bikers once more along my current route — but couldn't.

"Why? Why would you change routes?"

"I want to go through Iowa so we can add another state to our route."

It was about an extra 10 or 15 miles the way I now wanted to go, but I felt a need to do it. I hated having to lie to him.

"It's extra miles. Remember we said we'd cut across the corner of Nebraska, through Auburn into Missouri to save miles."

"I know, but I've changed my mind, okay? I want to change the route," I insisted.

"Okay. It's your walk. You change it if you want to," he sighed.

"Thank you. Now lie down and get some rest."

He slept for hours while I thought of my new route and hoped it would be better and safer for me in case my would-be attackers came back. "At least it has better-traveled roads," I babbled aloud.

"What'd you say?" Floyd sat up and asked.

"Oh, nothin'. Just thinkin' out loud. Sorry to wake you," I said, while admonishing myself for the babbling.

"Oh, that's okay. I'm feelin' a little better now."

"Think you can eat now? Maybe a little soup or something?"

"Not yet," he replied. "Maybe later."

• • •

The next afternoon we fell asleep in the Auburn rodeo grounds. Waking up from my nap, I felt a little tired and sick myself. After taking a couple of Tylenol, I emerged from our little home to find laughter about me as I watched all the cowboys and cowgirls getting ready for their rodeo events. Newcomers arrived, pulling their horses or homes on wheels.

"Howdy. My name's David," I said to a cowboy who was looking over the rodeo stock.

"Mine's Jim," he said.

"You ridin'?"

"No. I don't ride much anymore. I'm the rodeo bullfighter."

"Well, I'll be. I wrote a song once about rodeo bullfighters."

"I'd like to hear it."

"Well, I'm supposed to sing here today, so maybe you will." We talked a spell before I went back to check on Snicker and Floyd.

Floyd was up and ready to go when I came through the door.

"How ya feelin'?"

"A lot better, but our little buddy is still mighty sick," he said with concern in his voice.

"I wonder what's wrong with him, Floyd," I said as I laid back and started drifting into a sleepy state of mind.

"Don't know, but the vet in David City said to just keep givin' him lots of water and to watch him closely." Floyd left, and I drifted in and out of sleep for some time. Soon I noticed him peeking in at me with a smile as big as Texas.

"Do you want to ride in the Grand Entry, David?"

"Well, I hadn't thought of it, but it would be great," I replied with excitement.

"Good. I'll tell them you said yes."

"Wait just a minute, and I'll go with you."

Floyd introduced me to Hank, who seemed to be in charge and who showed me to my horse.

"Fifteen minutes," he said.

"What?" I asked as I stared at the huge black gelding who seemed a little fidgety to me.

"Fifteen minutes, boy. That's how long before we ride. You can ride, can't you?" he asked with a queer little smile.

"Yes, sir, I can. Is he a little spirited?"

"Just a mite," he said as he smiled again and walked away.

"Don't mind him. He's just trying to see what you're made of," said a young cowboy on a bay behind me.

"Well, I don't want to get on a rank horse and take a chance of gettin' dumped in the dirt. That's for sure," I exclaimed.

"He ain't rank. Just a high-spirited sort, but listens well if you get his respect," the cowboy explained.

"All right. Then I'll ride him."

As I stepped into the stirrup to mount, he sidestepped just a little, and I swung into the saddle. Hank looked back at me from up front, took a little pinch of chewing tobacco, placed it in his cheek and smiled a friendly smile.

We rode out with pride, holding Old Glory and circling the arena. I felt free on the black horse and wished I was at my brother's Bitter Creek Ranch. Soon all the cowboys and cowgirls were behind the chutes, ready to ride.

My mind drifted homeward again, and I suddenly missed the pungent smell of sage and the sight of a wheat field flowing in the Wyoming wind. I closed my eyes and could hear the sound of a rippling stream meandering down the canyons of the Big Horn Mountains. The image was vivid, and I could see my bobber begin to dance upon the water as a rainbow trout took my bait. The present sounds about me were lost as I pictured a lone coyote calling from a distant ridge — a haunting sound, but one I longed to hear. The smell of the livestock made me want to be on horseback with my brother, Jack, rounding up a few strays and talking of nothing that mattered — just being brothers. I could even hear the sound of creaking leather as I saw myself swinging up in the saddle on a crisp fall morning with the sun just on the rise.

I was so lost in my thoughts that I jumped when I heard my name announced. I was about to run to the camper to retrieve my guitar, but as soon as I turned around, there stood Floyd with my guitar in hand and a big grin.

"Give 'em a good one, ole buddy," he cried as I climbed the stairs to the announcer's box.

• • •

    I went to sleep later that evening with thoughts of the day and the songs that I had sung for these folks. They were good to me, and I had made some new friends.

    At 11:00 p.m., I awoke in a cold sweat with my breath coming in gasps. I began to vomit the minute I opened the door. My whole body shook as I tried to control the sickness. I felt as if I would die unless I gained control. My head was clammy from fever. Floyd never woke as I wrenched with pain from the vomiting. He had been so sick that he fell into a deep sleep for the first time in quite a while. A little after 1:00 a.m., I lay down again to try and rest.

    Headlights appeared in the park, and I wondered which cowboy had been out so late that night and if he was sick from his own type of poison. Several times in the night I awoke to relieve my sick stomach until there was nothing left to vomit. I still lay awake at 5:30 a.m., feeling as if every bull in the pens next to where we slept had run over me in the night.

    Floyd looked up at me and asked, "Are you restless, David?"

    "I could have died, and you wouldn't have even noticed!" I snapped, then wanted to take it right back. "I'm sorry."

    "What's wrong?"

    "I've been mighty sick all night, throwing up and burning with fever."

    "Boy, I wonder what we got. We've all been so sick."

    "I think I know. I think we've got food poisoning because Snicker has been down, too. He's been eatin' our leftovers. Makes sense to me."

    "I hope not, but it could be. I'll clean these utensils real good today. I'll boil everything. Jackie warned me to keep this stuff clean. We don't want Mr. Snicker or anyone else to be feelin' poorly," Floyd said as he patted Snicker gently on the head.

    "Probably a good thought," I said through an attempted smile. We talked for some time. I felt "weak as water," as my mother would say.

Rap, rap, rap was the sound on the side of the camper.

"Well, who the heck could that be?" I said to Floyd as he opened the door. I was face to face with my brother, Jack, and my sister-in-law, Ada. They had driven from their home which was 50 miles north of Gillette. .

"Well, I'll be darned. How'd you find us?" I exclaimed.

"I knew your route. We looked at the map and figured you'd be either here or in Nebraska City."

"Well, we're going back to Nebraska City today. We only drove down here for the rodeo. I'm changing my route and goin, through Iowa."

"Why's that?" Jack asked.

"Just to add another state to our trip," Floyd replied.

I wanted to tell Jack the truth, but I held it back.

"It's sure nice to see you two," I said. "I'm mighty sick to-day so don't know for sure if I can walk or not."

"What's wrong?" Ada asked.

"I don't really know. A virus or maybe a little food poison-ing from something we ate," I replied.

"Are you taking anything?" she asked.

"No, can't keep anything down right now," I said.

We sat around for hours and visited while I tried to feel bet-ter. About 3:00 p.m., Jack and I started walking from the point where I had stopped off. It was nice having him by my side. I was still sick and so was Snicker, but having Jack there made it more bearable. I knew if Frank and the fat one came back, the odds would be in my favor.

Floyd went on into Missouri while Ada made trips ahead of us, taking pictures of us along the way. Soon we had crossed over the Iowa state line and would cross the Missouri line if I could hold out.

"Sure seems strange crossing two state lines in just a mat-ter of hours like we're gonna do. I've been in Nebraska for a Whole month and then bang, we'll cross two state lines in no time."

We talked about my trip and what was to come. I looked at Jack and felt proud. He'd found his ideal ranch in Wyoming a few years back, and now he and Ada were working side by side to make it produce.

"You'd better chain that dog up, David. He's gonna get run over," Jack argued.

"I haven't had to chain him yet, Jack."

"You haven't been on major highways to speak of yet."

"Those back roads I've been on are more dangerous than this interstate. I've got lots more room to walk out here."

"Yeah, and lots more cars, too."

"He's mighty sick, Jack. I don't know what to do for him," I sighed.

"Get him some raw hamburger or liver."

"You think that'll help?" I perked up.

"Yep. Try it. I think he needs some raw meat."

I was willing to try just about anything since Snicker was going downhill. He normally ate dried dog food but had not been interested in it during his illness. Dogs always seem to go for raw meat, so I was certainly willing to give Jack's suggestion a try.

David Stewart

One sick puppy

We didn't make the Missouri line that day. We were too worn down to go the extra miles. Jack was ready to stop, too. His feet were a little tender from walking on the rocky shoulder of the road. He didn't like the shoes I had lent him to walk in, but he made the best of it.

The Rock Port, Missouri exit was where we settled that night. It was one of the few times we drove ahead at night to sleep. I hated it because the next morning when Floyd returned me to my marked point, I felt like I was backtracking.

"This is about how far we'll get tomorrow, Jack," I said

"Yeah. We're about 20 miles from our marked point. We might make a little more, but I'm not pushin' it these days."

We talked into the night about my trip.

"You're over halfway, David," Floyd said with pleasure.

Halfway, I thought. What a good feeling.

Five miles from the Missouri line, on June 12 (Day 44), Ada dropped Jack and me off. Several times I almost blurted out my encounter with Frank and the fat man, but I held it back. It took a long time to make the 20 miles to Rock Port. We stopped many times to visit and investigate old buildings.

The next morning brought a much better day for me. I was feeling almost up to par, more than I could say for my little buddy. He just lay around until I moved. Then he tried his best to keep up. He had bad diarrhea.

It was ever so hard to say goodbye to Jack and Ada, but I knew they had to get home and that I must move southward toward St. Joe, Missouri. They bought $66 worth of T-shirts and gave me $14 extra for gas before pulling out. I knew they didn't need all those shirts. They were just trying to help out.

I decided to take the day off and rest with Snicker since I was still ahead of schedule. I noticed that Jack was feeling a little under the weather before he left. I prayed for a safe trip for them as he and Ada drove away, and I watched until they were out of sight.

"David? You okay?" Floyd asked. He could see my tears and gave me a little pat on the shoulder. "Hard, seein' them go, ain't it?"

An old church near Rock Port

David Stewart

"Yes, it is. Sometimes I just want to quit and go home to my family and forget this whole thing. Sometimes I wonder if anyone will even care when I get to Nashville," I said insecurely.

"Sure they will, David. Sure they will."

I confided in my companion, "Oh, Floyd, I'm breaking up inside awfully bad. I've come a long way, but I might be all in."

He looked straight at me and said, "You ain't no quitter, or else I wouldn't be out here with you. You can make it!"

I knew he believed this with all his heart, but my body was crying out, "No, no, no! Let me rest! I've had enough!"

"It's going to get worse before it gets any better, Floyd. We haven't even hit real hot weather yet. They're calling this the drought of 1988 already. It's on the radio and it's bound to get much worse," I predicted darkly.

"Then I'll just have to stay close to you and give you water more often."

What was he feeling inside? Would he stay with me or one day say, "I've had it," and disappear? I think not.

"Maybe I can't make it. I've only come halfway," I whimpered softly to myself.

Floyd overheard me and said, "You know, David, there's some who think that a half glass of water is half empty, but the man who is no quitter knows it is really half full."

I smiled at him and replied, "We'll make it."

He nodded and asked me if I would like to see Rock Port.

PART 2
MISSOURI

12

The sufferings of Snicker

Rock Port was a small town. June 13 (Day 45) was the date of our day off, and Snicker and I were exhausted. A grocery store caught my eye as we moved down Main Street. "Pull in here, Floyd. I need some meat for Snicker," I said, remembering Jack's words and missing his company.

I had grown up working with Jack, and he had taught me much in life. I came from a Southern family that used a lot of old remedies. I remember my grandmother, my mother's mother, giving me old cures when I was young. Later, when my son, Chris, was cutting teeth, she said, "David, go out and kill me a chicken and bring me the warm blood. We'll rub it on his gums. It'll help him cut them teeth." My grandmother was blind but knew us all by sound.

"No, Grandma, he's okay," I said, as I took him and slipped out, knowing she was mad as a hornet.

I waited some time before going to see her again. She was still mad, but my son's teeth were all in. She held him and felt his face. "He's a pretty one, got big hands," she said.

I was smiling at the memory of my grandmother when I entered the grocery store. A lady recognized me from a TV interview and asked if I was the one walking to Nashville.

"Yes, ma'am."

"Where's your dog?"

"He's outside in the camper, ma'am. He's not feeling very well."

"Could we see him?" she pressed.

"Yes, ma'am, you can."

Floyd left the grocery store on these words and soon returned with Snicker in his arms.

"Oh, how cute! Just look at that face," the lady exclaimed. I smiled at Floyd and he at me.

"He's a charmer, that Snicker boy," I remarked.

"Could we get a picture of you and your dog?" the lady asked.

"Yes, you can, and I thank you for asking."

Snicker gave them his best, but I could tell he was feeling bad and soon excused him from the crowd.

Floyd and I talked on and on with these town folks as others Gathered.

Soon Floyd had Snicker tucked away in the camper.

"Can't leave Mr. Snicker in there long, David. It's gettin' mighty hot out."

"I know, Floyd. We'll be goin' soon."

I didn't want to leave all this kindness and human contact. These folks were my strength this day.

Floyd had disappeared for a time and as I stepped from the grocery store door, saying goodbye to my new friends, I spotted him across the street in a phone booth.

Always on the job, I thought with a smile. The man is truly dedicated.

He caught a glimpse of me and motioned me over to him.

"I've got Kathy Novak on the line from the News Record in Gillette, David. Talk to her."

I shook my head, but he insisted. I didn't want to talk to the press at that moment. It was as if I wanted to go and hide. He handed me the phone.

"Hello?" I said reluctantly.

"Hi, David!" she resounded joyfully. "Floyd tells me you've been ill."

I gave him a sour look as I replied, "Just a little. Nothing to worry about."

"We all worry about you, David. Gillette is following you with great interest and enthusiasm."

"That's so nice to hear, Kathy. Please tell everyone I said hello and that I sure do miss home."

I could feel myself getting homesick, and I think she sensed it.

"Well, I better let you go, David. I know how busy you must be," she said.

"Thank you, Kathy. Goodbye."

Hanging up the phone, I wanted to be home now more than ever. I could not help myself. I had to call Jackie. I asked Floyd to hold on for just a minute.

"Hello," came a familiar voice.

"Hi, honey. I'm in Rock Port. Did you get your song?"

"Yes, I did, and I cried. So did my mom," Jackie said.

"I'm glad you liked it," I said with joy in my voice.

"I love it, honey. Thank you."

We talked for a short time, and I stared toward home when we hung up.

"Feel like goin' to the local paper, David?" Floyd asked.

"Okay."

"About six weeks left, David. Only six more weeks."

"Not much if you say it fast, Floyd."

He chuckled, and off to the press we walked, but not before stopping to get the little guy with the cute face. We talked with the local press until I felt Snicker growing tired, then we found a shady place to camp.

"You know, Floyd, that was a neat little town."

"Sure was, David. One to remember."

We had our camper under a tree at the KOA campground, but the heat was finally upon us, and the flies seemed to be breeding before our very eyes.

"Snicker? Snicker?"

He looked up at me, his eyes drooping. "You're under it, aren't you, boy? Wish I knew what to do."

He tried to hold his head upright, but soon relaxed himself as I stroked him gently along his drawn and weary face. He seemed to be near death, and I was horrified at the thought that he might die because of me.

"I'm sorry, Snicker. I never should have brought you on this dreadful trip. I'll never forgive myself if you die because of something I yearn for!"

I bathed his face with water, and it seemed to be a comfort for a moment or two. I had no idea what was causing his illness, but suspected it could be a series of things. He had sustained shock from the two depraved animals in Nebraska and had inhaled insecticides when crops were being sprayed along the back roads. My mind began to ponder all the days gone by, wondering if it might give me more clues to the reason for Snicker's sickness.

"I suppose you could have eaten something rancid along the road, boy," I said softly as I placed two aspirins into his mouth and massaged his throat, causing him to swallow. He retched and I thought be would vomit, but he gasped instead, then swallowed hard as if he knew he must take the aspirin. I continued rubbing him as this seemed to be his only comfort. I offered him water, but he refused to drink. I took small amounts of the lukewarm liquid and eased it into his mouth, feeling sick myself at the thought of losing a dear friend. He eventually gave in to slumber. His breathing became so wan and hollow that at times I thought he was about to expire. I knelt beside the small and feeble pup and softly pleaded, "Don't wither on me, boy." The thought of continuing the walk without him was unbearable.

When he was finally at peace and seemed to be breathing

regularly again, I felt the need to strum my guitar. As I slipped away from his side, he moaned deeply but never opened his eyes.

The evening breeze was welcome as I sat with my guitar. Floyd was doing our laundry, but soon appeared with four people.

"These folks are from West Virginia," he said as he introduced the people.

"Been hearin' about you, young man," one of them said.

"They heard about you on the 'Ralph Emery Show,' David," Floyd said with excitement. Ralph Emery was a disc jockey for many years in Nashville and later had a program called "The Morning Show." He was also the star and host of a TV show called "Nashville Now."

"You mean Nashville Now," I asked.

"Yeah. They were talking about you the other night," he said.

"Well, I'll be!" I said with joy. That thought hung with me into the night as I sang for these folks and others who gathered about. I signed pictures and sold T-shirts for a spell before going to bed.

"I'm sure glad we met those folks," I said as I scribbled in my red book.

"Thought you would be. Thought they might bring you to a boil again," he said with satisfaction.

"You know me pretty well, ole friend."

"I just want you to be okay, and I know that it helps when you know people care about you."

I called my friend, Jim Isbell, in Nashville before going to sleep. Jim was playing drums for Jerry Lee Lewis at the time of my walk. He was also a producer and editor. I told him what the folks had said about seeing me on TV.

"I got you into Country Scene, David," he told me. Country Scene was a magazine published in Nashville.

"Wow! Thanks, Jim," I exclaimed.

"It's not much, but it all helps," he replied.

I couldn't figure Jim out. He never got very excited. He believed in me, though, and I was glad to have him as a friend.

Taking to the road called I-29 on June 14 was easy for me

after having spent time with the Rock Port folks, talking, picking and grinning. The new day proved to be a scorcher, though, and my pace slowed with the heat.

Snicker was not by my side this day. He just wasn't up to walking. This worried me terribly. I was giving him his medication and feeding him properly, but it just didn't seem to work. "He can't die, Lord," I cried out. "Please don't let him die."

I had studied my map and found the town where Buddy Boswell had his Union Mill Opry. Buddy was a man in his late 40s, with lots of personality. He conceived of, built and still operates his own Opry. When he isn't doing his weekend radio shows, he travels around and plays music with his family band. I had played a show with Buddy in Cheyenne some time ago. The guy who hired us skipped town and neither one of us got paid. Although I did not know Buddy very well, he had invited me to stop in and visit if I was ever in his neck of the woods in Missouri.

Floyd was about his routine once more, and I was alone to erase the miles that lay ahead, one step at a time. Sweat poured from my brow, soaking my shirt with the musty smell of my body. "I may not make it," I said to myself out loud, "but I would not trade these days for anything."

I was in farm country, that was plain to see, but the crops didn't look good because of the drought. To the east I saw a secondary road, and I decided to walk on it for a spell to see what adventures might come my way.

I came upon a farmer. His hat was low on his brow as I approached him. He was kneeling down near a fence post under the shade of a tree.

"Howdy. My name's David. Some call me the Walking Cowboy," I said with a smile.

"They do, huh? Why do you suppose they do that?"

I began to tell him my story. He told me his name was Clarence and that this was his farm.

"So you're walkin' to Nashville, huh? I read a little about it in the paper. Whatever gave you such a notion?"

I told him of that fateful night long ago at a truck stop where Jackie had asked me what I would do to sing on the Grand

Ole Opry.

In an attempt to impress Clarence, I tried to sound just like Jackie did when she asked that question. "My answer, Clarence, was that I would walk to Nashville, and here I am now, walkin' to Nashville."

He looked me over slowly, rolled the chew in his cheek to the other side and finally said, "Well, boy, do you think maybe she just wanted to get you out of the house?" he said, throwing back his head in laughter.

I was startled by his question, but was soon laughing right along with him. "No, sir, I don't think so," I answered through the laughter. "Well, I hope not anyway," I continued. We laughed some more.

"I'm just joking, son. You sure got a lotta brass to take off like that without knowing whether or not they'll let you sing."

"Yes, sir, but I want to show how much I love country music and hope they understand the why of it."

"Been a hot one, son," he said as he looked out over the parched fields. "This is my love, boy, this place. I've been here almost 40 years now with my missus. We've had good years and some not so good, but this one is downright bad."

I could see the hurt in his face as he went on.

"Is it all lost, Clarence? Will rain help?" I asked.

"Not much boy. It's pretty parched now. Rain could save a little, I suppose, but for the most, she's a goner."

When we finally parted ways, I watched him for a time as he rode the fields in his pickup. Then I took to the road again. Praying for his crops was useless, so I just prayed for comfort for him and somehow knew he had his comfort waiting back at the farmhouse in the form of his wife of 40 years. Occasionally I looked back, not knowing why, just looking back.

The next morning, June 15 (Day 49) I started my day talking to that darn machine again . . .

June 15 finds me in a little place by the name of Craig. I started walking late today: 7:30 a.m.

Snicker is still under the weather but wants to walk with me today. I don't know where he gets his strength. Somehow he is always giving to me, even in his time of weakness.

The Missouri sky is beautiful this day. The rain came upon me yesterday at about 5:00 p.m. and cooled things off. That coolness still lingers in the air of this morning as I step boldly. The landscape has once again changed dramatically from my past days to beautiful, rolling hillsides with rich farm ground and trees of many species. Trees are such a mystery. My home territory has very few, and here there are more than this land seems to need. Surely there are many deer to be found here, but not as easily sighted as in Wyoming. I also miss the soar of a lone eagle of a morning and the sight of a fox mousing along the back roads.

I began to pay special attention to my surroundings and to watch for wildlife. Soon I could spot a hawk in a tree and occasionally see a rabbit dart out of a hole and scurry into thick underbrush.

"You know, Snicker, we shall soon be in country with nothing but buildings. No wildlife, no trees or sagebrush; nothing but cars and more cars."

I shivered at the thought and wondered how Snicker would react to all the traffic. He had done okay in Cheyenne when we went through, but what of Kansas City and St. Louis? I dreaded the thought of such places.

The noon sun is so very hot above us now and Snicker is eating grass to help calm his stomach.

The flashing sign ahead of us read "Squaw Creek."

"Looks like a good place to rest, Snicker." He didn't care. Any place was fine with him. Parts of the huge truck stop area offered shade and rest for us, and we welcomed it.

"David, David, wake up," were the first words I heard.

"Huh?" I replied sleepy-eyed.

"I thought you might stop here. I've got the press and may-be even a TV station coming here soon from St. Joe and Mound City for interviews," he said rapidly.

"Great, Floyd. Where ya been all morning?" I laughed.

"Workin', David, workin'," he laughed right back. "If you don't mind, this will be our home tonight. After you're done walking, we'll just come back here."

"I don't mind. It's so darn hot,I'd sure like that sun to go down."

After my interviews, I walked until I could no more. We returned to Squaw Creek for the night.

"My name's Wendell Bailey, young man," were the words I heard as I looked up from our dinner table at the Squaw Valley truck stop. "I'm State Treasurer of Missouri," the voice contin-ued.

I stood up and replied, "Glad to meet you, sir. I'm David Stewart."

"Sit down, son. I know who you are. Seen you on TV so I took the liberty of introducing myself."

"My pleasure, Mr. Bailey."

"No, sir, it's my pleasure. I admire your courage."

We chatted with Mr. Bailey and his traveling companions for several hours before I excused myself.

Before retiring I called Buddy Boswell. "Hello, Buddy. This is David Stewart. I sang in Cheyenne with you a few years back."

"Yes, I remember, and now you're walkin' to Nashville. I been hearin' about it on the news."

"I want to stop by and see you, Buddy."

"Can you be here Saturday night?"

"I think so. I'll break my walk and drive in. How far are you off the interstate?"

"Not that far. I've already got the show booked. Don't know if I can work you in or not."

"That's okay. I just want to visit."

"Well, I've got Justin Tubb comin' in. Sure would you like you to meet him."

"I'll be there," I shouted, "with bells on!"

I lay awake thinking of what I might say to Justin.

13

A Foot Where a Face Should Be

The sound of a diesel engine chugging away in an almost cadence—like manner was something my senses had grown accustomed to over the weeks. As I lay in the dark listening to the train on June 16 (Day 48), I could not help wondering what Justin Tubb was going to say to me. Maybe he'd say nothing but hello. I hoped we could spend some time talking about music. The crisp morning air felt good upon my face before the sun came up to challenge me for yet another day. It was strange wanting the sun to go away. Only a short time ago I had prayed for its appearance. Is man ever truly satisfied? I wondered. "I think not," I said aloud.

Snicker seemed to be on the road to recovery. At least I hoped my intuitions were right about that. He'd sure had a rough time of it. There was a time when I thought he would surely die.

I was glad to be back on an interstate highway. The shoulders were so much nicer for walking. In many places there were secondary roads that paralleled the interstate, and they allowed me the freedom to change highways often. I walked on methodically. The humidity was heavy about me, and my feet began to burn.

"It's about 11 o'clock, Snicker. I wonder where Floyd might be. He's a worker, ole boy, a real worker. Well, if we don't see hlm soon, we'll leave a marker and go find some shade for a nap, boy. How's that sound?" Snicker cocked his head a little and did just a little bit of a dance for me. "You're gettin' better, boy. You've got a little spring in your step. What a sight to see! I surely must write about your recovery. Wait, I'll record it . . ."

Testing 1, 2, 3, ahem. Today, June 16, my friend, Snicker, is a little better in spirits, and I believe he's headed for recovery.

"Well, my little friend, I'm happy you're gettin' better," I said, as I rubbed my feet. They felt as if little pins were piercing them in every direction at once. The sound of the sweet morning was giving way to heavy traffic — traffic that I knew would only get worse as time passed.

A bird fluttered nearby in the thick brush, and Snicker's ears popped up. "Yep!" I said. "All the signs are telling me you're no longer swimming upstream, boy." I patted his head as he watched the lone bird.

Floyd found our mark on the interstate and came to the little place where Snicker and I had taken refuge from the blistering heat. We had managed to endure the heat and humidity as we tried to rest, but the pesky flies seemed to know just when we were about to drift away and prevented us from doing so.

"Hi, Floyd," I threw up a hand as he meandered toward us.

He was dressed in jeans, cowboy boots and a straw hat. Jackie had helped Floyd pick out a pair of good boots for the trip, and he was really proud of them. Floyd never had too much to say about anybody. Oh, he'd get mad at people now and again, but he always seemed to have a kind word for them.

"Hi, David. Nice little place ya got here," he replied.

"Pretty, huh? We just happened upon it."

A little roadside park displayed the beauty of which we spoke. If I had been driving, I would probably never have looked twice at this little haven, but to a man and his dog on foot, it was paradise to visit.

"Sit down, Floyd. Snicker is doin' much better."

"He looks better," he replied.

I watched as Floyd played with Snicker, just like a little boy on an adventure with his friend. "The rest did him good, David," Floyd said as he threw a stick, hoping Snicker would retrieve it. "I called my friend in St. Joe," he said tossing another stick.

"You did? Was he home?"

"Yep. He's comin' out on the road to meet you when you get a little closer to St. Joe."

"That's great. How did he sound?"

"Same as always," he said, then paused when he noticed that Snicker had no interest in fetching the stick.

"Same as always? You told me you haven't seen this guy in 30 years."

"Yeah, 30 years," he mused, as if it were just yesterday.

"Then how do you know he sounds the same as always?"

"Well, same as when I talked to him last. We've written a few times, Christmas cards and such."

We talked about many things in the shade of those Missouri trees, but I mostly just listened to his stories of days gone by. Then I moved on toward the south and St. Joe. Floyd came out again after a few hours and said his friend was coming out on the road to see us.

It was a grand reunion for those two old Army buddies. They shook hands along the roadside and exchanged slaps on the back.

"Mel Glenn, this is the Walking Cowboy," Floyd announced proudly.

"Floyd told me a lot about you on the phone today," Mel said as he shook my hand.

"Good things, I hope," I replied.

"Mostly," Mel said with a smile. "I've got you guys a room for tonight, and I want to take you out to dinner."

"No, you two go share an evening together," I said.

"Nonsense, I'm buying you guys supper. Floyd and I will have plenty of time to talk over old times," he insisted.

"Okay," I said. "It's a done deal."

I don't know how long they stayed out and visited along that highway. I didn't even see them go by me on the way to town. I was probably lost in thought. Sometimes my thoughts just seemed to grab the wind and race away like a balloon whose string had slipped through someone's fingers.

• • •

The sound of thunder echoed in the distance. It was only a few more miles to St. Joe, but cool rain would be welcome anytime. I imagined the feel and smell of the cool mist that I so wished for, and soon I saw a sign that read, "Jesus is Lord of our City." I smiled and said, "Look at that, Snicker. I love it, boy." He did not understand my enthusiasm but played right along as if he did, hanging on to every word I said as if each was a praise for him.

After supper that evening with Floyd's Army pal, we went back to his house. It was great hearing stories from 30 years gone by, and I wondered if anyone would remember the Walking Cowboy 30 years down the road.

"Come on down and see my work," Mel said as he stood in his basement entrance. In the room below was a kiln crafted by gifted hands. That was where Mel put into practice his desires of being an artist and a sculptor.

"You've got some nice work here, Mel," I said.

"Thank you. I sure love doing bronze work."

He talked for the longest time of his work as he and Floyd exchanged stories, sometimes offering different versions of the same ones. I watched those two men looking at each other all evening with looks of a good friendship that had never died. The miles and years had not mattered. They carried on as if it had been no time at all since they had last sat across the table from one another. I could see each one study the other when the other one's eyes were not upon him, perhaps looking for signs of age or maybe just signs of wisdom.

Soon we arrived at the motel that Mel had booked for us. I

thanked him for supper and the nice room.

"My pleasure, David," he replied as he handed me a plaque With a bronze arrow upon it.

"What a nice gift," I exclaimed.

"Glad you like it. Just keep on walking to Nashville."

I left them alone for their farewell.

• • •

Ring, ring, ring went the phone.

"Who could that be?" I wondered as I opened the door to our room. "No one knows where we are." That puzzled me as I leaped across the bed and grabbed the phone. I hoped it might be Jackie.

"This is the front desk! Is that your dog that's been barking for 2 hours?" he demanded. I looked at Snicker and he knew the call was about him. He held his head low and slipped into the bathroom.

"Yes, sir, it's —'

"Well, you better keep him quiet or you're outta here, buddy," he snapped.

"Sir, if . . . " I started to reply.

"There's no excuse for it, pal. Just keep him quiet."

Click — he hung up in my ear.

"Well, I guess he told me all right! Snicker, come here, boy."

First the nose appeared from behind the door, then a little more of the guilty face until his eyes were on me.

"Come out here, boy. Right NOW! Are you trying to get us kicked out of one of the few fine beds we'll have on this trip? Are you nuts, Snicker?"

He stood slumped at the shoulders, head hung to the floor. "Well, I suppose you're sorry. I'm just glad to see you alive and full of vinegar. Let's call the desk and bark at him, boy." The lift in my voice was his cue; he leaped up on the bed and lay his head on my leg.

"What am I going to do with you, Snicker?" I mumbled. His

ears perked as Floyd entered the room. "Our pal here is about to get us kicked out, Floyd."

"Yeah, I know. I just got my butt chewed down at the desk."

"One of us wasn't enough?"

"I guess we should just be glad we can stay. This beats that bunk all to heck."

"Your friend's really a great guy."

"Yeah, well, it could be another 30 years before I see him again," he sighed.

"I hope not. By the way, I'm in book two of my diary. Just started it. I figure I'm either over halfway to Nashville or I'm writing too big. Feels good to have all those miles behind me."

I thought about Floyd having no wife or child to share our adventures with. Sure, he had a home, but he lived alone. He never married.

He must really get lonely sometimes, I thought as I watched him make notes in his own personal journal. It was silent in the room. We had never discussed, compared or even read each other's writings. I believe it was because we were pouring out such personal feelings that we respected the privacy of the diary.

"Floyd, did I ever tell you the story about me thinkin' I had won $25,000?"

"No, what do you mean you thought you won?"

"Well, I was sure I had won," I said and told him the story as follows:

McDonald's had a $25,000 contest. You had to fill up a card with parts of characters. If you got all the parts: you won $25,000. Dawn was only about 8 or 9 at the time. I had been playing this game for a while and had all but two pieces of the puzzle. Earlier that day, I had stopped by for a bite and got some more pieces. Jackie was busy in another room, and Dawn was downstairs. I was alone at the kitchen counter and unveiled my hidden pieces.

The first one I pulled off fit one of my empty spaces. I

had four more tries to go. The next two were duds, but as I pulled the third one, I went crazy. "I won! I won!" I shouted. "Jackie, I won!" She came running and so did Dawn.

"What's the matter? " Jackie cried.

"Nothing's wrong. I won $25,000, honey! $25,000!" I shook the game card in her face. "See! I got 'em all. I won," I exclaimed. I was crazy with laughter, bouncing all over the kitchen while Jackie tried to get my card to verify my good fortune. 'No! You call 'em, jackie. Tell them I won! "I squeezed Dawn and bounced even more.

"Hello, is this McDonald's? My husband won the $25,000 prize. . . Yes! Yes, he did! . . . Okay, we'll be right down," Jackie said.

"What'd they say, Jackie?" I asked with excitement. They screamed, "In Gillette? Wow, somebody won in Gillette, I can't believe it! Come on down right away."

We all raced to the car, rejoicing and thinking of ways to spend the money. "Let's go to Florida. How about a new truck, honey?" Jackie exclaimed. "Let's all go shopping!"

"What happened then, David?" Floyd was up on the edge of the bed. "Did you get it in cash or check? What happened?" I continued:

So we raced through the doors of McDonald's, and I strode right up to that counter like a rooster in the hen house, grinning all over.

"Are you the winner?" the girl at the counter cried out. You would have thought it was written on my chest.

"Yes! Yes! I won!" I exclaimed. Suddenly everyone around us was applauding and shouting as I handed over my winning card. We were so excited that we could not be still.

"Sir. . . Sir. . . SIR!" the girl yelled.

"What? What do you need? My ID?" I asked excitedly.

"No, sir. You didn't win!"

"Whaaa, whaat?" I asked as my voice dropped.

"No, sir. You have a foot where a face should be," was the reply.

"A WHAT?" I shouted.

"A foot, sir. A foot, " she pronounced it very clearly so I would absorb what she had said.

I stared at that foot for the longest time. Then I looked right at Jackie, and we both started laughing uncontrollably, maybe to hold back tears or maybe because it was so embarrassing.

Dawn was fuming mad. "A foot? Mom! A foot?" she uttered in disbelief.

"Well, I didn't get a look at it at home, Dawn. It's Okay," Jackie said through her laughter.

"I am totally humiliated," Dawn cried out as we exited with moans and scowls at our heels.

"A foot — how could I have done that?" I said.

"I don't know! This is crazy," Jackie replied. We broke into laughter again.

"Stop it! It's not funny! I have to go to school, you know. Everyone will know about this," Dawn cried.

"No they won't," I said, but I knew how she must feel. I had embarrassed her in front of everyone. "I'm sorry, Dawn. I thought I had really won. We sure had that money spent, didn't we?"

"Dawn was mad for some time, but we'll still laugh about this for years to come, Floyd," I said.

"What a crazy story. Is it really true?"

"Sure is, Floyd! You can ask Jackie . . . Don't know if I'd mention it to Dawn, though, if I were you," I laughed.

14

Dream Walkin

As I headed out of St. Joe on June 17 (Day 49), I waved goodbye to Floyd. He was taking Snicker to the vet for a final check-up. We were afraid he might get sick again. Animals have a unique way of bouncing back, but I did not want to risk his health any longer.

Walking southward toward Kansas City, I reached for my recorder . . .

I have been up for several hours and have already talked to one reporter. I'm really tired, and the heat is getting bad. Floyd and I stayed up late tellin' stories last night. He seems to he concerned about my mental state. There are no sleepy little towns on this interstate. The landscape has turned to concrete around me, and the cars are getting thicker and thicker the further south I go. The traffic seems to roar on into the pit of night so that I awake to the sound of it. I shiver at the thought of Kansas City and even more of St. Louis. I looked at my map last night, and my next stop could be a place called Faucett. Floyd said there is a truck stop there. We will leave Faucett Saturday morning and drive eastward to Edgerton, Missouri, for the Union Mill Opry. I'm excited about meeting Justin Tubb.

As I put my recorder away, I decided to rest. I removed a sandwich from my pack and lay back to relax. I dabbed a Q-Tip into the New Skin and applied a second coat to my sore spots. It seemed to relieve the pain for a while. As I sat alone, I applied it several more times and ate as slowly as I could.

My thoughts drifted to Music City. "Ladies and gentlemen, welcome David Stewart," I imagined Grant Turner, the voice of the Opry, saying. Would I get to meet the legend? I pictured myself shaking hands with The King of Country Music, Mr. Roy Acuff.

"Hello, Mr. Acuff," I would say.

"Hello, David. Glad to have you here," he would reply.

• • •

Honk! Honk! The blast almost knocked me off the highway. I turned to wave, but the truck was way down the highway. Maybe I had been drifting out on the road or something. Gosh, where was I? Oh yeah, at the Opry. "Well, I may never get there if I get run over," I remarked to no one in particular.

"Today they should call me Dream Walker instead of the Walking Cowboy. I can't seem to concentrate on the road at all." I carried on with my dream walking and dream talking as the words of one of my songs drifted through my mind...

In the wings of the Grand Ole Opry
That's where I long to be
When they call out my name
And I take Center Stage
It'll come from the heart when I sing.

How many times have I sung those lines? How many?

•　•　•

Beep! Beep! There's Floyd, I thought. Must be bringing Snicker out to me. I wonder what the vet had to say.

The little motor home pulled onto the shoulder, heading right toward me. "That," I laughed aloud, "is Floyd's home, office and wheels."

People would always say to us, "That sure is a small camper. Aren't you cramped in that thing?"

Floyd's favorite reply was: "It's just like an egg-beater. When one of us turns, the other turns." Then he'd chuckle out loud.

I sat on the hood as soon as the little home on wheels stopped before me. Floyd scrambled out, all excited.

"I need you back in town!" he shouted.

"Why? Where's Snicker? Is he okay?" My throat was parched, and I felt like it was about to close. I could hardly breathe. I felt my heart pounding. "Where is he?" I asked with alarm.

"No. No." Floyd took my arm. "The little guy's okay. He's just not done yet. I've got you another interview. I thought you might need a little break for a spell, and you can talk to the vet yourself about the pup."

"Oh, man," I sank down on the pavement in front of the camper. "I thought . . ." My voice trailed off.

"I know, pardner, and I'm sorry. I should have thought about it and told you right off that the little guy was fine. I'm sorry."

"Look at us, Floyd! Now we're both a mess. All because my emotions got the best of me. An interview you say?"

"Yeah, they wanna talk to you at the station and spin your record."

"Well, let's get movin'."

I told the DJ about our day on the road. I babbled on so much that he probably thought I was losing it.

"You did fine," Floyd said reassuringly.

"I just seemed to babble."

"It sounded good on the radio out here. Let's go get our little buddy. You know, that little fellow hasn't missed many miles and wouldn't have missed a one if he hadn't got so sick."

"Well, now, Floyd, are you stickin' up for the little varmint? Sounds to me as though you're gettin' pretty attached to him," I teased.

He blushed a little around the ears — so much so that he turned his head and looked back at the road. "Well, it's hard not to like the little fella," he finally said with that little nervous chuckle of his.

Floyd, I found out, was a "hyper" type of person. I had never really noticed this before, probably because I had not spent a great deal of time with him in the past. He sure had a lot of energy — like a flea in a hot skillet!

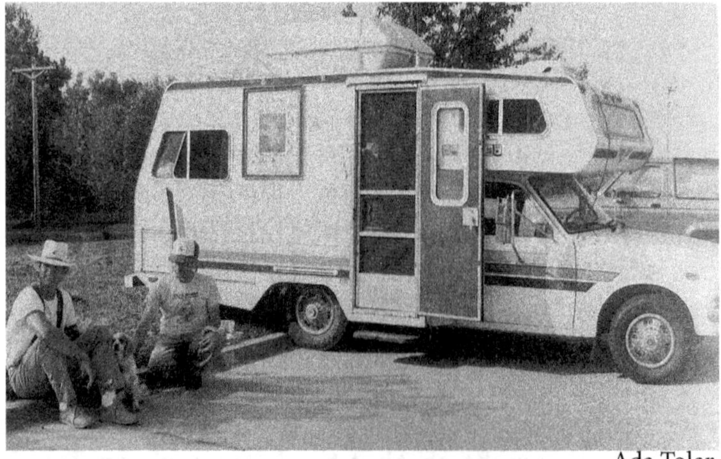

David, Snicker, Floyd and the trusty camper

Ada Tolar

The young receptionist at the vet's had already fallen for Snicker, and he was loving every minute of it.

"We just love this little guy," she said, as I walked in the door.

I smiled and reached for my wallet, then realized that Floyd had all the money. I was anxious to get back on the road. "Is he okay?" I asked.

The vet appeared and said, "He's okay. He has a little respiratory problem still, but for the most part he's okay."

"What do you think was wrong with him?" I asked.

"He's got an ear infection. This solution (he held up a bottle of medication) should clear it up. Just use it once or twice a day until it's gone. We gave him a bath and dipped him for fleas and ticks so he's raring to go. You know, I'm not so sure this little fella didn't have distemper and, if so, he's lucky to be alive."

"Distemper? My Lord. He's had his shots," I said.

"It's been a while, according to his tag."

"Did you give him another shot?"

"Yes, I did, just to be safe. I've got something else for you. It's an old coon dog remedy for his feet. You're going into scorching weather, and his pads are going to burn up. Put this on as often as you need to. Smells awful, but it works," he advised.

"Thanks, Doc. I've been worryin' about the heat on his pads. I've been noticing the tar on the road gettin' hot from the sun, and I know it's gonna get a lot worse."

"It sure is. You'd better protect your face and eyes yourself," he cautioned.

"I will. You got anything for my pads?" I asked with a laugh.

"No, I'm afraid I can't help you there," he said with his Missouri grin.

Floyd paid the bill, and we pulled away with Snicker acting like he had just been given a medal for bravery — must have been all the attention.

"David, we're about broke. That little bill was $28."

"How much have you got left?" I asked quickly.

"I'm not sure . . . maybe $15 to $16 at the most," he said without assurance.

"Great! Pull in at Dairy Queen. I need a blizzard," I exclaimed, unable to resist one of those thick, delicious milk shakes.

"Whatever you say, boss," he replied with a chuckle and that little cough of his that he assured me was due to allergies.

"Pull under that shade tree there," I said, pointing to the spot as if I had been there before. "Has Snicker been to the bathroom, Floyd?" I asked, wanting to dash through the door of Dairy Queen to get a Heath blizzard.

"Yes, outside the vet's office. In fact, he went on my tire," he said, looking at the pup.

"We'll be right back, boy. Get a little rest," I said as we climbed out of the vehicle. "What'll ya have, Floyd?"

"Just a cone," he said as if this were not a special occasion.

"You gotta have a blizzard," I exclaimed with emphasis on the last word.

"Okay, a blizzard," he agreed, checking out the young woman who was waiting on us.

"What kind do you want? Heath, M&M'S, Butterfinger?" I asked as I began pointing out all the flavors.

"That one," he said as I reached Butterfinger.

"One large Butterfinger and one large Heath blizzard, please," I said, anticipating the flavor after weeks of a bland diet.

Floyd took his seat and peered out the window while I waited at the counter.

"Eat it slowly. Enjoy every bit of it," would have been Jackie's words to me. I ate like a horse most of the time and too darned fast. I smiled at the thought of Jackie and whispered, "I love you." The young lady looked my way and blushed, and I felt the embarrassment run up my neck to the tips of my red ears.

"That'll be $3.29, sir," she said.

I could tell we were in the South with everyone saying, "Yes sir. No, sir." I really liked the lingo.

I motioned to Floyd as I savored that first gulp. He was still looking out the window at nothing in particular. "$3.29, Floyd," I finally said to get his attention. "You've got all the money." I had already indulged as if I owned this treat that was not yet paid For.

"And it ain't much, pardner."

I thought I detected a little irritation in his voice.

"Mighty good, David," he spoke after a spell of silence.

"I love 'em," I said, then paused. "What's on your mind? Anything bothering you?"

"No . . . only . . . we're about out of cash." He finally was able to release the words, although he did so with much restraint. At that moment, looking into Floyd's eyes, I could not help but wonder if he thought we would have to quit the whole thing because of money. Could it be that he was seeing something that I could not face?

"Don't worry, Floyd, the money will come," I said, not knowing if it were a true statement. "Jackie still has a little at home, and we have a credit card for gas."

"I know, but I'm feelin' a little guilty that you're havin' to give me money out here."

"My gosh, man, you quit your job to come with me. Do you think I could expect you to work for nothin'? You're bustin' your butt for me," I exclaimed, feeling in turn guilty that he had given up his job of installing sprinkler systems in order to join me on the road.

I could not believe he was worried that he was spending too much money, when all he did was look out for me. He blushed a little as he looked up and was about to speak.

"Don't worry," I said, cutting him off before it could be spoken. "We've made it this far, haven't we? This is the hardest thing I've ever done in my life, and not because of the finances."

He was silent and looked out the window once more, causing me to do the same.

I had not seen Floyd depressed too many times, or else I had, not paid close enough attention to notice. It's easy to overlook someone else's fears when you're carrying a load yourself.

"I'm almost done, and you're only just beginning, Floyd," I said to change the subject.

"I'm a slow eater," he said, with what looked to be an attempted grin on the corner of his mouth. "

"I've noticed that, and that's good. You'd probably live longer if that cough doesn't kill you."

I wanted to eat those words as I spoke them.

"I'm sorry, Floyd. I didn't mean . . ." I tried to apologize.

"It's okay, David. It's nothin' but allergies. I'm allergic to almost everything, probably even Mr. Snicker," he said, taking each bite ever so slowly.

"Oh, no! Not Snicker. Speaking of Snicker . . ." I said, leaping to the counter as Floyd chuckled behind me.

"One small cup of ice cream, please," I said as I turned to Floyd and winked.

"Good thinkin'. He needs one, too," Floyd said, knowing Snicker would love it. Floyd remained seated as I went outside. I wasn't quite sure if it was to finish eating, cough a little or it he just needed a moment alone.

15
Highway Hassle

I talked to my companion, while pondering over Floyd's financial worries. "We still have some daylight, Snicker. I'm glad to be out of that hot sun, boy. It must still be in the 80s."

Snicker stepped lively, as we walked on southward from St. Joe to wherever nightfall would stop us and leave yet another day in our backtracks. His ears were alert to every sound of the busy highway. In my heart, I longed for the back country that was far behind — the same land that I had prayed to be rid of.

I sat to enter a few notes this day of June 18 (Day 50):

> This land where I place my feet has
> much beauty. I have seen it day after
> day. The trees are full and I pick a
> leaf when I can, crumbling it
> between my fingers and enjoying the
> fragrance that lingers with me for a
> time. I know the heat will not cease.
> It is a drought year, and some of the trees that bring me shade
> may die like the crops I watch wither in the fields.
>
> Where I walk now is laid with much

*concrete. I can feel the closeness of
Kansas City with every step. There are
many people and with people comes
much progress. I have grown
accustomed to a small town
atmosphere and prefer it to large
populations.*

"How will we handle the big city, boy?" I asked, trying to picture where I might walk. "Kansas City will eat us alive if we're not careful. Please stay close to me," I said as I looked at the little guy whom I was asking to risk his life. I bent down to pet him. He placed his foot upon my thigh and gently lay his head in the palm of my hand. He softened my heart.

I looked up and had the strongest urge to leave the slab of concrete that was to take me somewhere new by twilight. The secondary road lay to my east and looked inviting. "Come on, boy. Let's go exploring," I said as I walked at an angle toward my destination, careful not to lose ground. He danced through the tall grass, bouncing and leaping over anything in his path, and sometimes scurrying after whatever little varmint jumped up ahead of him.

We had not been long upon the slightly crooked path when I felt a need to change my socks. The blister on my right foot had been a burden to me for most of my miles — only now it was no longer a blister but raw meat that was too tender to touch. I slowly applied lotion to the area. It burned something awful, but when dry, offered protection from infection.

I removed my scissors and cut the dried asphalt from Snicker's pads. He had picked it up from the shoulder of the road. I dabbed a Q-Tip into the concoction that the vet had given me. It seemed to relieve Snicker as I rubbed his pads. They were so dry that I applied the solution several times. "Pretty good, huh, boy?" I said, rubbing the small feet that seemed to take three steps to my every one. "Gotta keep you in shape."

"Let's move 'em out!" I finally bellowed, as if I were the leader of a wagon train heading for virgin territory. The trouble was, it was not virgin ground, and I feared the unknown.

I spotted a white car heading in our direction. It was the first to pass us on the side road. Not far off was the still ever-present roar from the interstate. "Boy, he's movin' fast, Snicker. Looks like he's over too far our way," I said, with caution mounting. The shoulder on which we walked was narrow compared to the one on the interstate. There was a shallow ditch of sorts that ran parallel alongside the road. I glanced at the ditch, then back at the oncoming car that seemed to be picking up speed. My senses seemed to be telling me something. For a brief moment, I felt fear. Was it Frank?

"Come here, boy." He hesitated, looking off into the brush at something that had caught his eye. "Snicker!" I shouted. My voice cracked, and he felt my fear and came to my side. The car was still approaching us at a fast speed and weaved to the shoulder as if the driver were drinking. I stood still, with Snicker close to me. I felt paralyzed for a moment, trying to evaluate the situation, trying to reach out to understand this unknown person. I bent and scooped Snicker into my arms. "He's coming right at us!" I yelled.

Without another thought, I dove for the ditch. Snicker flew through the air as I rolled over. My finger got caught in his collar, and the pain shot through me like a bullet. Snicker yelped as he hit the ground. When I fell, I heard the sound of tires roll over the spot where only a moment before I had stood. My heart beat frantically as I tried to stand upright. "Too far to see the license plate," I moaned, looking through the shimmering heat waves.

"Who was that idiot?" I cried out, holding my finger in my fist, tight enough to stop the circulation, but not the pain.

My mind turned to Snicker. "Snicker, come here, boy. Are you okay?" He came slowly, as if he had lost his breath when he landed. He wasn't quite sure why I had thrown him like I had. I checked him over as he neared my side, and he seemed to be okay. I could only rub him with one hand — the other hurt as if I had slammed it in a door.

I looked after my attacker, wondering if he would come

back and trying to understand the motive for this madness. "He would have run us down, boy. It's crazy. I can't figure it. Heck of a practical joke, tryin' to scare us to death." I couldn't shut my mouth and babbled incessantly until finally a lone tear appeared. I don't know if it was from fear or from the joy of having survived the insanity of someone I did not even know. I sank down and held Snicker close to my chest. "I can't figure it," I said again, searching for an answer.

My finger hurt with every movement. I placed Snicker to the side and tried to pull my finger back into place. It did not budge and began to swell. "I don't think she's broke, boy, but she sure is out of socket." The thought crept over me as I spoke, and my stomach felt like it might come to the surface all at once. My body ached as if the car had struck me head on.

Was it him? Could it have been? No, my mind's playing tricks. The heat is causing me to think crazy.

Those cold eyes had shown much hate as he had crawled on his bike and looked back into mine. Frank! Was he out to get me? The sweat began to pour from me as if I had been dipped in water. I wiped it away and could taste the salt from my body. It made me long for a drink. I drank slowly and tried to calm my thoughts. My breath was heavy, and my hand trembled. I poured some cool water over my finger, knowing I might run out of the precious liquid. "Get those thoughts of Frank out of your mind!" I shouted. "I must get to the interstate."

I stood and started for what I felt would be safety. "Come on!" I barked at the pup. He could not comprehend what he had done to make me talk to him in this manner. He began to shake all over as if he were out of control. I took him in my arms and headed to the interstate. More often than not, I looked over my shoulder the rest of the day, wondering why. Who could it have been? Was it only an accident? Surely not, or the driver would have stopped to see if I was hurt. It was no accident. That person or persons meant me harm. I thought long and hard about what had happened to me and still had it on my mind as I sat across from Floyd at the truck stop.

"Can I take your order, guys?" were the words that brought me to the present and let me escape my fears for the moment. The waitress was a pretty girl, and I watched as Floyd teased her a little. He blushed as she teased right back with a Southern drawl. He strained to understand some of her words that were clear to my childhood Southern ear. When he did not understand, he would grin and agree with an awkward chuckle that was a special part of his personality. I knew from the conversation that he had already been talking to this young lady before I walked in, and they had become friends. He made friends with everyone and told them all of my walk. He would hand them the address of the Opry and say, "Don't forget to write," with a grin.

To watch him was to know that he burned for this in his heart. It made me proud to listen to him. He was an honest man, never boastful. Well, almost never. I did hear him once tell a waitress, "He's doin' the walkin' and I'm doin' the talkin.'"

I stared out the window, lost in thought. The big diesels were pulling in for the night, and I knew I would drift away to their sound before long.

"Ready to order, David?" Floyd asked.

"Oh, yeah, I'm sorry. I got to driftin' back in time a little."

The girl stood with patience, and I wondered how long I had been in a daze and if they had been talking all that time or if they had just been waiting for me to order.

"I'll have a cheeseburger and fries. No, let me have a baked potato and soup. No butter on the potato and some water, please." My diet was bland, but I needed the carbohydrates. A cheeseburger would have sat in my stomach all night like a rock.

"Give me the special, and an iced tea, please, ma'am."

"Comin' right up, boys," she said as she hurried to the counter. We had taken up enough of her time. A waitress' job is hard with long hours, little pay and some awfully rude people to contend with at times.

"I believe we'll call it a short day tomorrow, if you don't mind. I'll quit walkin' around noon, and we'll head to the Union

Mill Opry," I said.

"I can't wait to meet Justin."

"Me, either. I sure hope we hit it off," I replied.

My mind would not let me go to sleep that night. My legs and feet cried out in pain as if I had just begun my quest. A crew of men was erecting a tent outside. I puzzled over its purpose until 2:00 a.m. I finally surmised it was for the Fourth of July fireworks. I had seen those tents before where they would sell fireworks at truck stops. I didn't know if I was right or wrong, but my conclusion let me finally fall to sleep.

Five o'clock found my eyes open once more and feeling as if I had been beaten in my sleep. I let Snicker out to claim every post or tire that needed his mark. I stretched long and hard, working on every muscle with great care for about 45 minutes. I allowed myself an hour every day for this ritual. The extra 15 minutes were for a bowl of oatmeal and to brush my teeth. I looked out at Snicker and saw he was close. I decided to lie back for just a minute since I was feeling tired . . .

"David . . . Wake up. It's gettin' late," I heard Floyd say.

"Wha . . . What's the matter?" I felt disoriented.

"You fell back to sleep. Snicker's up front on the floor. I saw you let the pup out this morning and fall back to sleep. I let him back in, thinkin' you might wake up. I decided you must have needed the rest since you didn't stir."

"What time is it?" '

"It's 8:30."

"8:30! I've gotta get movin'."

He smiled and said, "Don't push it too hard."

"I'll see you around one. Then we'll go for some country music," I said. The thought of getting to Buddy's and jammlng a little before the show sent me off at an even pace. I felt llke kicking my heels as I walked up the long ramp, so I did just that. Floyd was right; I did need those extra hours of rest. It did me good. I fumbled to turn on my recording device . . .

There are times I push too hard, trying to get in

an extra mile or two. I don't know what drives
me to do this.

I am beginning to learn patience. Nothing out
here goes fast, except the traflic and the nights I
look forward to. I still can't shake the thought of
not making it. I try to tell myself constantly that
the worst is behind. I have learned to comfort the
blisters. The shin splints come less often now than
in my earlier days. Surely I have encountered my
worst experiences.

With that said, I glanced behind me, wondering if I would
see Frank or if only his memory would haunt me. I prayed that the
thought of him would pass as I left him further behind — if
indeed I had.

Many thoughts ran through me as I walked along, counting
the mile markers. It was easy to lapse into a semi-conscious state
of mind. It helped to pass the time.

I heard a horn blast and looked up to see a woman waving
at me. It was the same woman I had seen pushing her big rig up
and down these highways for many weeks. She always waved, and
I could not help but wonder what her name would be. I waved as
she rolled by and gave me another blast of her horn. I smiled,
thinking if Floyd had seen her, he would have chased her down
and given her the Opry address.

I turned and moved on at a strange pace, sometimes moving fast and other times just meandering along. I touched my arm
where-I had been wearing my watch. I missed it and wondered
what time it was as I looked toward the sky.

"As of this day, I will not wear a timepiece again until this
is finished," were the words I whispered. From that moment on,
I played a new game wlth the sun. It helped to pass the time. "No
matter," I said, wondering why I bothered to whisper. "No matter!" I repeated out loud while the echo rolled away to wherever
echoes go.

Many miles stretched behind me. As I walked, I remembered the time I had discarded a mileage counter that Floyd had given me for my belt. The counter had started to annoy me because I was looking at it with every step I took. I gave it a fling somewhere in the prairies of Wyoming. Good riddance! I thought. In similar fashion, I often had the urge to uproot the mile markers that told me I was but a speck on a big planet. I eventually learned to ignore them by playing number and letter games with billboards. Now I had a new game: to guess the time of day. The sun was above me and I surmised it might be about noon.

"Twelve, straight up. What do you think, boy?" I asked. "Sounds good to me," I tried to mimic what Snicker's voice would sound like if he could talk. He only looked at me as if he thought I might be a little off center. I was off center! I had been talking to a dog for 700—plus miles.

I had come about 12 miles since leaving Floyd. Even without looking at mile markers, I knew. I sat to change my socks and had a peanut butter and honey lunch. How many of those darn things had I eaten? I looked up, thinking it had been about an hour since I had ventured a guess at the time. I figured it to be about 1:15 and wondered where Floyd might be.

Two sandwiches later, I had my answer as he pulled alongside us. He jumped out and raced across the median with fresh water.

"Sorry I'm late. Got tied up on the phone. You thirsty?"

"Not so much. One thing I like about Missouri is there's plenty of shade to go with the heat. What time is it?" I couldn't resist asking.

"Ten after one."

"I need a little more practice."

"What? I've got your watch. You forgot it this morning."

"You keep it. I'm guessin' the time from here on out."

I waited for his response, but he never asked why.

16

Just Lookin' for a Rainbow

The sign read "Kansas City, City Limits," and the traffic echoed a constant roar. Snicker sucked up close to my leg as if he were a part of it. It was Monday, June 20 (Day 52). I felt the need to record . . .

It's only 9:00 am. and the temperature has already climbed to 87 degrees. What will noon bring, and how will Floyd ever find me in this madness of people rushing to God knows where?

It has been two days since I left the interstate to see old friends at the Union Mill Opry.

There are a number of shows around the country that have taken the name of "Opry" from the famous and original Nashville show, then added their own namesake to the title. Buddy's Union Mill Opry was one such show.

It was strange to think that only a day's walk away was the small town of Edgerton. Not many people lived there, but it had some of the finest country music I had ever heard. I was nervous about meeting Justin Tubb. When we finally met, he was a true gentleman.

"I don't know if they'll let you sing on the Opry in Nashville, but you can sure sing on my radio show, the 'Midnight Jamboree,' when you get there," he said to me. The "Midnight Jamboree" is the second oldest show in Nashville, after the Opry.

"Thank you, Justin. That means a great deal to me.

"When do you think you'll make it into Nashville?"

"My plans are for the 22nd of July. I have plenty of time allotted. We've told the press the 22nd."

"Then you can sing Saturday night, the 23rd, on my show. A lot of folks will hear you, that's for sure," he said with pride, and rightfully so as he'd worked hard to make the "Midnight Jamboree" live on. He was not much for small talk unless it was about baseball; then he lit up. He was going to catch a game in Kansas City before returning home.

Buddy Boswell opened his heart and home to us in Edgerton, Missouri, and asked me to sing right before Justin came on. He had a packed house in the Union Mill Opry. The history of the place covered the rustic walls, and you could see the fruits of his labor in the family band that worked together with precision and love. It was great to open for Justin. I sang "In the Wings of the Grand Ole Opry." The crowd treated me well, and I got to meet a lot of wonderful people.

On Sunday we rested in the campground. The band had to leave early on a road tour, but we stayed on until about noon, returning to the Faucett truck stop once more. I pumped myself up emotionally to take on the giant city that was about to become a part of my life for at least two days. "Oh, the thought Of it, I cringed, while trying to imagine spending two long days walking through the traffic . . .

June 20, 1988. I will remember it for years to come. The temperature has reached 99 degrees, and my water supply has gone for the most part to Snicker. How he will endure the heat, I don't know. Floyd is somewhere in this place of many buildings, but I don't know where. I have no means of communication with him. I can't help but wonder what will happen if he has an accident. He is a bad driver in this traflic. Maybe that's being unfair. Our camper is hard to see behind but, all and all, he isn't very cautious. How would I know if something was to happen? If he were hurt badly, he couldn't even tell anyone where or who I was. . .

The fear of how I would conquer the next few days made my stomach sick. I could just quit now, I thought. No one would slight me for it. I had tried and had come a long way.

I imagined someone picking me up in a long white limo saying, "Mr. Stewart," as he opened the door for me.

"I don't understand. What's this all about?" I would ask.

"This is your limo. You have walked far enough for one man. I am here from the Opry to escort you the rest of your trip," the imaginary man would say.

Nice one, David, but they may not even know your name! That thought almost made me lose my breakfast.

A black cloud that had been following was now upon me, as if it had been waiting for the precise moment when I was weak. It suddenly covered me until I felt as if I would suffocate. Taking out my tape recorder, I tried to escape the emotion by talking it away. I spoke into the little machine, trying to hide it from the roar of trucks that seemed to be never-ending, blasting me backwards with every step.

Well, here I am in Kansas City. . . Kansas City. . .

I love you, Jackie. I wish you were here.

Finally they came! The tears! I didn't know why I had tried to hold them back — a manly thing, I guess. With the flow of tears came a peace, a relief of anxiety.

As I put my recorder away, I looked up to see a dirty yellow Nova ahead on the side of the road. Caution ran through me as we approached the vehicle. The man standing alongside the car was as dirty as the vehicle itself. I wanted to cross the highway to avoid contact, but the traffic was heavy. Snicker seemed to be as uneasy as I was. The man was dressed in jeans and a soiled white shirt. He was unshaven and wore dark shades.

"Howdy," I said with tension inside.

"Hi, I'm a little lost. Can you help me find Jefferson Street?" He spoke with a confident tone of voice.

"I'm not from these parts. I don't know anything about this city." There was something about him that made me nervous, and I wanted to move on.

He took a step closer and spoke again. "I've got a map in the car. Would you mind getting in and helping me find my way?" He had Missouri plates on his car, and I wondered if he was lying about being lost.

"No, I can't do that. I have to be movin' on. Let's go, Snicker." I moved out at a quick pace and heard him mumble something. I looked back after about 20 feet and saw him get in his car. He passed by at a slow speed. A car horn blasted as he moved out into the traffic. I had gone less than a mile when I spotted the car in the median, facing the opposite direction. As I got closer, he yelled out, "I sure could use some help."

I ignored him and kept on walking. He finally got in the car and headed away from me. I thought he was gone until I looked back to see him coming on my side of the road once more. He slowed down and smiled at me, then moved on. I was leery of what he might do and decided to pull up and rest. I kept careful watch as I nursed my feet. He never returned. I had a sick feeling that he was up to no good.

Soon Floyd was with me, and I was glad to call it a day.

Folding my diary and laying it next to me in bed, I looked over at Floyd. He was writing furiously in his own little book.

"This town scares me, Floyd. There's hardly any room to walk, and the traffic is so thick I can't even cross the road. We need a rendezvous plan. You can't stop on the opposite side of the road and get to me or me to you. So if you see me, honk and take the next exit. I'll take it, too."

"Okay. Whatever you think."

"Well, it's only a thought, but I know we don't want to cause a wreck or get run over. This is worse than I imagined. The times I have driven through here, it didn't seem so busy, but then again I wasn't on foot."

"I imagine it's a lot different from where you see it."

"I'm all worn out. The heat is sure a killer," I sighed.

"I feel bad that I can't get water to you," he confessed.

"The water's really no problem. I can take an exit, and most of these buildings have faucets so don't worry about that. Let's just concentrate on not having a fender-bender and on gettin' through this place."

"The TV people were upset because they thought I said you were on the by-pass today, and they couldn't find you."

"That's discouraging, but to be honest, at this point I just want to be on the other side of this city headin' east on 1-70!"

"I bet you do. Sure was a good time at the Union Mill, huh?"

"It sure was."

He seemed to know when to say the right things to change my mood from bad to good, and that night I fell asleep with good thoughts.

Before I left him on June 21, Floyd told me of a Union 76 truck stop to the east of Kansas City. We both agreed that would be our home for the night. We would rendezvous there if we lost contact.

Early that morning, I crossed the Missouri River, carrying a trembling Snicker in my arms. He'd made an attempt to walk, but the open grate that was the walkway across the bridge revealed the current below and made him nervous. It didn't do me much good either, I must admit. But even with fear in my arms and in my heart, I found I had to stop in the middle and admire the Kansas City skyline. There was a beauty about the town that I was able to capture from high above the water. I took a breath and lapsed into reverie for just an instant. I pretended it was Nashville and that my task was over.

"Excuse me!" a voice yelled from behind. I turned sharply around, startled, almost dropping Snicker who had just begun to feel secure in my arms. I thought the stranger had returned who had tried to get me into his yellow Nova.

"I'm sorry. I didn't mean to scare you," the man said apologetically.

"You sure did! I was lost in thought."

"I know. I parked on the other side of the bridge because I saw you standing here with your dog."

Puzzled, I looked at the bag he carried.

"I'm Dean," he said finally. "I'm a freelance photographer. I'm traveling the country, and I'd like to take your picture on this bridge."

He didn't know about my story and hadn't heard about my walk, and I elected not to tell him. I smiled inside and thought to myself: Maybe he'll be watching TV some night and see me and say, "Hey! I took his picture." The thought pleased me. He wanted to take my picture because I was on the bridge, not because I was walking to Nashville. It was funny. He never even asked why I was on the bridge. Maybe he thought I was jumping. Who knows? As I turned to watch him go, he was still clicking pictures of the skyline, then me, then the skyline again.

"Snicker," I said, "I've got a feelin' we're going to meet some interesting folks here." He agreed, or at least that was my interpretation of his response . . .

> *The drought of 1988 is what they're callin' it.*
> *Why'd I pick this year? Don't think I did. I think*
> *it picked me. It is my time.*

Snicker listened as I talked about trivia. I saw a pigeon trying to get in a hole some 6 inches off the pavement in the side of an underpass. Snicker's ears raised up, and I could tell he was waiting for my command. "Good boy, good boy. He means no harm to us. Let's see if we can help." I could see the bird's foot was broken as I lifted him off the ground. "He's trying' to get home, boy, but he can't quite make it."

I knew there was nothing I could do but place him in his nest. Maybe his foot would heal, I thought, as I walked away, trying to get Snicker away from him. Snicker's presence made the bird nervous.

I felt helpless. No one else even noticed as they buzzed by, but how could they? If they stopped on the highway, it would be suicide. Soon the feathered friend was miles behind us, and I knew that he would not be foremost in my thoughts anymore.

I looked to my right, and there was Floyd. He didn't see me. "What's he doin', Snicker? Look at him!" Floyd was taking I-70 West as I was about to take it east to St. Louis! "He's headin' for Denver, boy! Where's he going?" I thought of trying to cross the highway to get to him, but he soon disappeared from sight. I was walking facing the traffic, as I had done for most of the trip. I had been on the wrong side of the road when I came upon the guy in the Nova and was sorry for doing such a foolish thing. When I faced the traffic, I felt much safer.

I started up the off-ramp of I-70, eastbound once more, feeling frisky due to the change of highways. Little things sometimes changed my mood and kept me going, even when going on seemed next to impossible.

I turned and looked toward the west. "Where are you going, Floyd?" I shouted. "I hope he didn't decide to go home, Snicker." I frowned at the thought. It was now well above 100 degrees.

We walked until we could no more. The sun told me that hours had passed since last seeing Floyd. We relaxed in the shade of an overpass that provided a good view of I-70 in both directions.

No wonder I had not found the truck stop yet. The heat slowed us down, and I had to stop often to replenish our water.

Snicker's tongue hung low most of the time. The blisters on my feet were raw and wet. My feet swelled so much from the extreme heat that it felt like I was walking through fire at times.

> *I feel sick, so very sick to my stomach, and*
> *dizziness occurs more often than I'd like to admit.*
> *My feet hurt like hell! Two strangers approached*
> *me today. One filled me with fear; the other*
> *warmed my heart.*

Snicker kept looking upward from where we sat as if someone was above us. The overpass was very high and from where I lay against the wall, I could not see the ledge above. Curiosity soon got the best of me, and I began to climb upward on all fours. Snicker scurried on ahead like it was nothing, reaching the ledge and looking down at me. When I reached the top, a feeling of intrusion came upon me. The ledge was someone's home! It contained a blanket, a cup and a few possessions, probably the person's only possessions. "Come on, boy!" I said, "Let's go. Nobody's home."

We climbed back down to the shade of the overpass and relaxed for a while. I lay my head against the wall and thought about the homeless person who resided above us. I felt sleepy and at peace in the heat as I whispered my thoughts to the person we never saw: "I think that today you, me and Snicker are the same. We're all just lookin' for that ole rainbow." I thought all the rest of the day of the overpass that someone called home.

After the break, I trudged on to the east of Kansas City. The traffic was overbearing, and the heat was sickening. It almost destroyed me. I grew angry at the thought of having to face St. Louis.

Floyd finally showed up and told me that he hadn't been lost at all. I smiled as we walked together toward the cafe.

"I need to call home, Floyd," I said.

17
It's the Heat

I waited with anticipation as the phone rang several times.

Is she home? I wondered.

"Hello!" said the voice that I longed to hear.

"Hello, honey, it's me."

She laughed a little, then asked me about my days and if I had received the money she had wired. '

"Yes, I did. Floyd received it before he got lost." Floyd looked over at me with a stern face that told me he didn't approve of my saying he had been lost. "Well, not really lost," I explained, "only sidetracked for a while."

We talked until I felt my heart was filled with her presence. It was 10:20 p.m., and I knew I would sleep with Jackie inside my heart that night.

As I looked out toward the dismal city the next morning (Day 54), I was thankful to be alive. The cars had come so close that I had to keep my hands at my side for fear of hitting them or them me.

Floyd began buying three to four bags of ice a day to keep things at a temperature just under lukewarm. It was an expense we had anticipated. The ice had more than one use, at least for me: I put it on my shoulder and knees to relieve the throbbing pain.

"It's June 22. I will be in Nashville on July 22, in just one month — only one more month of this heat that may get even worse," I shouted. "All this for the privilege and honor of 3 minutes on stage. But don't forget what stage you long for: the Grand Ole Opry!" I uttered these words to myself with reassurance.

As I looked out at what lay behind me, I turned on my recorder instinctively . . .

> *I have traveled from freezing temperatures to a heat of 106 degrees. Nature has taught me much about not taking her for granted. I have learned to get up very early in this heat and get as many miles as possible behind me before noon, then rest, as I am doing now in the shade of a bridge on my way to Concordia, Missouri. The flies are like maggots. If I open my mouth, they find refuge.*

"Darn flies, huh, boy." He hated them and bit at them in vain as they buzzed about him in the humid climate that made the sweat pour from me in the darkest of shade.

"I don't know why you do it, boy. Why do you keep following me? You must think me nuts by now. Your pads have been iced over. You've been soaked with rain for days, blown off the road by winds and now you must suffer the indignity of these damn flies in temperatures you've never experienced in your life! What keeps you going? Could a dog love someone that much? If only us humans could be so true and faithful. There's much to be learned from you, Snicker."

He looked up, knitting his brow ever so slightly as if to say,

"You're okay, too." The expression in his eyes revealed many things. I stroked his head. It was all the attention he ever asked for. I fell asleep beside what I knew to be a true friend indeed.

By 5:00 p.m. the temperature was still in the 90s, but we moved out to gain a little more distance before the sun went down. Some days I walked during the early evening. The cool of the night felt fresh on my face and allowed my body a few extra miles before it rebelled.

The truck stop in Concordia was our home for the night — and a magnificent one at that. The place had everything from movies to tire irons. We paid for a shower at the truck stop, and the one I had before bed was much needed.

Living at truck stops and campgrounds had become a way of life for us. Floyd eventually learned that many truck stops provided truck drivers with a free shower in exchange for the purchase of diesel fuel. He would somehow work his magic and claim a free shower for me. Sometimes we were blessed with a motel room, but not often. Floyd would usually find us a spot for the night. If he didn't, we just pulled over and slept in the camper.

"Let's catch the news and see if you're on TV!" Floyd exclaimed.

"You go ahead, Floyd." I was tired and didn't care about TV. "I'm going to bed. The heat really got me today." Waves of nausea were with me a lot lately.

I wrote in my diary until sleep was almost inevitable. I spoke a few words on tape, then said good night to Snicker, hoping he didn't have any ticks and cursing myself for not checking. The night that fell around me would not allow me the peace I needed.

"I tossed and turned all night long until just before dawn," I said to Floyd as he rose with a smile and a look of refreshment the next morning. As I uttered the word "dawn," it carried me home for a moment to my daughter. It made me wonder if Jackie had been thinking of a beautiful sunrise, such as the one I was looking upon, when she had named her baby girl. She must have been, I thought to myself, for dawn is a beautiful sight to behold. Then my thoughts raced back to Tampa, Florida when Jackie had asked me if I would like to meet Dawn, She was 3 years old and pretending she was a bride with a towel draped about her head like a veil as I pulled up next to them on their way back from the neighborhood park. Jackie introduced us and Dawn said hello with a small voice.

And now she is 16, I thought with amazement. I had become Dawn's stepfather and grew to love her very much. She had lost her natural father young in life.

"You know I have two sons, too, don't you?" I asked.

"Yes, but I don't remember their names."

"Chris and Jimmy. They're fine boys. I just got to know them again a couple of years ago."

"I'm glad you got reacquainted. By the way, why didn't you sleep?"

"I don't know," I said as I pulled something from my hair. "A tick!" I screamed.

"What?" Floyd yelled. He hated the thought of them.

"A tick in my hair!" I said as I pulled it out. "They're overpowering us, Floyd!" I said with desperation.

"I'll spray everything. We'll have to spray the pup, again."

"Boy, Floyd, I hope that spray isn't hurting Snicker. We sure are putting a lot of it on him." I knew we must do something about the pests that subsided for a spell, then came to haunt us once again.

I thought of the tick fever that had almost killed me when I was a child, and I remembered Floyd's warning about Lyme disease. A sweat broke out upon my brow. I could do nothing about the blood-sucking pests but pull them from me.

"Floyd, please help me check Snicker at night. I should have last night, and that's what cost me a good night's sleep. The thing about ticks is just when you think you have them all, there's always one more."

"Just sleep for a while longer," Floyd said in a nearly demanding tone.

"Nope. I'm up now. I'll sleep through the heat of the day. See you in the shade," I said as I walked away from our house on wheels.

I chuckled to myself and thought of how well I slept some-times under a bridge, especially if I was fortunate enough to find one near a running stream or creek. "I sleep like a baby near run-ning water, much better than in a bunk," I said to Snicker, who seemed to sleep well almost anywhere except when he was sick. That old bunk I thought, is not long enough for a man of 6-foot 3-inches. Maybe that's what keeps me awake sometimes, having to curl up to sleep. Yes, that's it.

For some reason, I needed to rationalize why my body func-tioned so oddly at times. Talking to myself and reassuring myself seemed to be vital to my existence. The passing of time upon the

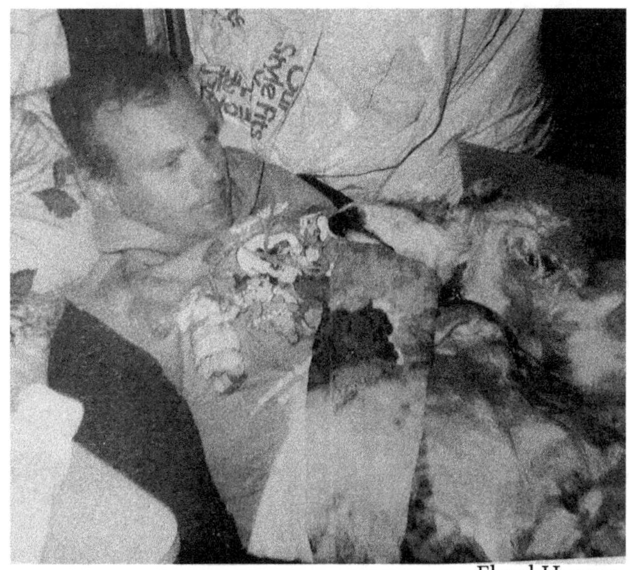

Camper cramp
Floyd Haynes

lonely parts of the highway caused me to ache for answers to all sorts of questions.

Walking and looking for the perfect spot, I finally had to reesort to an underpass with shade. It was the only bridge I saw. The place had no water to cool us and no soothing sound to lull me to sleep. The humidity was high, and the flies were so thick that they flew in my mouth as I breathed heavily. Every muscle in my body throbbed!

I had made a vow to myself to walk 25 miles this day. I faced seven more before the day's end. Lying with my back against the warm concrete under the bridge, I released my pack and began to moisten Snicker's face. The water bottle had about a pint left between us. Snicker and I had learned to fill up with water whenever we could. I had even learned to drink more than I thought I could ever hold at one time, and the method paid off. It had taken a while to learn some bitter lessons about this climate that was so strange to us. The heat in Wyoming was very dry compared to Missouri.

We drank a little to refresh ourselves, and I tried to remove my socks without feeling the pain of bending over. "Oh, man, Snicker. It sure is hot!" He looked at me as if that was an understatement.

I stripped down to my shorts and used my clothes for a pillow. The air between my toes helped make the heat bearable. I thought how nice it was to be off that hot asphalt that someone had long ago named the shoulder of a road. I was beginning to hate looking at the endless white lines.

I was all in for June 23. Nelson was to be our resting point for the night.

● ● ●

"Boonville" was the name I read before me on June 24 (Day 56). I had two things on my mind: Columbia, Missouri, and the friendly DJ named Butch Burrell, who called himself the "Ole Hound Dog." He had asked us to stop in for a visit when we got to his neck of the woods.

The noon sun was above my head at a temperature above 100 degrees. Snicker was trying to walk in the shadow that was cast just a little behind me. I paused beside the sign for a moment to look around for an oasis of some sort. Kneeling down to catch a little shade from the sign, I felt Snicker nudge me, trying to get his fair share of the seemingly cooler spot.

"Man, Snicker, it's hot!" He held a paw off the ground and

panted as if he would draw his last breath very soon.

"What's wrong, boy?" I said, lifting his paw.

"Ooohh, must be terrible, boy!" I tried to pull the tar from between his pads. I pulled gently then a little firmer until those sad eyes gave way to a yelp. "Sorry, boy. Guess I have to cut it out." I removed the small scissors from my bag and cut gently between his paws, trying not to hurt him. He lay as still as a sleeping child.

Shade, I thought with relish. Better find a cooler spot.

That cooler spot came some 45 minutes later, with no sweet babbling spring, but only the shade of some beautiful trees in a park near the highway. "There is water here, boy. No springs to bathe in, but we have ample water."

He remained calm as I worked again on the dried asphalt in his pads. "Dang, Snicker, this is terrible," I said, trying not to clip any skin and having to leave some asphalt in places. He slept well in the shade of those trees, his ears popping up from time to time. He dreamed and whined as if he were scared of something. Placing a hand on his head seemed to comfort him, and he would once again drift into peaceful slumber.

I spoke long into my recorder, occasionally cursing the flies, as I sat in that otherwise quiet place. I had heard a man once say that things don't just happen — we allow them to happen.

"How could I have allowed myself to do this?" I sensed a mood of self-pity coming on. With that realization, I began to laugh and yell, "I can make it!" I turned off my recorder, not wanting to ever be heard speaking in that frame of mind. Why? Why not just shout right into it or laugh or even cry?

Silence came over me and remained for a long time. I thought about my cousin, little Riley Witt, and his older brother, Chance. Chance had always called Riley "Ryebone" since his dad's name was Byrone. Riley had often recited a Bible verse to me during our lives. His little voice now came to me, whispering, "God cares about me." I finally said, "Yes, He does, Riley," then once again went to that silent space. It was a place I needed to go for peace of mind.

The temperature increased to 106 degrees. I rested through

the heat and walked well into the night to get the distance I wanted. The worst of the heat slipped behind the horizon with the setting sun. I watched it go down with greater respect than ever before, continuing towards Columbia, Missouri.

Around noon the next day, June 25, we climbed the stairs to the second floor in search of Butch's radio station. I had been thinking about making it through those doors for most of the miserable morning.

"I'm Butch, the 'Ole Hound Dog.' You must be the Walking Cowboy," he said as I walked through the door.

I felt a little de'jé vu at the moment as I stared at the happy man with long locks of hair and an attitude of friendliness that reflected all about him. He told me how happy he was to meet me.

"You've come a long way," he continued as he introduced me to his wife and young son. "It'll be about a half hour. You're just a little early for the show," he said apologetically.

"That's okay," I said with a smile. "I'm happy to be in such warm company."

My eyes wandered about, trying to take in the surroundings. The quaint place with high ceilings contained many memories in the form of old records hanging from the walls.

"I've an urge for a little food. Will I have time?" I asked.

"Sure. Half an hour to 45 minutes would be great. What are you hungry for?"

"Some carbohydrates. Any spaghetti nearby?"

"Yes, there is. I'll show you," a young man named Eli replied.

He was Butch's son.

"That'd be great. Hungry, Floyd?" I asked as I turned.

"No, sir. I'm staying right here and making some calls."

I could tell he was on cloud nine with all the media attention.

"Go on," he continued, "I had a late breakfast." I knew Floyd loved breakfast. Most mornings, he would head for a truck stop with several pay phones (using two at a time sometimes), pause for breakfast and visit with a waitress or two. This routine helped make his day brighter.

I walked down the street with the young boy at my side, and we talked about many different things. I smiled at the energy he displayed. Our conversation continued until it was time to go on the air with his dad. I had hardly ever been in such warm company.

The goodbyes came hard for me after a great interview with Butch on the show. I thought about Eli as Floyd and I sat in the parking lot of the local Dairy Queen. I opened the door, and Snicker leaped out at a dead run, heading for the nearest tree. He relieved himself with a leg in the air, looking back at me with a shameful expression on his face. I joined him outside and closed the camper door, sniffing the clean, outdoor air. "That camper's gettin' musty, boy. Needs a good cleaning." He lapped up the ice cream I had set before him, never looking up.

A while later, I opened the door of the camper and sat down on the passenger seat, placing my hand firmly in . . . "DOG CRAP! It's dog crap! Floyd, look at this! Snicker, how could you?" Snicker came at a run across the parking lot and began to turn in circles, trying to grasp the situation.

I was raging uncontrollably, like a madman. I tried to stop the anger, but could not. "Oh, Floyd. It's all over the place. My bed! Look at my bed! Snicker, you're a dead dog! I thought you said he went to the bathroom, Floyd," I barked.

"He did," was the reply.

"When? Yesterday? Look at this!" I screamed.

"Calm down. I'll take care of it," Floyd said gently.

I grabbed the comforter from my bed and rolled it into a ball, choking back the feeling of nausea. I opened the door and headed for the dumpster at a faster pace than I had used in days.

"No! No! Don't throw it away. It's Barry's," Floyd implored.

"I'll get him a new one," I grumbled.

"No! I'll wash it," he said, half begging and half demanding.

People began to gather and stare at the two men fighting over a blanket in the Dairy Queen parking lot, in heat close to 90 degrees. "It's the heat," I heard an old man say as he passed by like he had seen it before. His remark stopped me cold, and I glared his way. I looked around at the people with puzzled looks about them. "The dog . . . He messed up my bed," I stuttered, feeling like the fool that I must have appeared. They moved away, one by one to their respective vehicles, never saying a word, only looking.

"I'm sorry, Floyd. Look at me. I'm acting like a crazy man."

He looked at me for what seemed an eternity, then spoke with kindness. "Let's go to the truck stop. I'll wash these and clean the truck while you nap in the shade."

There was no reason for anyone to take what I had thrown at Floyd. I hated myself for losing control.

Snicker lay beneath the bunk, way at the back. There was no way he was getting near the man who only moments before had threatened death. He was playing it safe.

I walked through Columbia after my afternoon nap and quit around the 135—mile marker, then lingered in a hot tub. My body shivered with pleasure with every surge of the water upon my calves and shoulders. Floyd sat next to the pool of water, writing in his diary.

"Floyd, did that young man, Eli, tell you about having his own radio show?"

"Yes, he did, while you were on the air."

"I thought the interview went well. How about you?" I asked, knowing Floyd was pleased with his work this day.

"Two out of three ain't bad, huh, pardner?" he asked. "We got radio and TV today. I don't understand about the newspaper not turnlng up."

"I'm sure glad you were able to get us a room."

"The Chamber of Commerce did it. Sure are nice folks. I think I might step out for a while. Mr. Snicker's asleep in the room. He's not barkin'. I guess he figures he best be good," he said with a grin.

We had decided we would take June 26 as a rest day. I believed Floyd would be out for the night. I felt tired from all the heat and faced the mirror with horror, seeing dark bags and lines beneath my eyes for the first time. I wrote my thoughts before I lay to rest:

> *Diarrhea has set upon me again*
> *and nausea is present all too often,*
> *in waves that will not let me sleep for*
> *the longest time. I miss you Jackie.*

The sound of the door opening wakened me. Trying to be silent and not disturb my sleep, Floyd slipped beneath his sheets. I decided not to speak. As I lay awake hearing Floyd begin to snore, I wondered if he had had a good time, and my thoughts drifted once more to the Opry...

18

The Warm and the Storm

Sunday was a good day to rest. The housekeeper finally knocked at noon. "Maid service," she called as she entered. "Are you gentlemen staying another day?"

"No, ma'am. Just resting as long as we can," I answered as if apologizing.

"I saw you last night on TV. You're the one walking. Could you sign a picture for my daughter?" She asked as she handed me a photo.

"My daughter's a singer, and she is excited about what you're doing," the maid proudly proclaimed.

"Well, tell her I said to follow her dreams, ma'am."

"I'll do just that," she said with a smile.

Even though we had decided to rest that day, I wanted to walk a little more in the evening. I marked a spot five more miles to the east before returning to the motel parking lot.

Rested and full of new life, we both opened our eyes close to 4:30 am. the next morning, Monday, June 27 (Day 59).

"You'll be on the road by 5:30, David, if you've a mind to," Floyd said.

"I have a mind to. I'm feeling refreshed and renewed."

The morning was cool with almost a chill from the moisture that lay in the air. "That good ole morning dew," I said as Snicker searched and snorted in every hole he encountered. The traffic seemed light, and I could hear the birds sing and the crickets still exchanging sounds among themselves.

"I love it, boy. Let's get some miles in before that sun cooks our brains and turns our legs to putty."

There was a place ahead called Williamsburg that was my target for the day. "I wonder what we'll find there, my friend?" I asked of Snicker. He ignored me and went happily about his dog activities.

Over the course of many days, I had watched him go from a seemingly young pup to an exhausted old dog as the heat took its toll. "Will this be another one of those days? I heard the man on the radio say 'hot and humid' last night, Snicker, so it's bound to be another hot one." Snicker was enjoying the cool morning air.

"Let's walk 'em off, boy. If we get enough in before noon, it will be easy to finish out the day when it cools down." With that note, he began to pace me, and I felt a rush of love for the little furry guy with the speckled face.

Monday was basically long, hot and uneventful. To be more precise, it was uneventful until I phoned Jackie.

"I started a new song, honey. It's called 'Butterfingers' at the moment. It's about a guy who can't hang onto anything he puts his hands on."

"Where'd you get that one?"

"Floyd. He was talkin' about bein' a butterfingers, and I thought it was a good title. I'm just playin' with it some now."

We talked for quite some time before saying good night.

There was no light on in the camper, only the glow from the street lamp in the corner of the fast food parking lot that was our nesting spot for the night. I stared long at the pay phone on the corner as I wrote in my diary and thought about my conversation with Jackie. I wrote about her and hung on her name as I spelled it out.

The only "shower" I could find was the bathroom sink of the fast food place where we sat. I brushed my teeth several times, trying to feel refreshed, and washed as best I could in the sink, between interruptions from paying customers. I only had to clean up like this about a half dozen times along the way, either in a food establishment or a convenience store bathroom. I would wash my hands and face in the sink as quickly as I could, brush my teeth in a hurry, then take both wet and dry paper towels into a toilet stall for further "bathing." I would use the sink again to shave and wash my hair, then dry my hair under the hand dryer or with paper towels, excusing myself if people walked in. I got some strange looks, and it was awkward at times, but I got to where I could clean up in record time.

As the light went off outside my window, I felt pleased with myself for having already removed the ticks from Snicker. I knew he was grateful that I had not forgotten. Floyd had not yet returned. I was certain he would sit and drink coffee for a time with some new acquaintances. He loved to visit with people. I drifted off with Wyoming on my mind.

With the light of day the next morning came the reality of where I truly was — not in Wyoming, but in the Missouri heat. My thoughts drifted back to the morning I had crossed the Missouri River on a beautiful bridge just outside Columbia. The air was still as the birds soared with the down drafts from the high bridge. Huge rocks jutted out into the swift current, turning it ever so slightly. I had found a set of car keys halfway across the bridge and turned them over to Butch, the "Ole Hound Dog." I had been wondering about those car keys for days and whether the "Ole Hound Dog" had ever found their owner.

It was Tuesday, June 28 (Day 60), and I was going to

conquer it, I thought to myself as I counted the seconds that I stretched one leg and then the other. My recorder was lying beside me, and I reached for it . . .

> *Of late I have not weighed myself but know I*
> *have lost 20 pounds or more and am still*
> *dropping weight every day, no matter how much*
> *I eat.*

The highway looked never-ending as I peered down the long passage that lay before me. I wanted to turn south through the back roads of Missouri. The thought tore at my innermost emotions. After Kansas City, I did not want to face St. Louis. No matter how much I longed to, I did not take to the back roads. Perhaps it was because of my talk with Floyd that morning.

"There'll be less places for water along the back roads and probably no press at all. Let's stay on the trail we're on," Floyd said nervously.

"I don't know, Floyd. I may not be able to walk through the city again. It was too hard on us."

"I know, but let's turn just outside St. Louis. Highway 61 goes around, and we can get on the other side, cross the river and head for Nashville."

Nashville! He said a magic word there.

"I'll think about it, Floyd," I said, and he left it at that.

I had talked on the phone to my brothers, Jack and Jimmy. They were both concerned about my health and the reports of the heat. Jack had asked what he could do to help with publicity and suggested a newspaper ad in Nashville. "No ads in Nashville" was my order. I wanted to finish the walk and take only what press came out to cover my story.

As the miles mounted and my blisters called out to me, I gave in to rest. With a trembling hand, I turned on my comfort and spoke. . .

> *To my family and Floyd, I know I seem*
> *unconcerned at the outcome and just seem to*

*dwell on the day as of lately. I have tried so hard
to explain to everyone how I feel at the day's end
and can't even comprehend the way I get there
sometimes.*

*The only one who seems to understand now is
`Jackie. She can feel what I feel, it seems, and is my
rock when I grow weak.*

*Floyd, who understood early on, has got a fever
brewing in him now for the outcome. He
sometimes forgets what's at hand or so it seems.
But I know better because he has worked so very
hard.*

That night Floyd and I talked about my conversation with Jack about the coverage in Nashville.

"Not a bad idea," Floyd said when he learned of it.

"I know you all want it to be right, but I want to finish the walk with no prior communication with the Opry. Only then will I ask them to consider me, and I don't want to place any ads. I'll be satisfied with whatever press we get." Jack had already done so much anyway, including helping me through some bad times back in Iowa and Missouri.

Floyd and I sat alone for a few minutes. The air was still muggy, but we were cooled by the vent above our heads.

"Tell me about your other friend, Floyd."

"His name is Merlin Flair."

"I know that. You just introduced us." His friend had left the room for a moment. "Is he an old Army buddy?"

"Yes."

Floyd was not very talkative when it came to himself. You had to pry it out of him.

"Well, tell me, how'd you find him?"

"I didn't. He found me today while you were walkin'. He called back to Mel Glenn in St. Joe after hearing about it on the TV and came lookin' for me."

"Well, Floyd, this is reunion time for you."

Merlin came back and said, "You can come by our place. We live in New Haven."

I looked at Floyd. "South of where we're heading " he said.

I smiled, thanked Merlin and said, "Looks like we're still headin' east for now." Floyd appeared to be pleased with that statement. I knew he would have liked to visit his friend, but that he did not want to turn south yet.

I excused myself for the evening. "I'm going to rest, guys. Have a nice visit."

I don't know how long he stayed up with Merlin but Floyd was awake bright and early on June 29, burning for some action and fidgety because he could not call anywhere before 8:00 a.m. Then, suddenly, he spoke aloud. "David! Let's call Liz White. She's on the air early at WSM."

"Okay. You go call her and motion to me if she wants to talk to me." I sat over my oatmeal until he gave me the sign.

"Hello, David. Do you want to go on the air?" Liz asked.

"I sure would," I replied with excitement. We had become friends, I believe, through our communications during the many days I had been on the road.

"Aren't you glad we called?" Floyd asked after Liz said goodbye.

"Yes, I am."

Floyd had a way of helping start my day most times, and he really got me moving at 6:30 that morning.

• • •

The storm came so quickly that it caught me off guard. The days of constant heat had softened my senses to things around me. The lightning crashed about us with such fury that I shook, and Snicker whimpered as it cracked like a whip. I ran as hard as I could toward the rest area. It was closed! Under construction! Wet, cold and nervous about the ever-present danger, I raced for the bridge, scrambling to climb under it, throwing my pack ahead of me to try and keep anything dry that I could.

It was many years ago that I had gained my respect for lightning. I was in my early teens, playing softball with the church team. The rain came and people began to move to their cars, but the game went on. The lightning hit with a crash, striking the telephone pole nearest right field. I was in center field, waiting for the batter to swing. Every player went down, as if struck with the bat. I felt the electricity run through me and out my feet and elbows. People rushed to the field to assist the downed players. I sat up, shaking from the jolt. The players seemed to be okay, that is, all but one. The second baseman was down and convulsing. I heard someone shout to call an ambulance, and another yelled,

David Stewart

Shelter from the storm

"Don't let him swallow his tongue." I could hardly walk off the field, even with help. The ambulance soon arrived and took our man to the hospital. We all survived that horrid night.

The thought of that experience crept over me as lightning appeared in the sky and I clutched Snicker close to my chest. We shivered with every gust of wind and cringed at the sound of thunder. The immediate danger seemed to pass or at least ease a bit as I peered out at the black mass that moved slowly away to the west, leaving steady rain outside my shelter.

I saw the camper approaching and scrambled to where I thought it might come to a stop. Floyd barely saw us and slammed on his brakes. I was amazed he had not passed me by. Drying myself, I thanked Floyd for showing up.

"I'd like to say I knew you were in trouble, but I didn't. It isn't rainin' in town. I came after you for an interview," he confessed.

"No matter. You're a welcome sight." I had faced much inclement weather on the trip and was glad to have been rescued this time. We were cold, and it was a comfort to climb in the camper.

Floyd made calls after my interview. I slept like a newborn as the rain came to town and pattered ever so softly, smelling of freshness outside my window. After my rest, I walked until I was bone-tired, making some nice encounters along the way.

A kind lady stopped and talked to me in the late of day. "Hello," she said as she walked toward the interstate through the grass in high heels, carrying what seemed to be a book. It was indeed a book — her Bible. "Would you sign the inside page for me," she asked.

It seemed strange. No one had ever asked me to sign a Bible before. I had signed many things, but never a Bible. I hesitated as I looked into her eyes. "I want it there to remember to pray for you daily." The lump in my throat prevented me from talking as she asked questions. I could only nod for a time.

"You'll make it, and I will pray for you." With that she said goodbye. I wanted to hug her as she drove away.

Not long after the lady left, a man stopped to give Snicker

some dog biscuits. "Hello. You must be the Walking Cowboy. My name's Moxley, Gene Moxley. Can I give your dog some biscuits?"

"Yes, you can."

The man also shared some water with us. "I saw you on TV. I think what you're doing is great. I admire your kindness and love for animals."

I looked at him for a moment, then he explained, "Oh, I could tell from your interview with him in your arms. I could tell." He beamed while fussing over Snicker.

Later, a surprise from Gillette came just before my day was to end. Allen and Deb Connolly pulled up at about 6:30 p.m. on their way home from vacation. "We were on our way home, saw you on the highway and turned around," Allen said with a smile.

"What a nice surprise," I exclaimed. One more day and they would have missed me because I was changing my original route.

As usual, saying goodbye to someone from home was very hard to do, but they knew I had to move on.

Ten miles to my turnoff, I thought as night ended my walk. I shall start on Highway 61, a new road, within a few hours, come morning. That was the thought that began my rest that night. My hopes were to get around the city and onto I-55 before nightfall the next day. I knew I could make it, but I'd be doing some hard walking and would need an early start. Any change of regular routine would heighten my moods and give me renewed strength.

That night I reminisced. Thoughts of the great people I had met that day lifted by spirits. All the visiting, though, had put me 10 miles short of the turnoff that I wanted to reach before dark. I was tired and ready for rest. I knew the coming day would bring a new challenge.

19
Lost

The Union 76 gas station rest area soon became a mere memory of the night's rest stop as I turned onto the long route to go around St. Louis on June 30 (Day 62). I chose this detour in order to avoid the busy Interstate 70 along the eastside of town. Although the traffic was heavy, the shoulders were narrow and rough for walking in places. I felt more at ease here than on the interstate.

TV Channels 2 and 5 came out to us before noon. As I thought about the earlier part the day, I began to record . . .

The heat seems to be bearable today, but I haven't heard what the temperature is. I believe the extreme heat wave has let up a little, maybe because of the rain. I was nearly struck by a van

on a narrow bridge, and the news team captured
the excitement on camera. 'Wanna see it?" the cameraman asked
as I came near where they stood
along the road. "We have it on film," he said.
'No, sir, I saw it firsthand, " was my reply.

I visited with those men for quite some time. They were excited about my coming through St. Louis. The one named Al was a kind heart, and he talked of my story as if he had known me forever. I knew I had made a true friend in this man. I walked on with pride due to the way he spoke of me.

It was 6:30 and going on dark. "Snicker, we're lost, friend, and I'm nervous," I said to him as we sat across from a church. I had changed to Highway 141 and thought Floyd had understood where to find me. "I know I told him, boy," I said, trying to affirm it. "Well, I'm almost positive." More than three and a half hours had passed, and it was getting late. "I don't like this, Snicker. It bothers me."

I had made up my mind to crawl under the bushes behind the church and sleep there that night when a vehicle approached. A head appeared from the open car window. "Are you lost?" a woman asked.

I looked at her and her companion as I replied, "Yes, I am."

The man was probably in his 60s, and she must have been close in age. Both were dressed up. Their hair was gray, and both were smiling at me.

"We were going to church and saw you sitting here. We knew who you were. We saw you on Channel 5 News. Can we help?"

"I don't know. I'm separated from my support man. He's back on 61 somewhere. I'm a little nervous!" I confided.

"Well, get in, and we'll take you there," the woman offered.

"I can't, ma'am. I don't ride with anyone. That's our rule."

"Oh! Okay, we understand . . . Well, listen. You go down this road about one and a half miles. There are some lights there and a big parking lot. We'll get your friend and tell him where you are."

I felt joy and relief thanks to their offer of help.

"How will we know him?" the woman asked.

"He's in a little camper with posters about my walk on the side."

"Okay. You go on down there and be careful," she told me as they drove away.

I did just as she said, as if she had been my own mother speaking to me. If my mother knew where I was now, I thought as I headed for those lights, she'd be really upset. I smiled at the thought of my mother and was glad she didn't know where I was, at least not exactly.

Sitting beneath those lights, I thought the worst. What if they don't find him? What then? I didn't want to call Jackie yet and alarm her, but if I called, I could tell her where to tell Floyd to find me in case he called her.

"Oh, no! Please don't call her, Floyd!" I said aloud. "She'll be frantic." She had fears of something happening to me and had cautioned me about the cities. Oh, please, don't call her yet.

At that thought, I heard a horn blow. Floyd jumped out and ran to my side, embracing me.

"You're all right," he exclaimed with relief. He was jumping for joy and I was, too. "These folks brought me to you." He pointed to emptiness. "Where'd they go? They were right there behind me," he said somewhat baffled. I looked and they had vanished as if they'd never even been there.

"What were their names?" I asked.

"I don't know. They found me and told me how to get here. They followed to make sure I did not get lost. I never did know their names," he said with regret.

"Me, either. I never asked." They reminded me of guardian angels.

"Oh, no! I've got to call Jackie back!" he shouted.

"Oh, Floyd!" I yelled.

"I didn't know what to do, David! Let's get to a phone."

"Hello?" trembled a voice full of fright.

"Hello, honey. I'm okay."

"I thought you were dead in a ditch somewhere," she sobbed.

"It's okay, baby. I'm okay," I said with tears running down my face. "We're gettin' a lot of press," I said, trying to lighten the moment by changing the topic to some good news.

"I'm shaking all over. I thought you were dead!"

We both cried and reassured each other over the phone. Jackie and I were very close and had never spent much time apart. We liked being together, even working together. We sometimes fought but were in love all the time.

"You need to call the St. Louis Dispatch," she finally said. "They called here to find out where you were. The story's getting bigger every day."

"I know, honey. We're gettin' lots of press out here."

"Please be careful. I don't know what I'd do if something happened to you."

"I'll be careful." I had managed to keep my bad experience with Frank to myself, but not this one. It hit home.

I had met a policeman several hours before the arrival of the older couple who had volunteered to find Floyd. The policeman and I talked for a while, and he told me his brother was a detective in my home town. I thought he'd find Floyd so I wasn't too worried until the couple found me. Floyd told me no cop ever found him. Maybe I had given the officer the wrong road by mistake, but I had felt fairly certain of my directions.

That night I entered some notes in my diary about a beautiful girl I had met earlier in the day. As I wrote, I began to remember our conversation. She had dark skin and attractive eyes. She motioned for me to cross the road. Very leery, I asked her what I could do for her.

"Where you going?" she asked with what I thought to be a Mexican accent.

"Nashville, Tennessee."

"Why?"

"I want to sing on the Grand Ole Opry."

"I know Willie Nelson," she stated matter-of-factly.

"You do? Well, put in a good word for me," I replied jokingly. Everyone seemed to know a star.

She handed me $2. "That's all I can spare."

"I don't need it, ma'am." I felt embarrassed.

"It's okay. I want you to have it. Good luck!" And with that she was on her way.

"I hope to make it," I said to the back of her car as she drove away to I know not where.

"Snicker," I said, looking straight at him. "People are hard to figure sometimes. We'll probably never see her again, but she has touched our lives a little."

I continued to write upon a new page in my diary of June 30. My last words were:

We're in the parking lot somewhere on highway 141.

Floyd had talked with the local law enforcement about my plans to cross the river into Illinois, and they told him they didn't want me crossing the busy bridge.

"We'll just change our route some more," I told him the next morning.

"We can't."

"Yes, we can!" I replied. '

"They want to drive you over. It's only a short distance."

"No, Floyd. Remember, I'm walking every step of the way."

"What's your plan?"

Taking the map, I showed Floyd a route I had in mind. "We'll go to Chester, Illinois, by way of I-55 South. We'll cross there, go in the back way to Marion, Illinois, then be back on track the rest of the way."

"There's not much press that way, after we cross the river, probably not until Marion," Floyd complained.

"So be it, then! That's our new plan," I declared.

So on July 1 (Day 63), my route changed once more. I had to familiarize myself with the names of new places. My memory knew the old route, town by town. A change of route was ad-venturous to me. I made a game of it and in some strange way enjoyed the unknown aspects of it. By changing routes, I met a woman named Mary Priesak who happened upon me after the TV coverage had aired in St. Louis.

"Can you have lunch with me?" she asked kindly from tile distance I kept between her and myself, as I had done with other strangers until I felt comfortable.

"No, ma'am, I can't."

"Do you have time for a short talk?" she asked with much sincerity.

"Yes, I do." And so we spent some time sharing our lofty visions.

I was now 300 miles from my destination with almost 1,300 miles behind me. Jackie had told me in our last talk that, looking at my itinerary, she discovered we had included a day for June 31. We laughed and said no matter.

My home for the night was not known until I said I was tired at an off ramp south of Arnold, Missouri.

"Where to?" Floyd asked. "I don't see a truck stop so it looks like it's a parking lot tonight," he said as he pulled into a Holiday Inn.

I cooked up canned vegetables on our stove while Floyd explored our surroundings. He returned and opened the door to our little box with excitement.

"They gave us a room!" he announced. "They saw your story. The TV is really gettin' it out to the public."

A room, a hot shower, clean sheets and air conditioning — my mind was drawing pictures of paradise.

"Hey, Floyd. Good work!"

"It never hurts to ask," he said, and I knew he was proud of the little bonus sent our way.

I needed that shower so badly that I took an extra long one to compensate for another one I might miss.

20
The Rattler

Festus. As the word came to mind, I could not help but think of "Gunsmoke." I never missed an episode of that TV series and watched all the reruns. Now I was heading for Festus, Missouri, and it was another smoldering day. "Soon we cross the mighty Mississippi," I said to no one in particular. I was restless after walking some hard miles down I-55 on this day of Saturday, July 2 (Day 64), and longed for the back roads once again. My eagerness to cross the Mississippi was the driving force that carried me through the day. That evening I watched some children at play and felt at peace.

Sunday came with intense heat. I wondered if there would be lots of fireworks on the 4th. "I'll probably be in the sack, anyway," I spoke aloud, placing one foot ahead of the other and wondering how many steps I had taken, trying to do the calculation in my mind. But my mind would not function. "A bunch, boy. A bunch," I finally said to Snicker.

My sights were set on Perryville for the night. Floyd told me there was a KOA campground there, and I pictured their shower. "We shall stay there tonight, and then we head east by northeast to cross the river, boy." Snicker never looked up, he was hot, very hot. Water from the bottle seemed to help only temporarily. The heat was dreadful. Snicker's tongue hung almost to the ground. My eyes began to ache from the intense glare.

> *I have cut back on my miles a little and feel the plan we have is sufficient to carry us into Nashville on the exact day.*

My thoughts fell upon my children. Dawn would be coming to Nashville, and I hoped that Chris and Jimmy could join us. I would call them from Nashville.

> *I sure hope my mother will he sitting in the front row. I said it! Wow! I said it. I'm gonna be on the Grand Ole Opry! I have been apprehensive, but today I feel positive about it. I hope I can keep it up and not fall apart.*

Three miles from Perryville, my legs began to feel like rubber.

Why do things happen all of a sudden like this? I wondered and tried to remember what I had eaten that would cause the problem.

That night Floyd and I talked as I started the laundry.

"Hot as hell today!" he exclaimed.

"Not just that —- my legs gave up at times. My right knee has been acting up, too."

"Well, go on and shower, and I'll finish up the laundry."

•　•　•

"Good morning, America! I'm proud to be here," were the words I spoke with glee to the countryside on July 4. Floyd put an American flag on the antenna and started out toward Chester,

Illinois. I sat and wrote as he pulled away from me on the new
back road of Highway 51.

Always strive for the highest, hope for
the best and be proud of what you
are fortunate enough to accomplish

Chester, Illinois, would mark my arrival into another state.
So many days had passed since leaving home that it was hard to
look back on some of them. If I closed my eyes, though, I could
retrace almost every one of my steps.

The day was stifling, with the clouds allowing some relief and shade at times. The country was beautiful and rich, and
the crops were looking plush near the great river toward which I
trudged.

The drought had not been such a demon along the Mississippi. The river finally revealed herself to me after a long morning
in the sun. I stood in awe of this river that I was to cross and
wondered about her earlier travelers.

Across the river would be Floyd, waiting with a camera. We
recorded the crossing of state lines, rivers and some town city
limits. "He will be there," I said as I stepped to cross an old
bridge that shook as the cars crossed. It was the Chester Bridge. I
peered way ahead at the other side and smiled. "She's a toll
bridge, Snicker. I wonder if we have to pay to cross."

There was applause as I approached, and Floyd and two
bridge attendants snapped pictures. It appeared to be the changing of the guard, and one remained to watch the crossing. I was
introduced promptly to the two gentlemen with whom Floyd
had spent part of the day.

We stopped for a while on the other side of the Mississippi.
I looked out at a huge barge guided by a small tugboat and marveled at its grace upon the water.

"The press is coming soon, David," Floyd told me as I stood
beside a bronze statue of Popeye the Sailor. "The Home of
Popeye," it read, and told the history of Chester and of its famous character, Popeye.

"You know, Floyd," I said softly, not looking at him, "I took a picture of a sign that said 'Chester, Illinois, 13 miles,' at the same time a car passed me goin' about 60 mph."

He waited patiently for me to tell the story. I had a habit of pausing in the middle of my stories. "It would only take a car 3 minutes to go 13 miles at 60 mph," I continued. "It took me more than 3 hours to get that 13 miles."

That night I did not see many fireworks as I lay thinking about my day. Once in a while I could see red, blue, green, even white upon the darkness glaring through my window. I thought of the sunset pictures I had taken along the shore of the grand river. I jotted down some lines that were in my mind. I don't know if I had read the words long ago or if they were fresh lines:

Each of us has been given life
Like a chapter in a great book
It's up to us to turn the page
Lest we read the same, day after day.

Jackie had wired us some money, and it was much needed. I bought a newspaper. There was a picture of me in the St. Louis Dispatch. It was a nice big picture with a short mention of my walk. I smiled when I saw "AP News" written beside it. I knew Joe Edwards would see it in Nashville.

I read about an airliner shot down by an American warship in the Persian Gulf by mistake, and it saddened me.

6:30 a.m. was a nice time to relax and read, but I was late by half an hour already. I laid the paper aside and walked away from the outskirts of Chester, along a lonesome river road marked "Highway 3."

Frank came back to mind. Those cold eyes would be in every shadow of the lonely road. My stomach grew sick with bile.

The road is narrow and dark. The vegetation is
thick along this river road and for the first time I
want to carry my pistol. I don't know I just
feel uneasy this morning.

I know it's him. Those eyes of his haunt me and darkness and solitude bring on fear. I know this is to be a long and lonely back road for miles to come. You chose it, David! Now get movin'.

Snicker was alert to every movement, and there were many on our way that morning. Old shacks dotted the river in places, and weeds were grown up around them. Some newer places were there amongst the old. The humidity was high, but there was a slight breeze from the river and a smell of fish that I found not offensive but refreshing. The newness of it all was exciting and had my adrenaline going. In my heart, I wanted Floyd to stay close.

I had not gone far from the truck that day when I noticed its lights were on. I waved to alert Floyd. He only waved back, not knowing what I was trying to say, so I turned away to let the hours pass. As the day went by, I wondered why I had not seen him. The thought scared me. Many crazy images raced through my mind. There was a prison in Chester, and I thought of someone escaping and bringing him harm. Someone would stop. They'd stop for him if the battery was dead, I thought to myself.

Eighteen miles from Chester — more than 4 hours on foot — Floyd appeared and told me of his run-down battery. I was glad he was okay.

"Floyd, I can make Murphysboro tonight, so I'm pressin' on," I told him as I scratched along my belt. "Chiggers! I've got chiggers!" I could feel them in my groin area, too.

"I've got 'em, too. They must live along the river."

"Boy, I dunno, but we better get some chigger killer when we get to a town — or when you get there, I should say. Please don't forget," I urged.

"How can I? They're all over me," he moaned.

My diarrhea is somewhat better, but the ache in my. . .

I put my recorder away as I saw an oncoming vehicle. The

car came to a stop alongside me. My heart pounded like a drum.

"David Stewart?" the driver asked. "I'm from Murphysboro. I'm with the paper." The pain in my chest eased a little, and I breathed the tension out. I put the thought of Frank away talked to the man for a while. The conversation was not long enough and soon he was gone.

We began to walk on a little, when I saw an old barn and could not resist the temptation to explore it. Snicker was at my side as we stepped through the door into semi-darkness. We were greeted by the horrifying sound of a rattlesnake, and I froze stiff. I could not tell where it was or even the direction the sound was coming from.

"Snicker, get back! Get back!" He froze next to me, and I felt him shiver against my leg. My throat went dry, and I could feel my heart pounding in my chest. The killer snake could have struck at any moment. I bent over slowly and took Snicker into my arms, hoping I would not feel the fangs of the rattler. The entrance was only a step or two behind, but I was afraid to turn.

Suddenly I leaped backwards and sprawled on the ground outside. Snicker flew from my grasp, and we both broke into a dead run toward the road. Snicker was a step ahead as we jumped over a ditch and scrambled to what I felt was safety.

That night I realized how close I had come to danger, and I also thought of how close I was to my journey's end. Soon, David, soon you can rest, was my comforting thought.

You've made it one day at a time. "One day at a time." Those were five words that I carried with me for strength. "If I never get on that stage, I will be proud to have done this," I spoke to the darkness that crept upon the day of July 5.

"Tomorrow is July 6, soon to be July 22, a day I will remember and tell my grandchildren about." I wondered how many would I have. Three beautiful children could bring a man many grandchildren. I smiled at the thought. Jackie and I were not blessed with a fourth child but never gave up the hope that we still might be. The thought often scared me, but Jackie would say, "It would be a beautiful child." That made me wonder many times — wonder, with the want in my heart.

The rattler barn.

David Stewart

PART 3

ILLINOIS, KENTUCKY, TENNESSEE

21

Into Illinois

The sound of morning woke me gently. Rising, I looked out at the fog hanging over the hillside. I dressed and began to stretch, remembering the lady I had spoken to the night of July 4, on the river bank in Chester.

"The river's 17 feet below normal," she had said to the stranger on the river bank, while taking sunset pictures. That voice came back to me as my thoughts drifted to the big Mississippi that had carried so many people to new and wonderful places — and probably many to their death. She sure was down on her banks. There were barges run ashore up and down her and sandbars exposed here and there that were once hidden well below the black water.

The countryside of Illinois was a sight to behold. Even with the river low, the crops were green and plentiful, as were the trees that cloaked the rolling hillsides housing nature's wildlife.

It's more miles to Marion than I wanted to walk today, I thought with my first step on the cool morning of July 6 (Day 68). "There goes my average-mile theory all to heck, boy. I didn't think it would be as easy as I had thought these last few weeks."

After an hour, I decided to sit and write for a while. Snicker looked fine. A good bath the night before and a dip for fleas were his rewards for a hard day. He didn't like the flea dip at all — at least that's how he acted — but he liked the results. He was relieved to be rid of those little red monsters that ate at his skin, sucking blood from him as if he were their discovery well. The ticks seemed to be worse than ever along the heavily wooded area of the river that led me to Murphysboro.

"Somewhere, sometime, Jackie will be with me next week." I smiled at the thought. We had agreed to meet somewhere in Kentucky or Tennessee. Robin, Jackie's brother, had been in Wyoming for the summer and would help her drive to us.

It made me nervous to think about Jackie, her mom and Robin with us out on the road. How would we sleep everyone? Our money was almost exhausted again. No matter. Jackie's family was a tough lot and would make the best of whatever came. The money always seemed to come as we needed it.

I wrote in my diary for as long as I could. Then my thoughts turned toward home, to a telephone conversation I had with Jackie:

> *"David, Robin has come to Wyoming. He's got some problems," she said.*
>
> *"Is he okay?"*
>
> *"No." I could hear the pain within her. My dearest Jackie had many gifts, and the two that she excelled at were the gift of encouragement and the gift of giving to others — not material things so much as love and understanding.*
>
> *"He's got a drug problem, and I want to help him." There was desperation as she spoke about it. This was one of her little brothers, and the fear of Robin losing out to*

drugs was something neither of us could bear.

*"Bring him anyway," I said. Robin was a musician
and had a burning love for his music. He had fallen prey
to drugs as many do in all walks of life. But unlike many
who never ask for help and only vanish, he was crying
out for help.*

*"Thank you. I thought you would feel that way, but I
wanted to talk to you about it," she confided.*

*"Bring him with you to Nashville, Jackie. It'll be good
for him and I'll feel better that he's with you and your
mom."*

*"Mother's glad that he's here. She worries so much
about him and Mark."*

That phone call had been weeks ago and Robin was winning
the battle now.

"Robin built a fence at the store for us," Jackie had said
in our last conversation. "I showed him what to do and he did it.
You'd be proud." I could tell she was. I looked forward to seeing
Robin and talking with him about finding a path without a crutch.

As I walked on toward Carbondale, a college town west of
Marion, my thoughts drifted back to the river road and a little
place called Rockwood. It was just a small spot along the road,
and as I stopped to investigate, I spoke to the pup:

*"There's a store, boy. Let's stop and rest here."
Snicker stood at the door waiting, as I browsed for
nothing in particular, just trying to take in a little of
Rockwood's character.*

'Howdy, "I greeted the man who bent to pet Snicker.

"Hello. Your dog?" he asked

*"Yes, sir," I answered as I sat down on the porch,
looking across the street at the town's only other building,
the post office.*

*"You the one who's walking to Nashville?" he asked as
he spat to the south of us.*

I looked up at the man. He was a man who had lived

hard. I guessed him to be in his 50s, but was not sure. His pants were short on him, revealing socks that were sure to have been white at one time. Old tobacco stains lined the front of his T-shirt, and his hands were calloused and Dirty.

"Yes, sir. My name's David Stewart and that's Snicker."

"My name's Ben," he said, never offering any more than that.

"I'm pleased to meet you." I offered my hand, wishing I had my camera. The man who was stained with dirt had a photogenic look about him, a real presence. I could tell as he talked that he was an educated man, that he had faced some bad times and turned to the bottle for comfort, a comfort that was only temporary.

I liked Ben. We talked in the afternoon heat about country music. He knew his country music, all right. He named all the stars and told me he had all their records.

"Have you got a record out?"

"Yes, I have. Floyd has them in the camper."

"I sure would like to own one, " he said with a smile.

"Sure would like you to. Maybe he'll be along. If not, look us up in Murphysboro tonight."

My mind snapped back to the present and I realized that my finger was aching as if it had been jammed all over again. I had kept it taped the past weeks, and it had troubled me some, but not like this day.

I thought of Ben a lot throughout the day and of the stories he had told — some with sadness, some with laughter.

Other memories came to mind such as the night I walked into Murphysboro and first told Floyd about Ben. The conversation with Floyd went like this:

"I met him, David. He came to Murphyshoro today, ore you came in. He had a couple of friends along, and they all bought records. I sold T-shirts to some other

folks. We made $16 today."

"So you met Ben. What'd you think?"

"I liked him," Floyd said as he nodded his head in the aflirmative. "We've met some nice people. We're gettin' closer, buddy, " Floyd said with a content look.

"You talkin' to me or Snicker?"

"You," he laughed. "Both of you! He's my little buddy," he corrected as he picked up Snicker and gave him a hug.

Coming back to reality once more, I looked down at the hard pavement that plagued my feet with every step. I saw a penny and stopped to retrieve it. I was still finding at least one penny a day. It had become a ritual for me, looking for that penny. I suspected Floyd had dropped a few in my path at times, just to keep me at peace about it.

I had almost collected enough small tools to fill a tool box, from wrenches to small levels, hammers to screwdrivers. I'd found them all. I found them where people must have worked on a vehicle and driven away, inadvertently leaving tools behind — sometimes several tools together. I wondered about each tool I found. I picked up each one, wondering whether there was a story to be told about it or its owner.

"Twenty-some today, Snicker. I wonder what made me think we could do 15 miles a day and get by, boy? Maybe it'll average out as we get closer, and I can slow down."

He looked at me with those penetrating eyes, as if I had forgotten to acknowledge his presence.

"I'm sorry, boy. I meant to say we can slow down. I know you've come the whole way with me."

A car pulled to a stop as I was talking to my dog.

"Hello," a woman said as she crawled from the car, followed by a young Oriental man who was clicking pictures as soon as his feet hit the ground. "We're from the university paper," she explained energetically. "Can we have a few moments of your time, Mr. Stewart?"

"Mr. Stewart," I thought. This young lady's mother would he proud of her manners.

"David, ma'am, just David."

She seemed a little embarrassed and it showed in her cheeks, which were dotted with freckles and outlined with beautiful red hair that lay on her shoulders.

"Can we, David?" she implored.

I believe I had more fun with those two students than any other reporters on the trip. They were so in tune with what I wanted to do and hung on every word that I spoke about my aspirations. Thoughts of those two young people carried me for miles toward Marion, Illinois.

"We'll soon be southern-bound again, Snicker." The heat was with us after leaving the coolness of the river. The temperature was in the 90s, but felt bearable after the days in Missouri that sometimes flashed through me like a ghost from my past.

My stomach cried out in pain as I thought of the day ending. My finger would not leave me alone. All I thought of was Marion and the truck stop that Floyd assured me was on my route. "It's right next to the road, David, where this one meets the interstate. You can't miss it. I'll see you there," he had said. That was early afternoon, and I had not reached it yet. I'd been stopped a lot, though, and that had caused me to lose time. The last man to stop me was named Kirk, and he reminded me that I only had a few more miles to go.

"I don't want to hold you up. I know you're on a schedule. I just wanted you to know that I admire you."

"Thank you," I said, shocked at his words which came so sincerely. I watched him drive away in a small red truck. Tears came over me before I even knew they were there. I sat down and let it go — not so much tears of sadness, but mostly tears of joy for the stranger who had briefly visited me on a highway he knew well and I knew not.

I did know that just west of Marion, Illinois, I had met a man with heart — one I would never forget.

The next morning, July 7, I recognized the roar from the interstate as I looked toward it in the morning sun. My sleep had been erratic all night.

"What's wrong?" Floyd asked, as I paced back and forth.

"It's my finger. It's still really sore to the touch. I've also got a sore throat and a heck of a headache," I complained.

"Let's rest today and go see a doctor."

That thought remained with me that morning as I fought the call of the highway.

"I'll walk just a little today, Floyd, and rest in the shade. We'll come back to Marion this afternoon, stay here again, and I'll see that doctor. Maybe you can get me an appointment," I said as I walked away through the grass at an angle across the open field to the interstate.

I looked back towards Floyd, but he had already disappeared inside. I felt isolated again.

Why do these feelings come? "It's too early to feel depressed," I mumbled, but the depression never left me that day. It only intensified as did the heat.

At 1:30 p.m., while resting in a park, I heard a voice say over the radio, "It's a whopping 97 degrees out there, so be careful." I scoffed, "Be careful! What does he know of the heat?"

I jerked the headphones from my ears and shut off the radio.

The only doctor that Floyd found who would see me on such short notice was in an emergency room. Of course, I thought, that's the normal procedure, and that's where I sat, waiting to be called.

She was quite old, I thought, as I looked at the woman's face who sat across from me.

"Aren't you the boy who's walking to Nashville?" she asked.

The boy, I thought as I smiled at her. Well, I probably did seem like a child to her.

"Yes, I'm David Stewart," I said respectfully.

"Aren't you on the wrong floor?"

"No, ma'am, this is where they told me to wait."

"I think you are," she said. "The psychiatric ward is on the third floor." She let out a laugh that shook her belly.

I felt embarrassed, but laughed with her.

As quickly as she laughed, she became very serious and looked me straight in the eye. "Do you know Ralph Emery?" she asked as she raised her eyebrows.

"No, ma'am."

"Well, get to know him. He's a fine boy, and he'll help you. I watch him every day. You look him up."

I smiled and said, "Yes, ma'am, I hope I have the pleasure of meeting him. Yes, ma'am, I'll do that."

22
Nothing Broke

Nothing broke was the doctor's report that day of July 7 (Day 69). He X-rayed my finger and put a splint on it. "It's just a bad sprain," he told me. His advice for the sore throat was to gargle with warm salt water. "Throat infection, my foot! I believe it's all the dirt I've swallowed along with car fumes," I mumbled to myself.

Later that day, we rested in a public park. I sat still, feeling lonely for home and sorry for myself as I gazed upon a baseball game going on across the gravel road. The laughter I heard coming from the children didn't register. That is, it did not sound happy or cheer me up. It was nothing more than a distant sound to me.

"I'm gonna make it, and I'm gonna sing my songs!" I said with confidence. "I'll do just as the lady said. I'll find Ralph Emery and talk to him." He was a man who would understand my Opry obsession and how such determination can lead to positive results through perseverance. Ralph Emery had started out small and ended up with a very successful TV show and millions of viewers.

Floyd was resting. Occasionally I could hear him snore from beneath his shady spot. "He deserves the rest," I said quietly to Snicker, who was also in a peaceful state. Why couldn't I sleep? My eyes were tired, but my mind wouldn't slow down. There were too many things going on inside my head. If I could only turn the thoughts off and fall asleep!

"Energy, I need energy to go on," I said with fear in my heart. The doctor had offered me a prescription for pain but I refused It. You idiot! You could have been sleeping by now if you would have taken the pills, I thought. "But I can't afford to drain my energy with medication," I remarked aloud.

I wrote down my feelings as they changed from sadness to fear, and from excitement to paranoia. I wondered how many emotions there could be. "The human mind is very complex with too many emotions," I whispered, looking around for anyone who might be listening. Maybe the lady was right. Maybe I should have visited the third floor of that hospital, if only to talk to someone about my many emotions.

● ● ●

I found myself in Goreville at the end of a hot, humid July 8, but not to rest, for there was a noise of terrible proportion coming from beneath our moving home.

"What is it, Floyd?"

"I don't know. It started just before I found you."

"We have to go back to Marion."

"Think she'll make it back?" he asked with doubt.

"I don't know, but we better try before it gets dark."

The truck stop was again a welcome sight to behold.

"What're we going to do, David? It's Friday and everything might be closed for the weekend."

As I dialed Jackie's number, I went over our problem again in my head, knowing Floyd needed a vehicle to continue his work.

"We gotta have a car. I've got to go on to Nashville soon," he said.

"I know, Floyd. I'm calling Jackie."

She answered the phone. "Hello, honey, it's me. We've got some trouble. Can you come now, Jackie? Our vehicle is broken down, and we don't know what's wrong with it or how long it will take to fix it."

"I'll call Robin and see if he's ready. Maybe we can leave right away. Where are you?"

"I'm at the truck stop in Marion that I told you about."

"So you'll stay right there?"

"Yes, I've already walked to Goreville. I don't want to walk it over. I'll wait."

Floyd found a mechanic to look at the vehicle. "This one has to go to the shop," he said. "I'll call my boss and see if I can work on it in the morning."

"Oh, man. What's the problem?" I asked Floyd as the young man walked away to make his call.

"He thinks it's the rear end."

My heart sank. "How can we pay for a new rear end?" I wondered aloud.

"It'll work out. Don't worry. We've got other things to consider." That was easy to say but hard to absorb when I knew the outcome would be expensive.

"Yes," the mechanic said, as he returned, handing me directions to the shop.

"Well, if they can't fix the camper right away, we'll have you go on by car, and I'll leave Jackie and Robin to tend the vehicle," I stated to Floyd.

"Who's coming?" he asked with concern.

"Jackie, Robin and Betty."

"Where are we gonna put everyone?"

"I pondered on that some time back and decided not to worry about it."

Floyd spoke after a silence. "That was a nice girl we talked to on the road today. What was her name?" The "girl" he spoke of was a woman who had waved to me on numerous occasions from her giant rig. Today she finally stopped and said, "I've been seeing you for hundreds of miles, since Llncoln, Nebraska, Or further away. This is my last run this way for some time, so I thought I'd stop and ask what you're doing out here with your dog," I told her my story, and she listened with great interest.

She hadn't heard about my walk, and I wondered how many others didn't know.

• • •

By 9:00 a.m. on July 9 (Day 71), they had the wheels off and knew the problem. "It's a wheel bearing," the mechanic said. I sighed with relief to hear it wasn't the rear end. "I don't know about parts. It might be a problem. We'll have to call around," he warned.

Varnell, the owner of the garage, took me to his home and called a friend in Nashville by the name of Judi Martin. She was working at Bill Monroe's place and said she'd help get me some singing spots when I arrived.

"She'll help you. She's a good person," he said.

"That was sure a nice phone call. I hope the vehicle will be okay."

"It will, son. Quit your worrying."

He only charged me for parts that day and wished me luck. I put it on my credit card, cringing as the girl called in the charges, for fear they would exceed the limit. I shook a firm hand with Varnell as we left his shop.

I talked to several people back home, trying to reach Jackie to let her know we were back in business. She had already left with intentions of coming straight through. Probably about 24 hours on the road, I thought. It would be a long drive. I tried to figure when she and the others would arrive. It was actually too early to have them with me, and I felt stupid for having called her before knowing the verdict on the camper.

"What's done is done. It'll be good to have them here. Good for your emotional state," Floyd said.

"Yes, Jackie is good for me. I'm glad she's coming. Why

don't you go on to Nashville for a few days. Robin can drive the support vehicle, and you'll be free to forget about me for a while and concentrate on Music City."

"Are you Mr. David Stewart?" a woman interrupted our conversation. "You have a phone call."

It must be Jackie, I thought, as I raced to the receiver.

"David, this is Bob Miller," he said while laughing vigorously into the phone. "How the heck are you? I hear you have problems." Bob Miller was in Peoria, Illinois.

"How'd you know?"

"I called Gillette and they told me you were broken down and Jackie was on her way."

"Well, I haven't broken down yet, but the camper has," I laughed.

"You're doing well, David. Do you need me to send you some cash?" he asked, concerned, but trying to boost my spirits by keeping up the humor.

"No, we're fine, but I sure do thank you for asking."

I lay my head down, thinking of Jackie and that she would soon be with me. I knew I could face anything with her close to me. So many times a man takes for granted those who love him most. Her family, the Miller clan, knew about hard times and supported my cause. I was fortunate, I thought, to have family who cared so much about me.

Jackie arrived at 3:30 in the morning and tapped gently on my window.

"Good morning," she teased, as I jumped up and let her in while Floyd, Betty and Robin started to go for coffee.

Robin looked good and said, "I'm proud of you, Walking Cowboy." He and Melisa always reminded me of each other.

Robin said he wanted to walk 25 miles that day and started out early with Snicker and me.

"Is it possible to break your feet?" he asked in pain after we had walked several miles.

"I don't know, Robin, but I think it's time for you to quit for the day," I said with a laugh.

"Me, too." He waited for Jackie to come with relief in his

eyes, knowing he would soon be off the highway where I had to remain.

"Can I walk with you?" Jackie asked when she arrived, she laughed a bit at Robin, who laughed right back, went to the camper and was glad to trade places with her.

"Ask Floyd to join us in a few hours, Robin," I said.

"Okay. See ya later," Robin replied.

"Don't forget us!" I said, concerned about Jackie being exposed to the heat for too long.

Walking was exciting to them, but neither knew the danger they faced with the passing of the day. We were not supposed to be on the interstate in Illinois, and it worried me. When walking with no one but Snicker, I felt we would be left alone, but with someone with us, I felt we might get told to leave the main highway. We had not walked 2 hours when the rain came, cooling us, yet at the same time, drenching us to the very bone. Taking shelter beneath a bridge, I held Jackie to me, and we laughed and talked until the rain left us.

Robin came again after the storm and walked to the Ohio River with me. His feet were tender, so we took our time. Then Jackie joined us again. We were getting very close to Nashville now and talked about our arrival plans.

"You're only a couple of hundred miles out, right?" Jackie asked.

"Less than that. I'm past Goreville."

"Well, then, let's take the day off and find a nice campground. It's warm enough to sleep out, and we can do our laundry."

I didn't attempt to argue. We had plenty of time to make it to Nashville by the 22nd, so I rested some more on July 10. My throat was somewhat better, and my finger was hurting less than before. We camped in the Shawnee National Forest, and I felt at peace for the first time in a long time.

Floyd had decided not to go into Nashville quite yet. He wanted to get press in Metropolis and Paducah first, and he set out to do just that on July 11, leaving Robin on the road with me, and Jackie and her mother in the support vehicle.

Robin and I talked long about the effect of drugs, and he told me how being in Gillette for 2 months had saved his life. He was sincere. He had faced the devil head on and won.

After 10 miles, Robin turned to me and asked if we could stop for a short rest.

"You okay?" I asked.

Yeah, he said, trying not to reveal the pain.

"We'll cross the river tomorrow," I announced.

"We still have daylight," he said to me.

I looked at the river once more and replied, "Tomorrow's another day. This one is done for me."

23

We're in Tennessee, Boy!

On July 12 (Day 74), I crossed the Ohio River without human company. Of course, my faithful canine companion was near me, as always. I would not have it any other way.

Only 10 days left to go! I thought to myself that rainy day. Time to tape . . .

> *I'm bound for Paducah where I will rest for a spell before moving onward. The rain has been with me all morning, and I ache from the dampness. At first it refreshed me, but now it pulls at my every muscle.*

I asked Floyd to get a room in Paducah for the night so Jackie and Betty would have a place to rest. It was comforting to know they would be in a cool place.

The 2:30 interview went well and at 4:00 p.m. I made my way further south, leaving Paducah behind. Jackie walked with me for about an hour. We came upon two dead German shepherds on the highway. They had both been cut in half, not from being run over, but as if they had been surgically bisected.

"What is this, David? What happened to these animals?" Jackie asked with dread in her voice.

"I don't know, honey, but we better not hang around here."

We circled the two dogs cautiously, and Snicker began to move even closer. "Snicker! Get back! Get away from there!" I screamed. He came to my side and began to shake as if he were scared.

Jackie knelt and looked at the upper half of each dog, then at the lower half. She finally looked at me and spoke. "What could have done this? There's no blood, and they look like they were cut in half with something really sharp."

"I have no idea, Jackie. This is strange. They must have been killed somewhere else and dumped out here."

"But why?" she insisted. "Why would someone do this to such beautiful animals?" I ran it through my mind over and over, but could not find a rational answer. They both looked to be purebred shepherds with sleek, healthy coats. "They could have fallen off the back of a truck. I've heard of cults using animals for sacrifice. Or maybe someone killed them to sell as dog meat."

Still, the way they were severed had me puzzled, especially since there was no blood. "They don't even smell bad, so they couldn't have been dead for long."

"But how could they be cut so perfectly?"

Horrible thoughts crossed my mind, and I shared them with Jackie as she continued to question me. "Perhaps the dogs were frozen before they landed here. Maybe they were part of a lab experiment."

I looked around nervously, half expecting whoever had dropped the dogs to return.

"We better go, Jackie. There's nothing we can do."

Snicker was very uneasy, and the hair on my neck began to

stand on end as I thought of stories I had read about aliens taking animals for experiments and dropping them off in such places. My skin began to crawl. "Let's go!" I demanded abruptly, moving away from the carcasses. Jackie looked back several times. It was a sad scene and a mystery that we had no time to solve.

That night we returned to Paducah. Floyd and Robin took the camper for the night, and the three of us took the room. It was strange to have Jackie next to me after so long, but I will carry the memory of that night to my grave. As the years pass by, some time in the future we may sit upon a porch somewhere, rocking and remembering my journey and smiling about it.

With 140 miles remaining, I thought back to the first 100 miles I had walked in Wyoming and shivered a little at the idea of walking the final 140 miles in 10 days. It was a good feeling. My days would not be so long now. This was my reward for the hard days that had passed.

The heat and ticks were upon us south of the town of Paducah and made July 13 long and hard before I reached the Cumberland River. I stood for a long time, gazing at the river, wishing I could just float upon it to the heart of Nashville. My little boy nature came alive, and I began casting rocks into the water, occasionally waving at a passing car. I was done for the day and would go no further. The next day I would cross the river, hopefully not in the rain, but no matter, I would cross over her. For some strange reason, I preferred it that way, never crossing late at night. It was just a pet peeve I had.

Floyd was filled with joy when he found me.

"I got us a complimentary room back in Paducah. You ready to call it a day?" he asked.

"Ready is right. Take me home to Paducah for this night."

• • •

July 14 was marked on the itinerary as a rest day.

"David, this is hard, takin' our time like this."

"Yes, but I feel I'm gaining strength by not pushing it so hard. I'm down 30 pounds now. Just dropped the last 10 in a hurry."

"I'm goin' to Nashville soon."

"That's good. I think you're ready." And I really did. He had done great work, and I had full faith in his ability.

"Robin," I said, "tomorrow after you drop me at the river will you go to the Eddyville exit and get us a room for two nights? That'll be a good base as I walk to it one day and may the next. The girls can rest in comfort." I knew the rooms might be cheaper away from the big towns and we needed something cheaper, that was certain. Robin was enjoying being a part of the trip.

The morning of the 15th came with Jackie next to me. Floyd took me to the Cumberland River where I had quit the night before. I stood for the longest time. As I watched the sun come up, I stretched long and hard. Snicker was ready to move on. I was nervous about the Opry. The river lay before me and Floyd was miles down the road already. "Come on, boy, let's cross 'er," I shouted with a feeling inside me of being a pioneer on a journey across America. How many had taken this route from Cumberland to Nashville for trade or venture, some to stay, some to move on?

The heat climbed quickly that morning, and by noon it was 100 degrees. I still had some walking to do, but for a time I rested in the shade, occasionally knocking a tick from my hair, wishing I could dip myself as I had done Snicker so often.

"I came to walk with you," Jackie said, dressed in shorts, Nikes and a T—shirt.

"You might burn, honey," I cautioned her.

"No, I won't. I'll quit when I start burning. I can do that, you know," she answered with a grin.

We walked along that never-ending white line. An hour later we were hot and sweating like all get-out from the humid air that seemed thick enough to cut with a knife.

"We gotta take a break," Jackie said as I looked into her flushed face.

"You're awful red, honey. We'll stop at the next overpass."

"I wonder why my face always gets so flushed when I exercise," she commented.

"Exercise!" I chuckled. "If this is exercise, I have a fool-proof way to lose 30 pounds. I'll call it the 1,600-mile diet plan."

I removed the water bottle from my belt as we slumped back against the concrete. I hoped it would be cool, but it proved to be nothing more than concrete that offered a place to sit. Placing a little water in my hand, I wiped Snicker's face to cool him before drinking, then wiped mine with my cool hand and passed the water to Jackie. Before I could say more than, "Uh — hon — uh, Jac —," she had turned that water bottle up and polished off every drop of the water, wiping her mouth with satisfaction. She looked at me and smiled.

"That's all the water we had!" I said in astonishment.

"Oh, my gosh!" she cried. "I thought it was all mine. I'm so sorry." She was humiliated from having made that mistake, but surely not thirsty any more. She began to laugh about it some, as I licked my lips and tried to wet my throat, swallowing only dryness.

"What will we do now? I feel so stupid!" she exclaimed.

"Don't worry. I've learned how to do without water and so has Snicker. You needed it, anyway," I said reassuringly.

We talked of our plans for the future and of many things along that highway. Every time I looked at her, I felt a rush of love come over me.

July 16 (Day 78) came with more heat and ticks. It was Saturday, bu't every day seemed the same to me. I walked toward the Tennessee line with the Opry on my mind. I was getting nervous about the girls, and wanted to send them on into Nashville. Floyd had driven into Nashville the night before and tried to find me the easiest route to the capitol. That night I stopped about 10 miles from the line and could go no further. We decided I would cross the line the next day.

My plans were to make Tennessee on July 17; however, the new day came with thunder showers of immense magnitude. Because of this, Floyd and I decided it would be a good day to rest and recoup some more strength. My stomach still had problems, and I was just "plum tuckered out?"

Jackie called Dorothy Saypeck's house in Hopkinsville, Kentucky. Her daughter, Trish, lived in Gillette and was a friend of ours. She asked us to please look up her mother. "She'll feed you good!" she had told me with her Southern accent before I left Wyoming.

"Feed ya good," I remembered, as I pushed myself away from the table.

"Are ya full, honey?" she asked with her Southern drawl that brought back sweet memories of the South.

"Yes, ma'am," I said.

"There's plenty more!" she exclaimed as she passed me her famous Southern dish. There was a man named Dink Embry there from the Hopkinsville radio station; Miss Collie, a friend of Dorothy's; and Miss Collie's boyfriend who agreed to cut my hair.

"You need to have a cut, honey, if you're going to sing on the Opry," Miss Collie said.

The hospitality flowed from that home. If the rains had not come, we might have missed the experience.

On Monday, July 18, at 9:00 p.m., I crossed the Tennessee state line. I turned and looked back at the Kentucky sign that read "Open for Business."

"We're in Tennessee, boy!" I shouted to the wind while turning in circles, breathing in Tennessee air and feeling like the summit was in sight.

I asked that no one walk anymore with me (except Snicker, of course), as I needed to be alone while walking those last few days. I don't know why, but I felt the need and everyone respected my request.

"Clarksville will be home for a few nights, Snicker. We're very close now, but can't go in until Friday. So rest up, my friend. You've come a long way." In no particular hurry now, I slept long that Tuesday and only walked about 7 mlles before thunderstorms came. I had walked in plenty of bad weather on my journey, and was glad I could stop and rest through these storms. I was close to my destination and the miles did not matter anymore. I was pacing myself to arrive on Friday. When I saw Floyd, he was uptight. We were all nervous about the uncertainty of Friday.

"I want you to take the girls and go on into Nashville," I said, "Robin will stay with me."

"But, David, I don't want to leave you."

"You've done good work, and you need to be in Nashville now to continue it. Please take the girls to the Hall of Fame Hotel. The hotel agreed to give us a room for a few days. The girls will be comfortable there and can help you with anything you need."

"Take care of him, Robin," Jackie told her brother.

"I will, sis," Robin said with a smile, and they hugged good-bye. Soon they were gone, leaving Robin to look after my well-being.

"Let's go to Hopkinsville, Robin," I said before night came.

"Are we goin' back to those people's house?" he asked. Dorothy Saypeck had taken a liking to Robin and he to her.

"No," I laughed. "Tonight I want to buy a new hat for the Opry. I've got my credit card, so let's go."

I found a fine Resistol, shaped it just the way I like, then put it away.

"Let's see a movie Robin. Jackie left me some cash, too!"

●　　●　　●

Anticipation mounted with each step on Wednesday morning as I moved toward Music City. At times I walked almost in a strut, and other times I was barely able to place one foot ahead of the other. Constantly changing and uncontrollable moods were wearing me out.

I was startled to see a man standing near me as I looked up from changing my socks. I had not even heard his vehicle stop. He was a black man of 6-foot 4-inches, 225 pounds, dressed in a uniform that fit him to a tee. Scared, I started to speak, but he interrupted, "What are you doing on the interstate, son? You're not allowed out here." I told him who I was, and he knew about me. "They're talking about you a lot, cowboy," he remarked.

"Well, I'm only goin' to exit 31, then I'll get on 41A from

there if you'll allow it, sir."

He looked at me long and hard. "You be careful and, after, today, I don't want to see you on I-24."

"Yes, sir, you won't."

"Good luck," he said, removing his hat and ducking to get in the car.

"Man, snicker, are we full of luck or what?" Floyd had driven on the alternative road, 41A, and encouraged me to stay on I-24 as long as possible. "41A's narrow, David, and we don't want to take any unnecessary chances. I wish you'd take I-24 as far as possible." I had agreed to stay on I-24 up to exit 31.

"New Hope Road" was the sign I read at exit 31. "New Hope Road, Snicker." It rang in my ears for a time. I tied balloons on several posts for Robin to find me.

Robin and Jackie had missed me on the road a few days earlier. I had forgotten to mark my spot clearly enough. Floyd knew how to find me most times. After St. Louis, he seemed to be able to smell my whereabouts and come right to me. The marking of my spots with ribbons and balloons was a good idea, and I was glad Floyd had thought of it.

That night as Robin and I talked long in the camper, I told him I would do 15 miles on Thursday and save the remainder for Friday morning. He relayed the message to Floyd and Jackie.

The new highway was a winding one into Nashville, but I could take my time and was soon glad to have the extra time. Many folks had heard about the route and came to see the foolish "Walking Cowboy," some stopping to talk, some only to look.

"David?" Floyd asked as we sat alone that Thursday night of July 21 (Day 83). "Everything is lined up at the capitol building, and I took your record out to the Opry for Mr. Durham." Hal Durham was general manager of entertainment at the Grand Ole Opry.

I swallowed hard. "This is it, Floyd? Tomorrow I arrive."

Miles back I had crossed the Davidson County line and read "Home of the Grand Ole Opry." Some said I should quit there. I had made it. But I felt different. I wanted to walk to the capitol.

In fact, I would like to have walked right to the Opry, but I didn't want to offend anyone by doing so without permission.
The state capitol would be my final stop on a long journey to an uncertain outcome.

"You're supposed to call Liz White when you start out tomorrow," Floyd said.

"Okay, I'll do just that."

• • •

"Liz White, WSM," was the voice I heard at 6:00 a.m. on Friday, July 22, 1988. I could hardly believe it was the start of my last day (Day 84)!

"Hello, David! How are you?"

"I'm fine, Liz, and you?"

She laughed, "Well, I'm fine, but I didn't walk all the way from Wyoming! Are you ready for today?"

"Yes, ma'am, I am!"

"I'll see you at the capitol."

After the call, Floyd and I ate breakfast with my brother, Jack.

"There's some pretty bad spots up ahead where you're walkin', David. Looks like a rough neighborhood," Jack warned.

"You want to walk with me for a while?" I asked. He was excited to do so, I believe, and we set off toward downtown and the capitol. We lingered and visited at rest places along the way until Jimmy came to us and said the press was all there. I felt both elated and afraid at the same time.

"You better get moving," Jack said as he left me at the foot of the hill. Snicker and I made the last leg alone to a cheering crowd. I began to weep as Jackie came to me at the foot of the steps, my heart feeling as if it would burst. I held her close and we wept-together as reporters shouted questions from every direction. I had done it!

"I made it, Jackie!" I cried. "I made it!" She held my arm as we walked up the stairs to the roar of friends, family, the press and people who came just to see me.

Steppin' into Nashville   Ada Tolar

Floyd was the next one at my side with a hearty handshake and a tender hug to boot. "You did it, David!" He was crying, this little man who had become so big in my eyes. Pride rushed over me in great waves and at times I almost felt faint.

"David!" A voice came from behind. I turned. "I'm Joe . . ."

"Edwards!" we both said together.

I grabbed his hand and shook it for a long time. Joe had provided tremendous coverage, through Associated Press, from the very start of my walk. "Thank you" was all I could say to him.

"Feel like an interview in a bit?" he asked.

"You bet! Do you know Liz White? Is she here?" I asked excitedly.

"I don't know," he replied.

• • •

Dawn came to my side, and I held her close to me. She

Ada Tolar

With Joe Edwards at the state capitol

looked so grown up since I last saw her.

I looked around at an ocean of smiling faces and caught my sister-in-law Betty's eyes, filled with triumphant tears. Everything was happening at once. Little Tammy Gorton from Gillette, who was only a toddler at the time, sat in my lap as I sat down.

"Dave, when are you singing at the Opry?" she squealed.

"I don't know, honey."

Tammy's mother told me that Tammy cried almost every night while I was on my walk and would have it no other way but to be there when I arrived in Nashville. This child was one of the few people I allowed to call me Dave. I preferred David, but her nickname for me was used out of love.

The Chamber of Commerce presented me with a gold record and the Governor's office sent a welcoming assistant with congratualtions.

An associate of Liz White came up to me and said, "Liz couldn't be here, but will meet you later today. In the meantime, the station is waiting for a live interview.

Snicker lay down as if he knew we were done. Not caring about the crowd, he seemed to just want to rest. "You're done, boy," I said.

24
The Invitation

My mind was in a whirl. Jackie was screening my calls and Floyd was taking care of business as I spruced up at the Hall of Fame Motel. I was handed two telegrams: one from my dear aunts in Florida, and one from Governor Sullivan in Wyoming. There were flowers and call after call from all sorts of people.

Floyd returned and said, "We've got a news conference!"

My heart skipped a beat as I said, "A news conference?"

"They all wanna talk to you. This is the best way to do it. All at once."

The press asked me all kinds of questions, then a reporter wanted me to sing. I was ready for music and sang, "I'll Be Blue" to the press.

After the dust settled and most people had drifted out, a woman said, "Hi, David, I'm Liz White." She was a good-looking woman with a warm smile.

"I'm glad to meet you, Liz. Thank you so much," was all I could manage.

"You're welcome, David. Good luck!"

We talked for a spell, and she said she'd see me at the Opry. She spoke with confidence about me getting an invitation to perform. I could see in her eyes that she was happy for me.

I paced the floor until I could not put it off any longer. I had to know! All the reporters wanted to know what the Opry was going to do. I had to make that phone call, but I was afraid they would turn me down. I dialed Hal Durham's number with an unsteady hand. He was in a meeting and when he returned my call, I was out of the room. He said he'd call back.

Finally, it rang.

"Hello? . . . Yes, sir, Mr. Durham. This is David."

I sank into a chair, my heart beating hard. "Yes, sir, I did walk all the way."

We talked a while and he asked if I would like to sing on the Grand Ole Opry! He told me I could be on the Saturday night show, or else sing at a later date. There were a lot of people who had come to see me walk into Nashville — people from Florida, Minnesota, Wyoming, Illinois and Kentucky, so I chose Saturday night.

"He said YES!" I shouted, as I hung up the phone and kissed Jackie.

"What'd he say?" she asked with tremendous excitement. We were like schoolchildren and danced around the room.

"He said he had a spot for me tomorrow night and invited me out there tonight."

"Ooooh!" she squealed. "I'm so happy for you, honey."

The tears fell all over that hotel room as we cried and danced about, stopping only long enough to hold each other, then bounced around in excitement again.

I tried to reach Floyd by phone and had Jack and Jimmy looking everywhere for him, but to no avail.

"Oh, Jackie, I don't want him to be the last to know!" I exclaimed.

"I don't think he expected an answer so soon. I bet he's downtown unwinding."

As darkness came and we talked on and on about the Opry, I opened the curtain to view the city. In downtown Nashville there is a grand building that towers high in the air, and at night they turn on bright lights that display messages in huge letters. As I looked upon the city, the building lit up with a message that read, "One Day At A Time." Chills ran all over me. I looked at Jackie and began to break up inside. No one in the city knew my theme of "One Day At A Time," yet there it was.

"Thank you, Lord. I am finally here, and you gave me my heart's desire."

Later that night, Floyd stood with me backstage of the Opry. We were both frightened, but also very excited to be there. "Can I help you?" were the gruff words from Mr. Van Dame, who I had been warned was a "no nonsense man."

"Yes, sir, I'm David Stewart. I'm supposed to meet with Mr. Durham."

"Mr. Durham wants you to talk to Justin Tubb first," he said with a stern, Southern drawl.

I had told Mr. Durham that Justin invited me to sing on the "Midnight Jamboree" radio show. Mr. Van Dame wanted me to let Justin know I was singing at the Opry at 11:30 on Saturday night and that I might get to his show a little late.

"You walked all the way, huh?" Mr. Van Dame asked.

"Yes, sir, I did." The ice was broken between us.

Waiting a moment I asked, "Is Justin here?" with anticipation in my voice.

"No, sir. He'll be here right before he goes on," he said as he handed me a program and directed me to the Green Room with a smile.

• • •

A man sat with a crowd around him as I peered into his door. Mr. Acuff, the King of Country Music, was sitting not five steps away! My moment came and I approached Bashful Brother Oswald. He had been with the Opry for about 50 years and always wore big shoes, bib overalls and an old hat on stage. His real name was Pete Kirby, and he played dobro in Roy Acuff's band. I introduced myself to Brother Oswald.

He greeted me with a warm smile. "You're the fellow who walked all that way." He saw me watching Mr. Acuff. "You wanna go in and meet him?" he asked with a knowing twinkle in his eye.

"Oh, yes! Can I?"

He chuckled and said, "Come on," in a way only a Southerner can.

"Roy, this is the boy who walked here from Wyoming," Brother Oswald said.

"You don't say." He looked straight at me and asked, "How's your dog, Wyoming?"

I replied with a smile, "He's fine, sir, just fine." Brother Oswald winked at me, and I introduced Floyd to Mr. Acuff.

"I'm honored, sir." Floyd almost bowed. Roy Acuff shook Floyd's hand, and I held back a tear.

"You know, Wyoming, I walked about 50 miles on the railroad track one time, from St. Louis to a small town in Illinois, and wore out a pair of good shoes. How many did you wear out?"

To think that Mr. Roy Acuff would be interested enough in me to even ask this question! "Three pairs, completely, sir, and quite some wear on three more pairs of shoes." My heart pounded for hours, it seemed, after my visit with this legend of a man.

My meeting with Justin was brief, and he told me, "You sing on the Opry tomorrow night and come over to the Jamboree when you can get there. We'll be there." I was pleased with that.

The two greatest shows in Nashville, all in one night. Saturday night I would shine!

Mr. Durham told me to come early Saturday and rehearse with the band.

"You'll be on Charlie Walker's part of the show, David," he said and then left me to visit with the Opry family. Charlie Walker was an entertainer at the Opry. "Mr. Durham gets right to the point," I mumbled nervously. "I hope he likes me."

With Bashful Brother Oswald. Chuck Buell

Talkin' with Mr. Acuff. Ada Tolar

I met Mr. Jerry Strobel backstage. He was general manager of the Grand Ole Opryhouse and as Opry spokesman had made statements to the press about my walk. He was a warm man and wished me luck as we shook hands. I was beginning to feel at ease in my heart.

I did not want to leave the Opry that night, but knew I needed the rest. I had walked 1,600 miles in 84 days (including rest days), averaging about 23 miles a day at 2.5 to 4 mph. I had walked through seven states, usually from 6:00 a.m. to noon and then 4:00 p.m. until sundown, Monday through Saturday, through weather ranging from snow to 106 degrees and from 80 mph wind-driven storms to tranquil drought. I had lost about 32 pounds during the course of the walk, had walked through three pairs of sturdy shoes and had run the gamut of emotions.

Despite all this, there was not much sleep Friday night, only rejoicing and much talk. There were family and friends aplenty, and they were excited. The tickets for everyone had been bought, and everything seemed to fall into place.

"Jackie, I think I can have one person backstage tomorrow night," I said.

"Well, if you can, take Floyd. He deserves it and I want to be out front, anyway. I want to see your face."

So be it.

25

In the Wings of the Grand Ole Opry

The Opry security guard watched me as I approached to introduce myself.

"Well, I'll be!" he said aloud. "I'm Bobby Rose. Pleased to meet you. I just happen to have a little something here for you."

I expected a backstage pass or something.

"It's Mother of Pearl!" he told me proudly as he handed me a little cross. "Put it in your pocket when you go on." He winked and I noticed that he was closely checking the cars as they arrived. He knew most of the drivers and waved them on, but some he checked. Bobby had followed my story closely and was a great comfort for my nerves. He parked my car at the front of the building, then asked about my family.

"They're at the motel. They'll be here."

"I'll let 'em in when they get here."

"No need to. They're goin' out front," I told him.

He was aghast. "Call 'em and tell 'em to come to the gate. They can go on out to the front from back here. They've got to come backstage with you!"

I called Jackie and told her.

I sat at the back door with Mr. Van Dame, chatting about my walk and letting Floyd look about the whole area. I was gather-lng my thoughts and waiting for Liz White. She had called and I said she'd be there to talk to me.

"You that man who walked all that way?" a man of about 6-foot 7-inches asked me. I stood up and offered my hand.

"That was really something you did. I'm Big Jim Webb. I play steel for Del Reeves." I knew I'd never dispute the "Big" in his name. Not many men dwarfed me, but this man made me feel small.

He said, "Come with me. I want to introduce you around." I started to tell him that I was waiting for someone, but he took me by the arm and led me away.

"Thank God, a friend," I said softly.

"When do you sing?" He was a happy man who liked every-one, and everyone seemed to take to him. Big Jim took the edge away.

I thought about Bobby Rose waiting for my family. Jackie had agreed to meet me backstage, but she was not there, and it was getting late! Big Jim had introduced me to everyone in sight and I, in turn, introduced him to Floyd before he wandered away again.

Big Jim escorted me to my dressing room — number 4. I sat there amazed. What greats had sat in the chair I waited in? Dolly Parton? Randy Travis? Loretta Lynn?

Charlie Walker came through the door with his hand ex-tended.

"Hi, David. We're working together tonight." He was a gra-cious man, and I knew I would be at home with him on stage.

"Have you taught the band your song?"

"Yes, sir. Didn't take long at all."

"They're the best," he announced loudly. "What about an encore?"

"An encore?" He took me by surprise with that question, an encore at the Grand Ole Opry!

"Sure! You need to be prepared."

"How about 'Jambalaya' ? It's one of my favorites," I confided.

"Perfect."

At that moment, Liz White came in with tape recorder in hand. Charlie excused himself after greeting her.

"How do you feel?" she asked.

"I'm nervous as all get out . . . and excited . . . very excited!"

We walked around the Opry for a while. She asked me about this and that, mostly my emotions. I told her how Mr. Acuff had signed all of my old 78-rpm records. "He sang a line from every song as he signed each record with care. He handled them all with respect, slowly turning them over, knowing how delicate and precious they were to me. It felt great just to be standing there." Big Jim had left us alone, and it was a special time for me.

"Has your dream come true?" Liz asked.

"It's about to, Liz, real soon."

Jackie arrived a little late and found me in a state of nervous turmoil.

"Where've you been?" I asked, as she held me in the wings of the Opry stage.

"We got a little lost. I wish Mom could be back here," she sighed.

"Where is she?"

"I think she's taken her seat out front. I rode in a different car, and she didn't know we could come to the back."

It was getting close to the Charlie Walker portion of the show and Jackie said, "I'm going out front, baby. Like I said, I wanna see your face."

I stood in the wings next to Liz White as Charlie Walker spoke to the audience.

"We have a very unusual guest coming on tonight . . ." Liz touched the side of my arm. ". . . And it's a thrill for me to be able to introduce this young man. I see my friends, Mr. Hal Durham and Jerry Strobel, are both back here with us tonight. This young man has walked — I don't mean he hitchhiked; he didn't take any rides — he walked all the way from Gillette, Wyoming, to the Grand Ole Opry."

The crowd began to react to the words spoken by Mr. Walker. I could hear voices raising in approval, as if the crowd knew what was going to happen.

"Is anybody here tonight from the great state of Wyoming?"

The whistles rang out! The answer was more than he ex-Pected.

"Really? I had a great time out there. I went out to the One Shot Antelope Hunt last September. In fact, I'm going back again this September. I had a great time in Lander, Wyoming," he announced.

I looked over at Floyd. He winked at me and his face was all aglow. The palms of my hands were moist with sweat, and my heart pounded as if it would jump out of my chest.

". . . but 1,600 miles is how far he walked and I asked him, 'Did you walk in cowboy boots?' He said no, he walked in walking shoes. 'How many pairs did you wear out?' He said about three pairs. He told me how his thighs have just absolutely grown. I forget how many days — I'm gonna let him tell you about it. He's really a fine guy and he's talented and he writes songs and he sings and I know that he's delighted that the Grand Ole Opry people heard about what he was trying to do. He loves the Opry and he wanted to be here. I know you'll all give him a great BIG welcome here tonight. Ladies and gentlemen here is DAVID STEWART from Gillette, Wyoming! Walked all the way to the Grand Ole Opry! David!" '

The crowd welcomed me with shouts and whistles and I swear I heard my brother, Jack, yell: "Ya!"

The spotlight caught me at the precise moment I moved from the Wings toward the center stage. I was young. I was a winner I felt very alive and remembered Mr. Acuff sayin "Just luv 'em and they'll luv ya back."

"Thank you Charlie' I'm proud to be here, and I want to thank you folks who have been sharing a part of this trip with me.

Charlie Walker introducing me on the Grand Ole Opry   Ada Tolar

And I want to thank the Opry people. I just can't express how I feel right now. This has been a dream come true for me, and I'm gonna sing my tune that I wrote about the Opry. It's called 'In the Wings' and tells my story. I hope you enjoy it. Thank you so much . . ." I could barely get the words out.

I looked the crowd over for a familiar face, but saw none. I could hear someone in the crowd whistling and felt as if I was about to break down as I turned to the fiddler and gave him his cue. I looked down at the circle where I stood, the circle of wood that had been cut from the old Ryman Theatre where so many greats had stood. It was laid into the new floor. I dared not click my heels together for fear of waking up. I glanced at Charlie who smiled right back at me with a big Texas grin.

As the notes of the twin fiddles filled the air of the Mother Church of Country Music, I heard a small voice from stage right, "Mama, when I grow up I want to sing on the Grand Ole Opry." This was a young singer who had visions of her own. There was a part of my song where I addressed my mother. The young girl from off-stage did that part for me. She was nervous, and you could hardly hear her. I wondered how she felt. She too, was making her debut at the Opry.

I gathered all that was inside me and, with shaking voice I began to sing:

> *When they call out my name*
> *And I take Center Stage*
> *It'll come from the heart when I sing. . .*

The crowd applauded and I responded with, "Thank you." I prayed to myself, "Let me do this, Lord!" I was at the Opry, singing my song.

> *Can ya hear that lonesome whippoorwill*
> *I sing it sad and slow*
> *As a child with my friends*
> *I would pretend*
> *That I was the star of the show . . .*

My dream had come true! I was really at the Opry!

> *As my mind slips away to Nashville*
> *Somehow it seems so real*
> *I hear those lonely fiddles cryin' in the hills*
> *In the wings of the Grand Ole Opry*
> *That's where I long to he*
> *When they call out my name*
> *And I take Center Stage*
> *It'll come from the heart when I sing. . .*

The fiddles filled the air with a sweetness that identified my song, and the steel guitar echoed it. I took a deep breath and felt a tear on my cheek. I wanted to look back at Floyd, but kept my eyes on my audience. I swallowed hard as I knew it was time for me to come in again. My mother wasn't there, but she was in my heart . . .

When I'm home alone with the radio on
And George is singing a song
I get tears in my eyes when I harmonize
And I think of my dear mama's words

In the wings of the Grand Ole Opry
That's where I long to be
When they call out my name
And I take Center Stage
It'll come from the heart when I sing

In the wings of the Grand Ole Opry
That's where I long to he
When they call out my name
And I take Center Stage. . .

I spoke the last line.

It'll come from the heart. . . when I sing.

"God bless you. Thank you."
The crowd began to roar.
"David!" Charlie was chuckling. "David! How 'bout that! All right!"
I bowed deeply and started to leave the stage.
"Don't go away, David. Let 'em see you! Ain't that something! How about it!" '
The crowd continued to treat me well. Deep devotion and exhilaration overtook me. I was captivated by the magic and the passion of the moment. My knees were trembling, and then Charlie placed his arm about my shoulder. I felt like I would break down at any moment.
"All right, David. You know, I want to tell you something. I'm involved in a lot of things other than the music business, like golf and hunting, and sometimes I think perseverance is the greatest attribute that anybody can have because there are people, sometimes less talented, if they've got the heart and desire,

Singing on the Opry...   Ada Tolar

...and later at the Midnight Jamboree   Ada Tolar

they're gonna make it, and I guarantee you with what you've done, you really want it. I know you do and they love you. I asked you if you'd do an encore for us. I know they want to hear it (the crowd came alive again in an affirmative manner) and you suggested 'Jambalaya.' I can't think of a better one."

Charlie held my arm and gave me assuranace that I was okay. He winked an I turned to the band.

"Whatta ya do it in? C? Is that all right?" I nodded at Charlie and turned back to the audience.

"Hank has been a great inspiration to me for many years — Mr. Hank Williams. 'Jambalaya,' ladies and gentleen." The band came in as if I had been singing with them for years and the Carol Lee singers were right behind me.

"Luv 'em, luv 'em and they'll luv you back." Those words from Mr. Acuff kept running through my head as tears filled my eyes, and I sang from the heart.

• • • • • • • •

If one advances confidently in the directions of his dreams,
and endeavors to live the life which he has imagined,
he will meet with success unexpected in common hours.

Henry David Thoreau (1817-1862)

THE BUSY BEE
Since 1927
BREAKFAST. LUNCH. DINNER
CAFE
OPEN 7 AM
HOTEL
OCCIDENTAL

Heart and Sole :

the road I chose

Epilogue

For a man who walked from Wyoming to Nashville, Tennessee, David Stewart doesn't get to travel much these days. He and his lovely Jackie have anchored themselves to an old hotel in the Wild West, The Occidental. That old hotel has had its day—replete with famous customers like Butch Cassidy, Calamity Jane, Buffalo Bill, Teddy Roosevelt, and Owen Wister whose Virginian finally got his man at that very same hotel.

The hotel got its man too—David Stewart—and now it's "having its day" all over again. David and Jackie welcome travelers from all over the world to the hotel and its historic saloon.

But the real magic happens in the far corner of that saloon. The same dream that drove David to walk over 1500 miles still drives him. Countless hours in that corner have created a culture of music and community that is world-renowned. In 2006, David started The Thursday Night Jam. From humble beginnings, that jam has now become an incubator of musicians who will be playing bluegrass and living their dreams long after David lays down his guitar. In that corner, pickers from all over have joined together for hours of spontaneous music-making. Age doesn't matter, but tuning does.

My shy daughter Morgan was just a kid when she started playing at the Jam about ten years ago. She found out that first

night she was actually standing in one of the greatest corners
in the whole world. Growing up in that saloon, playing upright
bass right next to David, she now regards him as one of her best
friends. Nowadays, David often invites her band to join him as he
opens for professional bluegrass musicians who have traveled all
the way from the South to little ol' Buffalo, Wyoming, dreaming of
playing on the stage in David and Jackie's Occidental Saloon. Turn
around is the fairest play.

Karen Blaney
BigHorn Bluegrass Camp Director
David Stewart Fan